Mike
Bailey

Printed in the United States of America

First Printing, 2017

ISBN-13: 978-1977810908
ISBN-10: 197781090X
AISN: B07622Z296

Michael Bailey/Innsmouth Look Publishing
www.innsmouthlook.com

Cover illustrations Copyright © 2017 by Patricia Lupien
Cover design by Patricia Lupien

Book production by Amazon Create Space,
www.createspace.com
Edited by Julie Tremblay

The Adventures of Strongarm & Lightfoot
Blades of Glory

ACT ONE
In Which Our Heroes Heed the Call to Adventure and the Payday it Promises

ONE
A Day in the Life

If you will indulge me, my friends, let me tell you about cockatrices. You'll understand why I'm doing this in a few minutes.

The cockatrice, taxonomically speaking, is a bird, but most birds would take offense at being mentioned in the same breath as so loathsome a creature. Cockatrices are strange and ugly things that might, to a distant viewer, appear as a malformed turkey or exceptionally large gamecock. A closer inspection would reveal distinctly serpentine features, such as fine blackish-green scales running down the creature's head and elongated neck as well as down the length of its whip-like tail.

Not that getting close to the noisome animal is something any sane soul would recommend. Aside from a pungently musty stench often likened to the pit of a long disused public outhouse, the cockatrice possesses a foul temper — pun not intended, I assure you — and an unusual offensive capability. Their beaks, curved and sharp like an assassin's dagger, exude a toxin capable of immobilizing a full-grown man within seconds and, in sufficient quantities, killing him by causing paralysis so complete it arrests his heart. As a curious and truly unique side effect of the venom, the victim's skin turns a sickly gray, which gave rise to the myth that cockatrices — or cockatrix, if you prefer — turn their prey to stone.

Despite this handy ability, which allows them to easily subdue a potential meal of superior size, cockatrices are cowardly things that prefer to put as little effort into their hunting as possible, especially when hunting alone or in small numbers. They tend to avoid anything that looks like it might be more effort than it's worth, e.g., human beings, and will resort to consuming small animals or even scavenging other animals' kills before picking a fight. Only when their numbers are vastly superior will they consider swarming upon a man. Fortunately, under normal circumstances a cabal of cockatrices is fairly small — a half dozen or so. Acclaimed naturalist Desdemona Quesp, widely considered Asaches's foremost expert on cockatrices and other esoteric avian species, once recorded a cabal of an even dozen making its home in the woods south of the elven metropolis City Lyth — but only the once. Following her discovery, she jokingly suggested cockatrices are such repulsive creatures even they cannot stand themselves in any significant number.

Imagine the esteemed Professor Quesp's surprise, her shock, her scholarly exhilaration upon learning cockatrices are perfectly capable of gathering in much larger numbers — say, nearly one hundred strong.

Alas, Desdemona Quesp did not make this paradigm-altering discovery; Derek Strongarm and Felix

Lightfoot did — though not intentionally and not at all by choice.

You see, Derek and Felix had been hired by Oliver Prande — owner of Prande Poultry, the largest and most successful chicken farm in Bemo — to rid the woods surrounding his property of a cabal of cockatrices that had in recent weeks taken to raiding his coops. The partners were offered a reasonable reward for what struck them as a reasonable job — reasonable, right up until the moment they succeeded in tracking the cockatrices to their roost deep in the woods and found it absolutely overrun with the filthy beasts.

As I said, cockatrices are not by nature bold, but they are perfectly capable of drawing upon the wellspring of courage that flows most freely when the odds are overwhelmingly in one's favor. Emboldened by the profoundly lopsided cockatrice-to-human ratio, the creatures responded predictably when accosted in their home, erupting in a frenzy of beating wings and cries that have been likened to the screech of a hawk, if said hawk had a massive hairball caught in its throat.

Derek and Felix in turn responded predictably and ran like hell.

My apologies; I should have noted that this strategic high-speed withdrawal also included their young charge David, the current alias of the former Randolph David Ograine, youngest son of Malcolm Ograine, high lord of all Asaches — *former* by dint of the fact he is believed by the world at large to have died during his quest to slay the mad lich-lord Habbatarr (which you would already know if you'd enjoyed my first tale featuring the duo of Strongarm and Lightfoot. Why you'd pass on such a thrilling epic and join their ongoing adventures now is beyond me).

It made a sort of sense that David, as the son of a renowned leader, should lead the charge to safety, and lead he did, his youthful stamina and a healthy dose of terror-induced adrenaline compensating nicely for his comparatively shorter stride. For a time, he impressively outpaced his older companions, but only for a time, and then the strain of his flight caught up to him with a vengeance, and his pace plummeted from a sprint to a stagger.

Fortunately, Derek was right there to scoop up the faltering lad and sling him over his broad shoulder like a sack of potatoes — a position David had found himself in once before. He hated it then, and he hated it now, but the sight of the cabal weaving and bobbing through the trees like a living wave crashing through the pilings of a pier convinced him to endure the indignity.

"Shit!" Felix panted. "The woods are thinning out!"

"That's not a good thing?" David said.

"No! The trees are the only thing slowing them down!" Derek said. "Once we hit open ground, they'll catch up!"

As if to confirm this, the cockatrices began to close the distance as the forest became less dense, and by the time the trio reached open ground in the form of a vast grassy plain, the beasts were close enough that David could catch occasional whiffs of their powerful fetor.

"*Igi au'sum!*" David cried, casting his ever-reliable Finger of Flame spell. The quick spray of magical fire went astray due to the vigorous jostling that came with being Derek's cargo and thus failed to immolate their pursuers — David's express intent — but the flash of white-hot flame startled the cockatrices well enough to allow Derek and Felix to re-extend their lead.

"Derek!" Felix shouted.

"I see it! David, hold on!" Derek said.

"Hold on for whaAAAAAAAAAAAHHH!" David squealed as Derek released him, and he found himself suddenly airborne. He spun like a coin returning to the hand that flipped it, the light blue of the early summer sky above trading places with the darker, less inviting blue of a large body of water. He sucked in a breath before hitting the lake, but the impact immediately drove that air from his lungs. He held onto what little he had left as he desperately climbed and clawed toward the murky gleam of sunlight playing on the water's surface. He broke through with a gasp that doubled as a scream, a cathartic release of the mortal terror that had been growing in his belly since sighting the cabal untold minutes earlier.

A second cry caught in his throat as he gazed skyward and beheld a roiling black cloud silhouetted against the late morning sun — a cloud that flapped and screeched as it drifted out over and then fell into Red Clay Mine Pond. In their fervor to catch their prospective meal, the cockatrices pitched themselves over the edge of the cliff overlooking the great pond with reckless abandon, forgetting that their capacity for flight was, shall we say, suspect at best — but certainly stronger than their ability to swim. The foul fowl hit the water with a series of dull splashes, and one by one, amidst a cacophony of panicked shrieking and a frantic beating of their sodden wings, they slipped beneath the surface. A grayish-green froth bubbled up from their watery mass grave and settled into a noisome, oily film.

"Well," Felix said, "that worked out."

"Rather nicely, yeah," Derek agreed.

"Are you two insane?!" David wailed. "We almost got killed by a mob of chicken monsters and fell off a cliff!"

"It was a small cliff."

"And all the cockatrices are dead thanks to that cliff," Felix added.

"Maybe not *all* of them. We should double back to make sure the roost is clear."

"Yeah, probably."

"Madmen. Both of you, madmen," David said.

"Oh, quit bitching, kid. You were the one who wanted to come with us."

That point, David could not argue. In the weeks immediately following his harrowing experiences at Castle Somevil-Duur, David was perfectly content to remain in his room in his de facto home at The Perfect, Ambride's premier gathering spot for adventurers seeking gainful (if not necessarily honest) employment, sleeping or reading or practicing his spells while his elder companions took to the ongoing task of keeping their little collective financially solvent. This involved them setting out for sometimes days at a stretch and, more often than not, returning with tales filled with narrow escapes from certain death. The seasoned heroes, well accustomed to facing their own mortality on a regular basis, brushed these experiences off with a laugh, yet David was unable to find the humor in their stories. They only served as stark reminders that the day could come when one of them — perhaps all of them — would never return.

The dreadful thought gnawed away at his contentment until he was no longer able to enjoy his self-imposed solitude. Every day alone turned into a grim vigil; he took to sitting in the tavern awaiting his friends' return, always refusing offers of food or drink because his stomach was too knotted with worry, his head filled to overflowing with bleak scenarios that all came to the same bleak conclusion. There were days when his relief upon a companion's return was so great, he was almost overwhelmed by an impulse to hurl himself across the room to deliver a rib-crushing hug.

Almost. If nothing else, David still had his dignity.

When Derek and Felix secured their contract with Oliver Prande, David jumped at the chance to join them — an impulse he now regretted and continued to regret as he and his partners trudged back to the cabal's roost, his wet breeches insistently wedging themselves between his nether cheeks.

Finding no lingering cockatrices, the companions declared their job completed and hiked back to Prande's farm. The men attempted to renegotiate their pay based on the greater-than-anticipated size of the cabal, but Prande held fast to their agreed-upon terms, arguing he had no idea the roost was so large. Nevertheless, a pang of guilt compelled Prande to offer the trio lodging for the night in his impressive manor. He also invited them to join him for a sumptuous dinner — chicken, of course — as a token of his gratitude. David, who'd had his fill of anything remotely galline, picked around the poultry and filled up on vegetables and bread before turning in early.

Sadly, his bedroom proved a poor refuge from the day's experiences. He slept fitfully that night, and when he did sleep, he dreamed of flying over an endless ocean on crude wings constructed of sticks and leaves while pursued doggedly by thousands upon thousands of greenish-black roosters with blood red eyes, their angry squawks sounding disturbingly like human voices. And yet, he found the nightmares almost preferable to the constant murmur of thousands of chickens clucking outside his window and the low miasma of their excrement floating on the air — and to a gnawing sense of discontent much like he felt whenever he laid awake in his bed at The Perfect, keenly aware of how lumpy his straw-filled mattress was, how scratchy his woolen blankets were, how the sounds of raucous revelry from the tavern below wafted up through the floorboards, and how particularly heavy rains would sneak in through the roof to drip drip drip on his nightstand. This was not the world in which he was raised, far from it — and yet, it was the world he chose after he learned the former was founded upon lies and betrayal.

In these quiet moments, the former Randolph David Ograine wondered whether he made the right choice.

Derek, Felix, and David set out in the morning and, after taking breakfast at a local tavern, made the journey back to Ambride on foot, their pockets a little heavier with gold than when they arrived, but only a little.

Such was life nowadays for our noble heroes. No

major calls to adventure had come through The Perfect since their return from Somevil, which meant finding other means of earning a living until someone had need of a qualified party of heroes for hire. This would happen eventually, they reasoned, but for the nonce, all they could do was bide their time and make the best of their available opportunities.

Winifred had managed to secure an unexciting but steady job at an apothecary, where she employed her skill as a healer mixing tinctures and salves. She also joined the local healers' guild, which served the community by providing emergency medical care, most often to working-class residents who injured themselves on the job. She quickly became a much-prized asset due to her magical abilities, which only two other healers within the guild possessed, and not to the same degree of skill as the kind elven woman with the ever-present warm smile.

Erika, meanwhile, had followed Derek and Felix on the adventurers' path, sometimes joining their small missions, sometimes taking jobs on her own. As an elf of the Clan Boktn, a race with a reputation for violence — an overblown reputation, but a reputation nonetheless — her very existence tended to attract offers that fell under the umbrella of the so-called dark trades, which came with generous paydays but required the contractors to compromise their morality — assuming the contractor in question in fact possessed a personal code of ethics to begin with. Erika had received her fair share of shady offers, and though they'd all been well within her wheelhouse as a brutally efficient warrior, she'd turned nearly every one of them down without a moment's hesitation. In one case, she savagely beat her potential employer and very literally dragged his semi-conscious body to the nearest constable's office for a lawful arrest and summary prosecution.

And then there were Derek and Felix, who accepted whatever above-board drudgework came their way, even when it fell outside the broad realm of adventuring. Money was money, after all, and they needed every coin they could acquire to keep their heads above water, if barely; lodging and food was a slow, constant drain on their combined resources, and they were relieved to simply break even week to week.

Relieved — not *happy*.

I mentioned all this not only to bring you, my friend, up to speed on the recent events in our heroes' lives but to kill time while Derek, Felix, and David made their hike back to The Perfect, which was long, uneventful, and wholly uninteresting. You're welcome.

It was early evening by the time the men stepped foot inside The Perfect, which was as busy as ever, filled to capacity with adventurers recuperating between jobs, a handful of assorted laborers, and one or two of Ambride's more well-to-do residents who found the publick house's rough-and-tumble atmosphere uniquely charming. Greeting them at the door, as always, was The Perfect's resident mascot and chief peacekeeper Bullmoose, a stout, towering black mastiff.

"Hey, buddy," Derek said, grasping two handfuls of the dog's generous jowls and giving them a hearty shake. "How're you doing? Huh? How you doin'?"

Bullmoose responded with a throaty bass *whurf*. He offered a similar greeting to Felix, who slipped the dog a half-eaten piece of jerky before moving on. And then David entered. Bullmoose lowered his head ever so slightly, and a growl rumbled deep in his throat.

"What?" David said. Bullmoose *hurrf*ed, blowing hot, moist, jerky-scented air in his face. "Come on, what did I ever do to you? Stupid animal," the boy mumbled as he skirted past the mastiff.

"He's not stupid," Derek said, taking offense on Bullmoose's behalf. "Bullmoose is a very intelligent dog."

"Then why does he always give me a hard time?"

"Like he said," Felix said, "Bullmoose is a smart boy."

"Derek! Felix! Over here!" Winifred called out, waving from a table in the center of the spacious tavern. She rose to greet each of them with a hug, as her custom demanded. No friend of Winifred Graceword ever went un-hugged. "How was the job in Bemo?"

"We got chased by chicken monsters," David said with a false air of pride. "And then we fell off a cliff."

"Same-old same-old," Felix said, sighing contentedly as he took a seat.

"Where's Erika?" Derek asked.

"Out on a job. She expected to be back this evening. Oh! Before I forget," Winifred said, reaching into a small leather satchel lying on the table. "This came for you today, Derek."

Winifred handed Derek a rectangle of cheap, stiff parchment that had been folded in on itself to create a packet and sealed with a blob of yellowish tallow. Derek grinned at seeing his name — his true name, Derek Bla'smith — written across the front in a delicate script.

"Letter from home?" Felix said.

"Uh-huh," Derek said, breaking the waxen seal. His smile took on a melancholy quality as he read the missive, but joy remained strong in his eyes. "Mom says hello to everyone and hopes you're all doing well."

"Aww," Winifred said.

"How's the family doing?" Felix inquired.

"Everyone's fine," Derek reported. "Things have been busy at the shop. Brownie's about to drop another calf. Granddad got into another argument with Councilor Staph at the tavern."

"My Gods, the epic adventure that is your family's lives," David drawled. "However do you stand to be away from it all?"

Felix was never above delivering unto David a stiff backhand across the arm when he felt it warranted, and David had grown to expect getting smacked now and then, but he was utterly unprepared for Felix jumping out of his seat and reaching across the table to slap his shaven head.

"Ow!"

"Watch your mouth, you little shit," Felix snapped, drawing the attention of half the tavern. Bullmoose, ever vigilant, wove his way through the patrons, ready to intervene.

"Felix, stop," Derek said. "It's okay."

"It is not okay, Derek. What he said was *not* okay, man."

"Felix. Let it go."

Felix, reluctantly, sat back down.

"I'm going to my room," David mumbled, and

he slinked away.

"Yeah, nice apology!" Felix shouted after him.

"Okay, enough," Derek said. "I think he got the point."

"Doubt it. The kid does not learn."

"He's learning," Winifred said, "but not as quickly as he could. He's not doing himself any favors spending so much time in his room all alone. He needs to get out more."

"Glad to hear you say that," Erika said, joining the group — or rather, she attempted to do so, but Bullmoose sat in front of her, blocking her path. Sighing, Erika stooped until her face was level with his — she did not have to bend too far — and allowed the black beast to run the dripping slab of meat that was his tongue up her face, chin to forehead. Satisfied, Bullmoose resumed his post at the front door.

"That dog," Erika grumbled, wiping her face on her sleeve.

"It's sweet," Winifred said.

"Welcome back. Winifred said you had a job today?" Derek said.

"I was asked to convince someone to strongly reconsider his choices in life," Erika said, offering nothing more. "We need to talk about David. Winifred's right —"

"I love it when you say that," she chirped.

"— we need to get David out into the world more, and not just so he can learn how to live in it."

"I agree. I've been cutting him slack because he's still a little shaken up from the siege and from — um, his transition to civilian life," Derek said, taking care not to let slip any revealing details of David's origins, "but it's not doing him any favors."

"Yeah, well, carrying his deadweight ass around isn't doing us any favors either," Felix griped.

"And that's the other problem; David *is* dead weight," Erika said, waving Derek quiet even as he began to speak in the boy's defense. "He's not contributing, Derek. We have four unreliable incomes and five reliable expenses, and that needs to change."

"No, you're right," Derek conceded, "but what would he do? I don't say this to be cruel, but he doesn't have much in the way of useful skills."

"I don't care what he does. I don't care if he has to mop floors in a tavern or muck out stables or —"

"Ooh! Ooh! I have an idea! I have an idea!" Winifred said, bouncing in her seat. "Maybe he could find a job with the academy?"

"Oh, hey," Derek said, "that is a good idea."

"I know!"

"The work probably wouldn't be too strenuous, he'd be someplace he might actually find interesting..."

"It has potential," Erika said. "He'd have to keep his own abilities under wraps. If anyone learned he can work magic, they might think he's a spy from one of the other academies."

"So we'd have to trust David to keep his mouth shut?" Felix said, laughing. "So much for that idea."

"Let's not write it off so quickly," Derek said, rising. "Someone order dinner for me. I'll go talk to him."

Derek went upstairs and knocked on David's door. He knocked a second time after the first effort was met with stony silence.

"What?" David said.

"It's me. I need to talk to you."

"...Okay."

Derek entered David's quarters, a tiny room filled almost to capacity by a bed and a small nightstand. Derek had to squeeze into the corner to close the door behind him. David pulled his legs up to give Derek room to sit on the end of his bed.

"David —"

"I'm sorry," he said immediately.

"What?"

"For what I said downstairs. I don't know what I said, exactly, but I'm sorry."

"Well, thank you."

"Do you...is there some kind of problem between you and your family?"

"No, no. The problem isn't with my family, it's with...it's complicated." David nodded. "That's not why I'm here. We think it's time for you to find work."

"You want me to get a job?"

"We think it'd be good for you. You spend a lot of time alone in this closet," Derek said, looking about and wondering if the room had indeed been a storage closet at one time (it had). "You'd get out, meet new people, learn a useful skill — and to be frank, you need to start contributing to the group."

"*You want me to get a job?*"

"We need the money. We're living payday to payday and we're not saving anything for a rainy day. Besides, we've all been supporting you ever since we left Oson. Do you think that's fair to us?"

The boy frowned. "No. But what would I do? I don't really know how to do anything except work magic."

"Funny you should say that. Winifred had an

idea I think you'll like. Tomorrow after breakfast, you and I are heading over to the academy to see if they have anything for you."

"The academy?" David said, perking up slightly.

"Yeah. It probably wouldn't be anything glamorous but you'd be someplace interesting, and it wouldn't be shoveling manure in a stable. That's a plus, right?"

"Definitely."

"Now, you'd have to keep your own skills secret while you're there and pretend to be a normal kid —"

"I can do that."

"Can you? Serious question, buddy, because the academies tend to be secretive and more than a little paranoid. If they found out you're a sorcerer yourself —"

"I can do it," David insisted.

"All right."

Derek invited David to return to the tavern for a proper dinner, but he firmly refused, claiming he was more tired than hungry, and he wanted to go right to sleep. Derek accepted this answer, albeit reluctantly, for he suspected lingering embarrassment over David's earlier transgression might be the real reason he chose to remain in seclusion for the rest of the evening.

But this would be the last time the young man would close himself off from the rest of the team, Derek told himself. Tomorrow David would find gainful employment and thus regain something he'd not had in several months — humble, perhaps, but meaningful nevertheless:

A purpose.

TWO
The Ambride Academy of Magic

As I noted in a previous story (which you'd know if you'd read it), magic is a relatively new field of study in the world of Ne'lan. The ability to wield magical energies was discovered about four centuries prior to the tale I now relate and has been slow in its growth and evolution, largely due to the fact these energies are powerful and primal — a force of nature in the truest sense. Tapping, manipulating, and controlling magic is hazardous under the best of conditions, and thus all efforts made toward expanding mankind's knowledge have been, wisely, deliberate and methodical.

As is often the case with academics, likeminded scholars of the magical arts gathered to discuss their respective discoveries and experiment with new techniques. Over time, these gatherings developed into formal partnerships, and out of this, the academies were born. However, this is about where the sorcerers' cooperative spirit ended, and things took a competitive turn. Research and experimentation led to conflicting, contrasting, and contradictory hypotheses between the academies, which led to heated disputes over which approaches were best, which led to rifts and rivalries that continue to this day. The academies withdrew into themselves and became insular, and the general public began to view them with curiosity, suspicion, and sometimes outright fear.

And yet, some host communities regard the academies with great respect by their host communities, and the Ambride Academy of Magic is one such place. Even though its members were at heart every bit as secretive as their contemporaries, they recognized the value of maintaining a positive standing among city officials and residents. By presenting an open, friendly façade and cultivating a reputation as a scholarly institute dedicated to the pursuit of knowledge and learning, the academy found it could conduct its work without drawing undue attention or scrutiny.

An aside: only those outside the academy refer to it as the Ambride Academy of Magic. Those within find the name gauche and simply refer to it as "the academy," and so shall I for the remainder of my tale. It's always wise to stay on a wizard's good side.

The academy called a massive, rambling stone mansion its home. It took up several city blocks and surrounded on three sides a central courtyard large enough to stage an army preparing to march. The most southerly wing overlooked the Maan River, which snaked through the center of the city, and it was there that Derek and David entered the academy, stepping into a great foyer with a high arched ceiling. They crossed the foyer, their footsteps echoing dully off the stonework, and approached an unassuming man in dreary gray robes. He sat behind a lectern perched atop a dais, and from this vantage point, he could look down his nose at visitors without having to tilt his head.

"Good morning," he said, his tone neither welcoming nor dismissive. "May I help you?"

"I hope so," Derek said. "This is my squire David. He's looking for work."

The man's eyebrow twitched. "You introduce him as your squire and yet you say he needs work."

"That's right. My name is Derek Strongarm. I'm an adventurer for hire by trade but, well, work's been on the slow side lately, for both of us."

"And you thought to bring your boy to the academy to find him a job — doing what, exactly?"

"Whatever needs doing. Surely your scholars are too busy with their own work to worry about things like sweeping the floors or serving meals."

"There are any number of taverns in Ambride in need of swept floors and served meals."

"True, but I thought a job with the academy would hold his attention better. My squire has always had an interest in magic."

The man leaned over the lectern to gaze down at David with dark, narrowed eyes. "Has he now?"

"You have to admit, to a layman it's fascinating stuff," Derek said, expertly concealing his growing concern that he and his friends had not thought this out as well as they'd believed.

"A layman," the man said with too much emphasis on every single syllable. He settled back into his seat. "We have no need for *laymen* here — real or alleged."

"Ah. You think David might be a spy from a rival academy."

"The thought had crossed my mind, yes. It

wouldn't be the first time another academy attempted to infiltrate our ranks."

"But it would be the first time they attempted something so clumsy as to walk through our front door and ask for a job."

Derek turned. A woman clad in dark red academic robes emerged from a side door. A small, neutral smile played on her lips. She was not an old woman by any means, but age was starting to make its presence known; faint crow's feet became visible as she approached, and a thin streak of gray sprang out from a head of auburn hair.

She surveyed Derek over the top of a pair of pince-nez spectacles and said, "If your squire were a spy, this would either be the cleverest means of slipping him into our academy, or the most idiotic."

"He's not a spy," Derek said, "but I think this might have been a dumb idea anyway."

"Let's find out. Follow me."

"Madam Roust," the man at the lectern said, the start of a reprimand.

"I'll take responsibility for them, Bodd." She gestured. "This way, gentlemen."

After a moment of uncertainty, Derek and David followed their unexpected host through the door from whence she came, through a series of corridors, up several flights of stairs, and into a room that occupied an entire top floor, a room that seemed to be half library and half warehouse. Sunlight poured through stained glass skylights, casting a chaotic, broken rainbow over tables and shelves and display cases, over books and wooden crates and objects ranging from a rusty oil lamp to an ornate suit of bronze armor to a dragon's skull. If there were any method to this madness, Derek could not detect it.

"My name is Elzbet Roust. This is my office."

"Your office is very impressive," Derek said.

"It's a disaster is what you mean," Roust said. "My specialty is artifacts, not organization."

"Artifacts?" David said.

"Items that have been imbued with magical properties — and I don't mean pedestrian fare such as swords that burst into flames on command or boots that silence their wearer's footsteps. I speak of antiquities possessed of great power."

"I see," Derek said.

"No you don't," Roust said, not unkindly.

"No, I don't. Why are we here?"

"You said the boy was looking for work. I could use someone to help me keep things tidy around here."

"Not that I'm complaining, Madam Roust, but just like that? Five minutes ago your man downstairs was basically accusing us of being spies."

"Bodd is too distrusting for anyone's good. The fact of the matter is, the academy is in dire need of servants, attendants, assistants, and has been for some time, but Bodd turns away everyone who dares to inquire. He's convinced they've been sent by a rival academy to steal away our secrets."

"I've heard the rivalries between the academies can be pretty fierce."

"Not untrue, but the use of spies has fallen out of fashion. The academies have become more focused on developing their own bodies of knowledge rather than stealing someone else's. Much better use of everyone's time, I say. To my point: I could use an able body, quite desperately, and you, lad, appear to have one. What's your name?"

"David, ma'am," he said.

"David...?"

"I don't have a last name, ma'am."

"He's an orphan," Derek said. Lying as a rule was not his forte, but with this particular falsehood, he'd grown comfortable enough to state it convincingly. The truth was close enough to the lie.

"My condolences," Roust said. "What say you, David? Does the idea of sorting and labeling and cataloging and unpacking and repacking appeal to you?"

"Yes, ma'am," David said. "And I know how to read and write, if that's helpful."

"It would be at that. I'll pay you a goldie a day to start, and you may start immediately if that's acceptable to you and your master?"

"It absolutely is, Madam Roust," Derek said, sealing the deal with a handshake. "I appreciate this."

"If the lad lives up to my expectations, the appreciation will be all mine."

"Show her what you've got, buddy," Derek said. "I'll see you tonight."

"Now then," Roust said, leveling an appraising gaze at her new assistant. "Where to begin? Ah, I know. I'm looking for a particular item: a human skull engraved with elven runes. According to legend, it's a vessel for the soul of the wizard Reginald Lostyr and possesses the ability to transmute elements in alchemical fashion."

"Wow. Neat," David said. "Um, where is it?"

"Somewhere in here," Roust said with a sweep of her arm, indicating the considerable width and breadth of her office. "I remember taking it out of its crate and setting it down somewhere. Find it for me. There's a lad."

David marveled at the seemingly endless piles of parchment and stacks of books, at the towers of boxes and the pyramids of crates, at shelves that reached to the ceiling and rows of tables that stretched from one end of the floor to the other, and let out a sigh.

"Sure," he said. "No problem."

It took David four days to locate the skull, but along the way, he managed to sort and organize a not insignificant portion of Madam Roust's staggering collection of curiosities. It might have been the proverbial drop in the ocean, but it marked the cleanest her office had been since she first came to the academy, and for this, Roust was greatly pleased.

(It took but a cursory examination of the skull to determine it was utterly devoid of any magical properties, a discovery that disappointed Roust and David in equal measures.)

To his surprise, David took to his new responsibilities readily and quickly grew to enjoy his time with Madam Roust. She was mercurial and tended to jump between projects without rhyme or reason, which meant his duties could abruptly change minute to minute, but she was never dull — nor was she ever unreasonable or unkind. Demanding, yes, but always fair and always civil.

Roust in turn was delighted to have the young man as company while she worked, for it was her habit to think out loud and having someone else in the office to act as a sounding board made her feel a shade less eccentric. David took care not to say anything in response that might betray his own knowledge of things magical, as limited as it was, but the questions he asked in feigned ignorance often succeeded in driving Roust's thought process in revealing new directions.

Along the way, David gleaned a wealth of information about magic in general and magical artifacts in particular — including the fact that legitimate artifacts were extreme rarities, much more often than not the stuff of myth. Of those items that proved genuine, their powers were typically overstated.

"Last year I studied a mummified hand purportedly once attached to a revered priest of the god Victor," she told David one day as they took lunch at her desk. "Legend had it that anyone who possessed the hand would become invulnerable to all physical harm. All it did was fill its possessor with a false bravery that bordered on reckless abandon — which I learned the hard way when I decided that banging my own hand with a mallet would be a fine way to test the theory."

"Ooh," David said, wincing sympathetically. "Have you ever found anything good?"

"Nothing especially paradigm-shifting or earth-shattering, no," Roust said plainly, "but perhaps that's for the best."

"Why do you say that?"

"I've heard about some items that, if they indeed exist, would be quite dangerous in the wrong hands. The Sword of Magnus Brong, for example, allegedly grants its wielder godlike powers as long as its bloodthirst is slaked. A scrying crystal once used by the mystic Zika Tanmouth allegedly foretells the future. Oh, my, the list goes on and on. The Sarcophagus of

King Delian the Mad, the Might of the Shattering Hand..."

David sat bolt upright, his eyes widening.

"You've heard of the Might of the Shattering Hand?"

"My friends Erika and Winifred, they're elves. I heard them talking once about Artemisia Renn the Shattering Hand."

He ended the lie there, remembering a piece of advice once imparted to him by ace dissembler Felix Lightfoot: less is more. Don't say more than you have to and don't oversell it.

"The Might of the Shattering Hand is a suit of magical armor. The stories are frustratingly vague as to its abilities, but they claim that a worthy elven warrior who wears the armor would be able to command the four elven clans. That has been interpreted to mean that its wearer would be the one to reunite the clans Artemisia Renn exiled from Wihend centuries ago." Her mood darkened ever so slightly. "It's also been interpreted to mean that its wearer would lead the unified clans in the final war against humankind Artemisia Renn intended to wage."

"The what?"

"Artemisia Renn was by most standards a sound ruler, but she was also a rabid nationalist. She wanted her people to remain independent and resisted all efforts to integrate Wihend with the rest of Asaches because of its overwhelmingly human leadership. She believed that joining humankind would be the first step toward the extinction of elvenkind, and she was ready and willing to pursue her own extinction agenda in the other direction. This is supposedly what caused the rifts to form between the clans and ultimately led to Renn exiling them from Wihend. If they wouldn't stand behind her as one people, they would be one people no more."

David rolled this story around in his head for the rest of the day and on into the evening as he sat with his companions for dinner.

"You okay, buddy?" Derek said in between forkfuls of a juicy rare steak. "Awfully quiet tonight."

"I'm fine," David said. "Just thinking about some of the stuff I learned today from Madam Roust."

"Like what?"

David hesitated, recalling Madam Roust's warning that the Might of the Shattering Hand — now in the custody of Winifred's sisters at Temple Ven — could be the catalyst that rekindled a long-dormant race war. An image arose in his mind unbidden, of his longtime protector Erika Racewind clad in the ancient armor, and a knot formed in his belly. The Might of the Shattering Hand fit her a little too well.

"Stories about a bunch of different artifacts," he said before scooping a generous helping of garlicky, buttery baby carrots into his mouth to ensure it would be too busy chewing to say anything more.

"I'm so pleased you're enjoying your new job," Winifred beamed.

"Too bad it doesn't pay more," Felix said.

"That's not the point," Derek said.

"I thought that was exactly the point. A goldie a day isn't doing a thing to help keep us afloat."

"Give him some credit, huh? He's contributing. He's trying."

"He's sitting right here," David said. "Hey!" he

cried as a man in a herald's livery rudely used his bench as a stepladder in order to reach their dinner table. "What the hell?"

The man, ignoring David's protests, cleared his throat theatrically and said, "Ladies and gentlemen! If I might have a moment of your time!"

"Get off the table," Fenster Dott, The Perfect's proprietor, said from behind the bar, his normal speaking voice a match in volume for the herald's shout.

"I will in a moment, good sir, but first I —"

"Off the table."

The herald's composure slipped, and he said with an indignant sniff, "Do you mind? I'm trying to make an announcement."

"Last warning. Off the table."

"Look, I just need a minute to —"

"Bullmoose!"

The mastiff's meaty front paws slammed down upon the edge of the table, and he let loose an explosive *BWHOOF!* The herald shrieked and pitched to the floor, arms spinning like pinwheels. Felix brayed with laughter and rewarded Bullmoose for his service with a generous piece of turkey from his plate.

"Good boy," he said, giving the dog a loving thump on the side.

Derek, stifling a laugh of his own, rose to help the herald up. "Thank you," he said sheepishly.

"I strongly suggest apologizing to Fenster before you try that again," Derek said. The man nodded and, giving Bullmoose a wide berth, went to Fenster to make amends.

"After all that, his announcement better be damn important," Felix said.

The herald returned from the bar, duly chastised, and stood in front of the fireplace. "Ladies and gentlemen? Your attention please?" he said plainly, his sense of showmanship extinguished. "My name is Gerald Ilkfurth —"

"Gerald the herald?" Felix snickered under his breath.

"Shh," Derek said.

"— and I hail from the city of Woeste. I'm here to put out a call to adventure to any able-bodied men or women interested in a lucrative contract. This would be a recovery job, but beyond that, I have no more information to offer. The city council will hold open auditions for adventurers at the end of the week, at noon sharp, at city hall."

"What do you think?" Derek asked his companions.

"The whole thing is too vague," Erika said. "No details about the job, no specifics about the payout..."

"It's a contract with a city council, though. They almost never commit to a specific reward up front," Felix said. "They're going to try to get the best people possible for the lowest price possible."

"Maybe so, but we'd have to rent horses to make it to Woeste within the week, and buy supplies for the trip, and maybe pay for lodging while we're there, and there's no guarantee we'd even get the job. We could wind up losing money."

"We definitely won't make money if we don't try," Derek countered.

"I think we should go. I have complete faith in our qualifications and believe we stand as good a chance as anyone to land the contract," Winifred said.

"I say nothing ventured, nothing gained," Felix said, "and let's face it: it's not like there've been a wealth of options lately."

"I agree," Derek said. "It's a risk, but that's the nature of this business."

"I'm not thrilled about it," Erika said, "but okay. David?"

"Huh?" said David, who hadn't been paying attention to the deliberations.

"Do you want to go with us or would you rather stay here?"

"Oh. Um. I don't know? Do you want me to go with you?"

"Of course we do," Winifred said.

"Not really," Felix said.

"It's your decision, David," Derek said. "If you want to come with us we're happy to have you, but it would mean taking time away from the academy, so if you'd prefer to stay here, that's okay."

David chewed on his bottom lip. "Can I think about it?"

"Sure, but we'll need to hit the road tomorrow morning, so we'd need a decision by then."

After dinner, David went directly upstairs to ponder the matter. The temptation to stay in Ambride and continue working for Madam Roust was powerful, but it came with a gnawing sense of guilt. He'd be here, safe and sound, while his friends would be out risking their lives, and in part for his benefit. Felix was right: his contributions were well intentioned but, for their meagerness, ultimately hollow.

His mind made up, David stuffed his belongings in a beaten leather backpack, taking care to conceal one item in particular by wrapping it in a ragged, thread-bare shirt he held onto for that very purpose.

Madam Roust would understand, he told him-self. She knew he was foremost Derek's squire and that responsibility came first. Surely, she wouldn't dismiss him for honoring his obligations.

Would she?

THREE
Welcome to Woeste

She would not, David learned to his immeasurable relief.

Before departing, Derek accompanied David to the academy to plead on the boy's behalf, but Madam Roust needed no convincing. She understood where David's first loyalties laid and granted him an open leave from his duties in her office. She wished them both a safe and speedy journey and gently demanded that David share with her every detail of his adventure upon his return. He happily agreed.

The companions left Ambride at mid-morning and headed west upon the Grand Avenue, a heavily traveled road that began at the capital city of Oson, terminated in the western city of Wecride, and passed through many cities and towns along the way.

Woeste, a metropolis second only to Oson in size and population, marked the approximate midway point along the Grand Avenue, and for this reason, the city was regarded as a critical trading hub for all Asaches, for industries both law abiding and, unavoidably, illicit. Woeste had developed a reputation as a haven for the latter, but this was overblown and unde-served. Yes, there were streets that were best avoided at night, there were those within the city government who held questionable alliances, there were establishments that only the very brave or very foolish patronized, but let us be honest: such could be said of any large metro-politan area. Woeste was not unusual in that sense.

It was, however, unique in its means of govern-ance. Large city-states were ruled by a warden, a lord or lady whose authority was unquestioned and abso-lute and, typically, inherited from the previous warden. Some wardens allowed for the existence of local coun-cils to manage day-to-day affairs, offer advice on larger issues, and act as proctors for the general populace, but ultimately, the wardens answered to no one — other than High Lord Ograine, of course. Smaller municipali-ties beholden to a larger territory were usually man-aged by governors who acted as extensions of a war-den's authority, and the smallest of communities were often overseen by mayors or some other minor func-tionary who served as subordinates for a neighboring governor. Woeste by all rights should have had a war-den of its own, but the city abandoned wardenship as a means of governance following the death of Lord Ulys-ses Kilnmar, a despot whose name remains in history books solely to serve as an object lesson to future gen-erations. Kilnmar was petty, self-serving, vindictive, controlling, and abusive, and during his reign he nearly drove Woeste to citywide bankruptcy. He died unmar-ried and childless and thus had no heir to assume his mantle, so the citizens of Woeste seized upon this rare opportunity to form a government by and for its people and, in theory, ensure that no single unworthy ruler ever again held the reins of power.

This move scandalized the wardens' court, which moved to maintain its preferred status quo by inserting a new warden of its choosing. Woeste pushed back, hard, almost to the point of threatening open rebellion; at which point, the court chose to back off rather than risk a civil war. The court permitted Woeste to attempt direct democracy and self-rule, indulging this flight of fancy the way a parent might indulge a child declaring his intent to run away from home and join a traveling carnival, and the wardens fully expected the populace to come crawling back to them on hands and knees following the complete and utter failure of its grand experiment.

More than a century later, the wardens' court was still waiting.

"It's an interesting city," Erika said as their weary horses crossed the border separating Orh Grato from the outskirts of Woeste. "Politically, culturally, gastronomically..."

"Ohh, some of the restaurants and taverns here are *soooo gooood*," David said, his mouth watering at the mere memory of a two-inch-thick steak he'd enjoyed during a diplomatic trip to the city. He was eight at the time, too young to understand the significance of his family's visit to a territory too recalcitrant to treat with the respect afforded other territories, but too vital to Asaches's economy to wholly ignore.

"You ever visit the pub down the street from city hall?" Felix said. "They brew their own beer on-site and they have a stout that's absolutely —"

"You've been to Woeste?" Erika said.

"I've been to a lot of places."

"Did you leave on good terms?"

"No one here's out to kill me, if that's what you're asking."

Once across the border, the companions headed due north. They reached the edge of the city proper around mid-afternoon and stopped at the first inn they encountered intending to secure rooms but found it to be fully occupied. Such was the case at the next four inns and publick houses at which they stopped.

When they met with similar results at inn number five, the party decided to pause for dinner before setting out once again, and it was during their meal they realized why there were no vacant rooms anywhere. Four men clad in battered leather armor and rusty chainmail populated a neighboring table. A man in something akin to scholar's robes and a woman in partial steel plate loitered near the fireplace, enjoying its soothing warmth. In a far dark corner, three sets of hooded cloaks huddled around a table and whispered conspiratorially.

"It looks like every adventurer in Asaches is here," Derek observed.

"Is this normal?" David wondered. "Do this many people always turn out for a call to adventure?"

"I've seen some heavy turnouts for big contracts, but nothing like this," Felix said. "Either everyone thinks there's a huge payday attached to this job or they're all as desperate for work as we are."

"Either way, it's bad news for us," Erika said. "This is a lot of competition to overcome."

"First things first," Derek said. "We need to find someplace to stay tonight."

Felix took a draught of his beer. "I might have a solution."

"Here we are," Felix said, pausing in front of a small gatehouse, beyond which stood a tall manor house with a sharply sloped roof that sprouted no fewer than six brick chimneys. As they approached, Erika took note of a sign on the gatehouse, to the right of the gated entrance, a red oval encompassing the name PINCEFORTH HOUSE rendered in gilded lettering.

"You want us to stay in a brothel?" Erika said, mildly scandalized.

"This is a brothel?" Derek said, peering through the wrought iron fence that surrounded the property. The building sported a fresh paint job — ivory white with deep blue accents — and was absolutely immaculate from the top of its tallest chimney to the precisely trimmed hedges at its foundation. The house cast an elongated shadow across an emerald lawn, lush and meticulously manicured and absent of a single dandelion or patch of crabgrass.

"It's not a brothel," Felix said. "It's a house of hospitality."

"Can you pay the people who work here to fuck you?" Erika asked.

"If that's what you want, yeah."

"So it's a brothel."

"It's a *house of hospitality*," Felix insisted testily. "Come on."

Felix sauntered up to the gatehouse and offered a wave and a cheery greeting to the man behind the gate, a dark-skinned gent taller, broader, and thicker than Derek.

"Mavolo, my man," Felix said.

"Felix Lightfoot," Mavolo said humorlessly. He unlocked the gate and stepped out, his face stony, then embraced the thief as though embracing a brother, though a smile never appeared on his lips. "What brings you back to Woeste? You here because of the call?"

"That I am, and I hate to impose, but it appears every room in the city's spoken for."

"No imposition, my friend. You know you're always welcome at the Pinceforth House." Mavolo stepped aside and gestured toward the open gate. "You know the way. I'll see to your horses."

"Thanks, buddy. Appreciate it."

Felix led his friends down a path of crushed stone and up to the front door. He walked in without knocking or ringing the brass bell that hung to the right of the door. He paused in the mudroom to diligently wipe his boots on a mat of woven straw.

"Clean feet, people," he said. "Giuliana likes to keep her house tidy."

They did as told and followed Felix inside.

The foyer was warm and fragrant with the aroma of fresh flowers, and candles set into wall sconces filled the room with a cozy glow. The atmosphere, Derek thought, could only be described as welcoming. As they entered, a woman seated at a high writing desk near a closed set of pocket doors looked up from writing something in a leather-bound ledger. She blinked once and did a small double take, and then a broad smile spread across her face.

"Oh my Gods," she said. "Felix Lightfoot."

"Hi, Liana," Felix said.

Giuliana Pinceforth clapped her hands together, hopped down from her chair, and hustled across the foyer to welcome Felix with a warm hug. Her dwarven heritage was obvious in her height, or lack thereof, which forced Felix to bend down to return the embrace.

"Oh, my lad, my lad," she said, her voice hitching. "You've been gone too long."

"Life's kept me busy," Felix apologized. "How's my favorite lady doing?"

"Oh, well, quite well." She glanced past Felix as if only now noticing that he was not alone. "And who are these lovely people?"

"Liana, this is my partner, Derek Strongarm, my friends Erika Racewind and Winifred Graceword, and the kid is David, Derek's squire. We're in town for the call and I was hoping maybe you could put us up for the night? I hate to ask, but —"

"And why do you hate to ask, eh?" Giuliana said, giving Felix a playful swat. "Is my house no longer good enough for you, Mr. Lightfoot?"

"Your house will always be too good for me."

"As it so happens, you may well have the entire place to yourselves. Our regulars seem to be preoccupied with the considerable influx of visitors to our fair city — none of whom I'm about to let in unvetted, I'll have you know," she said to Felix's companions. "This is an exclusive house, open only to men and women of good standing."

"Then how did Felix get in?" David said half-jokingly.

"Felix Lightfoot is a good and true friend of the Pinceforth House. He is always welcome here," Giuliana declared, "as is anyone he calls friend in turn.

Ladies, gentlemen, my house is at your disposal."

With that, she crossed the foyer to push open the pocket doors and reveal a grand parlor, the central feature of which was a ring of loveseats and full-length couches artfully arranged around an unusually large, high table that, when called upon to do so, doubled as a small stage. Pairs of matching easy chairs populated the corners, providing somewhat more intimate seating for guests. Small end tables of hand-carved mahogany were strategically placed to provide guests with a place to set their drinks and pipes. Iron sconces wrought to resemble winged faeries in flight emerged from decorative pillars ringing the room, their hands cupping spherical candles that emitted a pleasantly sweet yet musky aroma. It was a stunning room.

So too were its occupants, a score of women and men in silken robes, all of whom were unbearably beautiful. They were human and elven and dwarven, tall and short, lean in build and generously curvaceous, blond and brunette and redheaded and clean-shaven, pale-skinned and dark. There were masculine women and feminine men and those who defied conventional concepts of gender. They stood, sat, and lounged artistically, as if posed that way to present the prettiest possible tableau for their clientele.

"Oh my," Winifred cooed breathlessly. "I had no idea your home was so...delightful."

One of the ladies, a lass with chestnut brown hair gathered in a loose knot atop her head, rose from a couch upholstered in lush red velvet, her eyes wide.

"Felix?" she gawked.

"Hey, Kat," Felix said, at which point the girl abandoned all pretense and bolted across the room to throw herself into Felix's arms with a delighted squeal.

"I thought something had happened to you," she said, her voice breaking. "I hadn't heard from you in so long."

"I'm sorry about that, kiddo. It's been a crazy year."

"Well, then, you have a lot to tell me, don't you?" Kat said. She stepped away from Felix, wiped the happy tears from her cheek, and put on her best, if dampest, hostess face. "You must be Derek. I'm Katarina."

"Hi, Katarina," Derek said, taking her proffered hand. He almost let it slip his friend had never before mentioned her, not even in passing, but instead offered a safe greeting of, "It's nice to meet you."

"My lovelies," Giuliana said, stepping forward to address her people, "for those who have never had the pleasure, this is Felix Lightfoot. He holds a special place of honor here at the Pinceforth House, and he and his friends shall be afforded every courtesy and indulgence during their stay. Kat, dear, why don't you see to their rooms?"

"Of course, madam," Kat said. "If you'll follow me, please?"

Kat led them out through an open side door into a small hallway and then up a lushly carpeted stairway to the second floor, along the way passing a series of paintings in the romantic style depicting scenes that stayed on the tasteful side of the line separating the erotic from the pornographic.

"Will any of you be sharing a room?" Kat asked.

"No," the company said as one.

Kat led them down the hall, toward the back of

the house, and opened a door seemingly at random. With a sweeping gesture, she said, "Derek, please have this room. You may leave your belongings in here and then join us down in the main parlor."

"Thanks," Derek said, gawping at a bedroom finer than any he'd ever stayed in before, finer even than his guest quarters in Castle Somevil-Duur. Tasteful wood paneling lined the walls, from which hung more of the suggestive artwork such as he'd seen along the stairs. A small brick fireplace, currently dark, sat near the foot of a stout four-poster bed, from which dripped heavy velvet privacy curtains. They were a perfect match for the curtains hanging in front of the room's sole window, which overlooked a backyard that dwarfed the front. A modest cottage — for a caretaker, Derek surmised — sat in the far corner of the property, tucked under an ancient, towering tree, the branches of which were curiously barren for this time of year. It was the sole spot of dreariness he'd seen in this island of opulence.

Derek stripped out of his armor — a brigantine coat that had been gifted to him by Lord Paradim of Somevil, along with assorted mismatched pieces for his arms and legs — and opted to change into fresh clothes from his pack instead of the plush fleece robe hanging from an open wardrobe. He sat on the edge of the bed to peel off his boots and socks and fell backwards into the comforter, caught unawares by the bed's luxurious thickness. He laid there for a while, debating whether to get up and join his friends or stay right where he was, in the middle of this gloriously downy-soft cloud.

With a sigh, he finished slipping into fresh socks, put his boots back on, and went downstairs. Winifred had already returned and was busy chatting up the hosts and hostesses, her attention flitting from person to person in giddy indecision.

An elven woman with tawny skin and ebony hair, marking her as Clan Alrive, approached Derek with a smile. "Mr. Strongarm, I'm Felisia Fairweather, the concierge," she said.

"Concierge?"

"Madam Pinceforth's second-in-command, if you will. I'm to see to your needs, whatever they may be. Shall we start with a drink?"

"Uh, sure. That'd be great."

"This way, please."

Felisia did not walk; she glided, her stride slow, smooth, and deliberate, like that of a jungle cat. The long, form-fitting silk dress she wore in place of the traditional hostess's robe swished back and forth about her feet, conjuring in Derek the image of a mermaid slipping through the water. She led Derek through the main parlor and into a small salon that served as the house's bar.

"As you can see, we have a wide variety of libations," Felisia said, understating the matter by a magnitude. Glass-front cabinets lined every wall, and bottles filled every cabinet. "Much of our selection is from local crafters but we have imported selections as well, if that's more to your liking. Tell me, Mr. Strongarm," she said, sliding behind the waist-high counter. "What's your pleasure?"

"For you to call me Derek, for a start."

"Derek," she purred. "You strike me as a basic, down-to-earth sort of man. One moment." She turned to the row of wooden kegs sitting behind the bar and poured a nipperkin's worth of a dark amber brew into a small pewter sampling cup, which she presented to Derek. "I think you'll find this barley wine to your tastes. It's strong, robust, straightforward but not simple..."

Derek sipped the drink, letting the flavors play on his tongue before swallowing. "Oh, yeah," he said.

"I'll have whatever he's having," Felix said, entering with Kat on his arm. He stepped up to the bar and leaned over to give Felisia a kiss on the cheek. "Congratulations are in order, I hear. Kat said you're the new concierge."

"I am, and thank you," Felisia said. She glanced past Felix to Erika, who did a double take in awe of the staggering selection of spirits. "You look like a woman who enjoys a good whiskey. Give me a moment to take care of these gentlemen."

Felisia poured the beers, and once the steins had been set down in front of her first customers, she emerged from behind the counter and fetched from a cabinet a glass bottle half-filled with a rich brown liquid.

"Twenty-five years old," she said as she poured out a dram. "Intense, has a good bite, surprisingly complex."

Erika took the glass, gave the whiskey a gentle swirl, sampled its bouquet, took a sip, and let out a tiny sigh.

"Can I get you something else, Miss Racewind?" Felisia asked. "Or some*one?*"

"All I want is to get off my feet and sit on something that isn't a horse," Erika said.

"This way, then. Derek, if you'd care to join us?"

"You coming?" Derek said to Felix.

"You go," Felix replied. "I promised Kat some stories."

"Okay. If I don't see you again tonight, make sure to be up nice and early tomorrow."

"Will do."

Felisia brought Derek and Erika to yet another parlor, this one small and intimate. Two easy chairs sat before a fireplace waiting to be lit. Felisia attended to that task, plucking a length of dried straw from a glass vase atop the mantle, lighting it on a nearby candle, and touching the flame to a mound of excelsior on the floor of the fireplace. It caught immediately and licked up to caress a pyramid of bone-dry logs.

"You two settle in," she said. "I'll be right back."

"I have to admit, this is not at all what I expected," Derek said, sitting. He sank into the cushions.

"No," Erika agreed, taking the other chair. She swirled her drink in its glass and took a hearty swig.

"My mother would have a fit if she knew I was spending the night in a brothel."

"She would?"

"Mom's a little old-fashioned."

"Does that mean you won't be, ah, *partaking?*"

"No, but that has nothing to do with it. You know me. I'm not really much of a...oh, what's the word? Hedonist?"

"Close enough."

"What about you?"

"Nope. I'm good. Besides, I want that bed all to myself."

A host entered, carrying a small tub of steaming water. "Miss Racewind? I'm Dale," the well-muscled man said, flashing a snow-white smile. "Felisia asked me to attend to you."

"Attend to me?" Erika watched with something akin to horror as Dale set the tub down and lowered himself to a knee before her, gently taking one leg in his hands.

"If I may?" he said.

Erika looked to Derek for guidance. He shrugged. "Okay," she said.

Dale's nimble fingers unlaced her boot and slipped it off. He then removed her hose, repeated the procedure with her other foot, then placed the tub in front of her.

"It's a hot mineral water bath," he said. "Please, go ahead."

Uncertain at first, Erika eased her feet into the water, the temperature of which could not have been more perfect — hot enough to be instantly soothing, not hot enough to scald.

"May I refresh your drink?" Dale asked. Erika handed him her half-empty glass. "Be right back."

"I don't know how anyone can live like this," Erika grumbled.

"Waiting on people hand and foot?" Derek said.

"No, getting waited on hand and foot. Being constantly fawned over and pampered and having your every whim indulged? It's awkward."

"You didn't get this kind of treatment when you worked for High Lord Ograine?"

"I was a servant, Derek. Yes, I had status, perks, and privileges most of the staff didn't, but at the end of the day, I was the help." She frowned. "I'd rather be a servant and work for a living than have everything literally handed to me on a silver platter."

"I get that," Derek said. "That reminds me, where's David?"

"Asleep, probably. As soon as he saw his room he dove right into bed."

"Good. I don't think a place like this has much to offer a kid like him."

"I think it might have too much to offer."

Dale, a fluffy white towel draped over one arm, appeared at Erika's shoulder and offered her a fresh whiskey. She mumbled a thank-you as she took the drink, hoping the host would consider his duties to her fulfilled and go away. Instead, he pulled up an ottoman and sat in front of her.

"How are you doing?" he asked, smiling his perfect smile.

"Fine," Erika said.

Dale lifted one leg out of the hot bath and gently patted it dry with the towel. "I'm told you're a professional adventurer," he said casually as he dried Erika's feet.

"Um, yes."

"You must have some exciting stories to tell."

"I guess." Dale laid the towel aside, grasped Erika by the ankle with one hand, and pressed the palm of the other into her instep. "Oh, no, wait, this really isn't necessaAAAAAHHH!"

"You okay over there?" Derek said.

"Uh-huh," Erika whimpered, sinking into her seat as Dale strategically applied pressure to knots and aches that, until this moment, she was unaware she had.

"People are always surprised by how much tension they keep in their feet," Dale remarked.

"*Gnyuhhh.*"

Derek, increasingly uncomfortable with the moans escaping Erika's lips, rose. "I think I'll leave you two to get better acquainted," he said.

"Don't you dare leave," Erika panted.

"Ask her about her weapon collection," Derek said to Dale. "She loves talking about that stuff."

"You're a dead man, Strongarm! A dead maAAAHHHAHAHA!"

Erika's cries followed Derek down the hall but, mercifully, faded by the time he returned to the main parlor. Winifred, he noticed, was gone, as were Felix and Kat.

"Just me, then," he said to himself, wandering back toward the bar, where Felisia greeted him with that suggestive smile of hers.

"Derek," she said.

"Mind if I hang out in here? The back parlor got a little, um...crowded."

"Please do. Do you need anything? A refill on your drink, or —?"

"No, I'm okay, thank you."

"This is your first time in a house of hospitality, isn't it?"

"Is it that obvious?"

"You seemed a little overwhelmed."

"I guess I am. I'm not used to such..."

"Extravagance?" Felisia suggested. "I understand. You strike me as a man of simple means."

"I grew up on a farm. We never had anything fancy, but we were happy."

"Tell me, Derek Strongarm, what led you to

leave your happy farm life to become an adventurer for hire? If I may ask?"

Derek couldn't prevent the frown from forming. "Circumstances beyond my control."

"I'm sorry, Derek. I didn't mean to make you uncomfortable," Felisia said, the apology coming not from a diligent hostess coddling a client but from a person expressing sincere regret.

"You didn't," Derek said. "It's just something I don't like to talk about."

"Then we won't talk about it. We'll find something more pleasant to discuss," Felisia said, adding with a smile ripe with intent, "or do."

"Actually, I wonder if you could tell me something."

"I'll try."

"The call for adventurers the city council put out. We don't know anything other than they're looking to hire people to recover something. Do you have any idea what the deal is? I imagine a woman like you has her ear to the ground."

"Oh, that I do," Felisia said as a mild boast, "though I fear I only know so much that might be of use. A few weeks ago, a band of raiders stormed Woeste. They caused no small amount of damage to the city center, and to the archives in particular."

"The archives?"

"A repository for documents and items of historical value."

"That's an odd target."

"Isn't it, though? Rumor has it something was stolen from the archives but no one seems to know what that something is."

"I doubt that. Someone always knows something."

"Very true. Then perhaps it would be better to say, anyone who knows anything is exercising considerable discretion. I wish I could be more helpful."

"Me too," Derek said, downing the last of his beer. "I should go to bed. It's going to be a long day tomorrow."

"If I might accompany you?" Felisia said. She led Derek back to his room, her arm entwined with his. "Do we part company here, Derek Strongarm, or would you like some companionship for the evening?"

Derek smiled. "I'm going to say we part company here."

"Alas," Felisia said, but she took no offense at his answer. "Will you and your companions be returning tomorrow?"

"I suppose that depends on how things go for us."

"For the sake of you and yours, I hope they go well." Felisia stood up on her toes and placed a soft kiss on Derek's lips. "That is in case I don't see you again."

She turned then and went downstairs, slowly, granting Derek ample opportunity to change his mind and call her back.

He considered it.

FOUR
The White Butcher Comes to Woeste

Derek awoke with the rising sun as he always did, but he lingered in the sinfully indulgent bed for as long as his bladder allowed, and even then, he got up grudgingly.

Once dressed, he crept downstairs and wandered around the empty parlors and hallways in search of a kitchen, which he eventually found in the far back of the house — along with a bleary-eyed Kat, who stood at a cast iron stove frying a thick slice of ham and an egg.

"Derek, good morning," she said cheerfully.

"Morning. Oh, that smells good."

"I can make some for you."

"Please, don't bother."

"It's no bother. It is my job to take care of our guests, after all."

"I'll be fine with some coffee, if you have any. And honestly, I'd be much happier if you treated me like a friend than a customer."

Kat smiled a smile free of intent or ulterior motive. "I can do that. Any friend of Felix's is a friend of mine." She gestured with her spatula to an iron pot sitting at the back of the stove. "Mugs are in the cabinet to your right."

"Thanks." He took one and filled it to capacity. "Can I ask you something?"

"Sure."

"What did Felix do to earn this kind of treatment? I've seen him get warm welcomes at other —" He paused and searched for a polite term. To refer to the Pinceforth House as a mere brothel struck him as insulting. " — establishments, but never like this."

"He's never mentioned me, has he?"

"No. I'm sorry."

"No need to be sorry. I understand why he might not want to talk about it. The circumstances weren't exactly pleasant."

Derek couldn't help feeling wounded at this. Felix knew all the sad details of his lowest moment; why wouldn't he share with him the tale of the Pinceforth House?

"Well?" Derek said.

"All I'll say is that Felix did this house, and me personally, a great service." Kat scooped the ham and egg up out of the skillet and slid it onto a plate, which she then handed to Derek. "If you want the details, you need to ask Felix. It's his story to tell."

Derek sat in the main parlor with his coffee and waited for his companions to rouse themselves. To his surprise, David was the first to arrive — wide awake, packed up, and ready to go. As Erika theorized, he'd had gone right to bed, fallen asleep immediately, and for the first time in a long time, slept the sleep of the just.

Felix joined them a few minutes later, after a quick visit to the kitchen for a cup of coffee and some dry toast. Soon after that, Winifred came downstairs with a bounce in her step and a wide grin on her face, which she ascribed to the attentiveness and generosity of her evening's companions.

"What's keeping Racewind?" David said.

"Maybe she found a friend for the night?" Winifred wondered.

"I doubt it," Derek said, though deep down he doubted his doubt. Dale had succeeded in eliciting from Erika moans of delight of one variety, after all; it wasn't outside the realm of possibility she'd enlisted him to inspire other ecstatic exclamations. "Maybe someone should go check on her?"

"Maybe *you* should go check on her," Felix said.

"Why me?"

"Because of the four of us, she's least likely to kill you."

Conceding that perfectly valid point, Derek headed up to Erika's room and knocked on her door. Receiving no response, he knocked a second time, more firmly, and braced to run away. He was no fool.

"What?" Erika snarled from within.

"Hey, it's me. You okay?"

"I'm asleep. Go away."

"You have to get up. We need to get going."

"You take care of it. I'm staying here."

"Erika, come on. Erika? Oh, for..." He opened the door and peeked in. From the doorway, he was unable to determine how many bodies were buried beneath the mound of quilts. "Erika?"

"*Whaaaaat?*" she groaned from somewhere within her cozy cocoon.

"It's morning," Derek said, daring to enter. "You have to get out of bed."

"No I don't. I like this bed. I like it more than I like you."

"Unfortunately, you can't audition for the city council from your bed."

"Bet I can."

"Erika," Derek sighed, "we're facing some stiff competition for this job and having High Lord Ograine's former personal bodyguard with us is going to carry a lot of weight. We need you there. Please get up."

"I hate you."

"I know you do. Now come on, up and at 'em."

"All right already!" She threw off her covers and jumped out of bed, as bare as the day she was born. "There! I'm out of bed! You happy now?"

"No!" Derek cried, slapping a hand over his eyes. "Gods, Erika!"

"You wanted me out of bed, I'm out of bed. Now get out so I can get dressed." Erika spun Derek around and aimed him toward the door.

"Oh, sure, *now* you don't want me seeing you naked. I do not get you."

"You're not meant to. Go. I'll be down in a minute."

Derek felt his way into the hallway and went back downstairs. "She overslept," he reported. "She'll be right down."

"Uh-huh," Felix said, smirking. "She had someone with her, didn't she?"

"No."

"Come on, man, you're beet red. You walked in on her, didn't you?"

"She was alone," Derek insisted.

"Whatever you say."

Erika joined them presently, dressed and armed and armored. "Give me a minute," she said as she fought to whip her hair, a frazzled spray of white, into its customary braid.

"Turn around," Derek said.

"Why?"

"Because otherwise we'll be here all morning. Turn around." She did as asked. Derek finger-combed through her severe case of bed head and with practiced speed and ease wove her hair into a tight braid. "There you go."

"Huh. Nice job," Erika said, admiring his handiwork. "Where did you learn to do that?"

"I grew up with three sisters. I also know how to lace a bodice and hem a skirt."

"Well, if I ever need you to do anything like that —"

"We'll know you've lost your mind and need us to put you down like a mad dog," David said. "Can we go now?"

"Not quite yet," Kat said, interposing herself between the companions and the foyer. "You don't get to sneak out of my life twice, Felix Lightfoot."

"Wouldn't dream of it," he said, taking Kat in his arms. She held the thief tightly, whispered something into his ear, and briefly redoubled her embrace before reluctantly letting him go.

As they filed out, Kat seized Derek by the arm

and said to him, as if demanding from him a solemn oath, "You keep Felix safe."

"I always do," he said.

Satisfied, she nodded and released Derek to the day.

After taking breakfast at a nearby inn crowded with fellow adventurers, the company proceeded into the very heart of Woeste, to city hall itself, a tall, stately structure constructed of granite blocks each as high and wide as David was tall. Turrets stood at the building's four corners; a bell tower rose up in the center of its front façade; and a magnificent dome capped the central mass. A sprawling open courtyard sitting in its morning shadow was already buzzing with activity as adventurers from across Asaches gathered to make their final preparations and to scout the competition.

"Wow," Derek marveled, taking in the crowd. "I haven't seen a turnout for a call like this in some time."

"Don't mistake quantity for quality, my friend," Felix said, unconcerned. "Besides, you know how these things work."

"I don't," Erika said.

"Nor I. I've never participated in a call to adventure," Winifred said. "What happens, exactly?"

"Someone will lay out the job in detail — what they want us to do, what they'll pay, so on — at which point half the people here will leave because it's too dangerous or doesn't pay enough," Derek said. "After that, the contractor will call us in for a quick face-to-face. Sometimes they'll hire a party outright, sometimes they'll try to get their prospects into a bidding war to knock the reward down..."

"There ain't gonna be no biddin' war," a tower of a man said, looming behind Erika. He grinned, displaying a mouth full of brown teeth (well, not *full* of them; his mouth held teeth and gaps in equal numbers). Relatively fresh scar tissue, pink and smooth, crinkled about his eyes. "My mates and me're gettin' this job, see? You be wise to clear out now, save youselfs the humiliation."

"Right, I forgot about this part," Felix said to Erika. "This is when the blowhards and braggarts go around trying to scare off the competition. Would you care to do the honors?"

"Absolutely," Erika said, turning to face her would-be tormentor — who blanched at the sight of the elf and staggered back, his mouth slack in mortal terror.

"The — you — you're —" he stuttered before at last blurting out, "the White Butcher! The White Butcher!" and plowing through the throng like a renegade bull — a bull that screamed like a small child startled by an exceptionally large spider.

"What the hell just happened?" a nonplussed Erika said.

"I don't know, but I'm going to find out," Felix said, breaking off. "Stay here."

"I always knew you were scary, Racewind," David said, "but that was impressive even for you."

"The White Butcher?" Derek said.

"No idea," Erika said, now keenly aware that every other adventurer in sight was staring at her, many with curiosity, some with fear. A woman in a rusty mail hauberk, half her hair missing to heavy scar tissue — the aftermath of a severe burn — made brief eye contact with Erika before skittering away. When Felix returned minutes later, smiling excitedly, a wide moat of empty space had formed around his friends.

"You beautiful, bloodthirsty bitch, I could kiss you," he declared.

"What'd you find out?" Derek asked.

"Oh, you are going to love this. We have in our presence none other than the White Butcher of Castle Somevil-Duur," Felix said with a grand gesture of presentation.

"I'm the what?" Erika said.

In making his gentle inquiries among the other adventurers, Felix had learned that mingled among their numbers were assorted mercenaries who had participated in the ill-fated Siege of Castle Somevil-Duur. They'd witnessed Erika's brutal slaughter of the invading force's leader, the assassin Ruined Isys, and by some perverse miracle, escaped the subsequent fiery holocaust that consumed the throne room and so many of their compatriots. In the days and weeks following that massacre, the survivors spoke in fearful, guarded whispers of the demon wearing an elven woman's skin who had rained hellfire down on Ruined Isys's mercenary army and continued to hunt them in their nightmares.

"Um, excuse me? Point of order?" David said, raising a finger. "I was the one who rained flaming death down on those mercenaries, not Erika."

"Beside the point, kid," Felix said. "Erika's the one with the reputation, and it's literally scaring people off. Guys, this is our ace in the hole and we need to play the hell out of it."

"Assuming Erika doesn't mind being portrayed

as an unstoppable hell-spawned killing machine," Derek said.

Erika shrugged. "Whatever."

At Felix's insistence, Derek worked up a pitch that emphasized Erika's credentials and quietly rehearsed his speech until a man in fine gray waistcoat, a purple stole of office draped across his shoulders, appeared on the back steps of city hall.

"I think it's almost show time." As Felix said this, he watched an old man in scholar's robes bustle up to the vested man and engage in a brief but vigorous argument. The city official ended the row by leaning in and poking an emphatic finger into the old man's chest. He used that same finger to dismiss the old man, who stormed off with a scowl etched deep in his features.

"Ladies and gentlemen! If I may have your attention!" the vested man cried. The courtyard fell silent. "I am Benson Traymon, city councilor, and I've been charged with conducting preliminary interviews. I'll begin by providing you with the details of the job for which we are hiring. If you find neither the job nor the pay to your liking, or I dismiss you, please leave immediately. Thank you in advance for your cooperation."

Traymon withdrew from a pocket a folded piece of parchment. He consulted it for a minute, nodded to himself, and then folded it up and tucked it away.

"Recently, our fair city was besieged by a band of raiders, about twenty people strong," he began, his voice loud and clear and each word precisely enunciated, like a classically trained stage actor delivering his lines to the cheap seats in the back of the theater. "We thought this a simple raid, but as we assessed the damage, we learned that the raiders had stolen from our city archives an item of great historical significance to Woeste: an iron mask that once belonged to our last warden, Lord Ulysses Kilnmar. While its monetary value is negligible, it is a truly irreplaceable piece of our heritage, and the city council is willing to pay five thousand gold for its recovery."

"Five thousand?" David said.

"Wait for it," Felix said.

"We believe the raiders have established a base camp west of the city," Traymon said, adding a dramatic pause before concluding with, "in the Gray Necropolis, approximately one day's journey through the Monolith Forest."

A murmur rippled through the gathering. Out of the corner of his eye, Derek spotted a party of four warriors, two men and two women, huddle together. One of the men shook his head, and then the quartet made a quiet exit.

"Looks like the location's a deal breaker for some folks," Derek said. "Don't suppose anyone knows anything about the Gray Necropolis or the Monolith Forest?"

"Heard the names a few times during my last visit," Felix said. "Lots of rumors and legends about them. Gods know what's true."

Traymon gave the gathered adventurers a few minutes to arrive at a decision, one way or the other, before continuing. "Please remain in your groups," he said to the remaining parties. "I'll meet with you all in turn."

"What do you think?" Derek asked Felix.

"Not sure. The over-under feels a little wonky."

"The over-under?" Winifred said.

"It's a rough formula adventurers use to determine how legit a job is," Derek explained. "If it feels like the client is offering to grossly over- or underpay you based on the stated risk and/or value of the item they want you to recover, chances are something's off. They might be downplaying the danger or the value of the objective."

"Considering what we know of the job, do you think five thousand is too high or too low a reward?"

"Not sure," Felix said, "but my gut tells me our man Traymon is withholding info."

Over the course of the morning, Traymon worked his way through the prospects with a speed and efficiency not normally found in bureaucrats. He spent no more than three minutes with any given group, and the company found their optimism growing as Traymon ruthlessly winnowed down the field of candidates, sending away six parties for every one he directed toward city hall.

At last, Traymon reached our heroes, whom he surveyed with a cool, dispassionate, and critical eye. "And who might you be?" he inquired.

"I'm Derek Strongarm. This is my squire, David, and these are my partners: Felix Lightfoot; Winifred Graceword of the Clan Lyth, formally of Temple Ven, sister-in-service to the goddess Felicity; and Erika Racewind of the Clan Boktn, former bodyguard to High Lord Ograine —" He paused for effect. "— the White Butcher of Castle Somevil-Duur."

Traymon arched an eyebrow. "I see." He stepped up to Erika. "Would you be the same Erika

Racewind who accompanied our late Lord Randolph Ograine into Hesre?"

"I would," Erika said, adding with a nod toward her friends, "and they accompanied me."

The other eyebrow went up. "If you'll proceed to the council chamber," he said.

Felix waited until Traymon had moved on before pumping a victorious fist. "Yes!"

"Easy, pal, that was only the first hurdle," Derek said.

"Come on, man, you saw the look on his face. We got this job locked up tight."

"Far be it from me to dampen anyone's optimism, but pride goeth before a fall," Winifred warned.

"Uh-uh. No way. We got this in the bag."

Felix reiterated his supreme confidence upon entering the council chamber and beholding the remaining competition thus far, five other parties of varying sizes and compositions. They in turn leveled critical gazes at the companions, taking their measure before returning to whatever conversation had previously occupied their attention.

They moved toward the center of the council chamber, which occupied the domed heart of city hall. Derek turned in a slow circle to take it all in. Rings of bench seating rose up at a steep angle from the edge of the main floor to the outer wall, much like the seating one might find in a coliseum. A low stage marked the front of the chamber, and upon this stage stood a series of seven lecterns, one of which was curiously short.

"That's what's known as a Blusterer's Foil," David said, noting the stage setup. "The concept is to keep meetings and hearings brief by forcing the council to stand. They're less likely to indulge in lengthy speeches or deliberations if they're not allowed to sit."

"Huh," Derek said, reexamining the stage through the lens of this new information. The squat lectern must be for a dwarven councilor, he reasoned — and he was instantly proven wrong when the council strode out onto the stage.

"Oh, shit," Felix said. "Shit. Shit!"

"What is it? What's wrong?" Winifred asked.

"Remember what you said about pride going before a fall?" Felix said miserably.

Derek followed his friend's gaze to the man leading the procession, a man with a hard face and hard eyes and a hard, humorless smile. His flyaway white hair would have presented as comical on anyone else, but on him, it lent an air of madness. His attendant, a tall woman with a warrior's build, pushed his wheeled chair across the stage and placed him behind the short lectern, then faded back a step to assume a protective position.

"Shit," Felix cursed again, pulling up the hood of his cloak and turning his back to the council as its infirm member scanned the prospects.

"Talk to me, Lightfoot," Erika said, "what's wrong?"

"The guy in the chair? We have a history."

"How bad of a history?"

"Bad," is all Felix said.

"It's okay, we can work around it," Derek said. "He's one man. If we can win over the other six, we're good, so let's focus on that."

Traymon returned, the seventh and final band of adventurers in tow, and then joined his fellows on the stage. A silver-haired woman wearing a stole of office adorned with three gold stripes at either end stepped up to the center lectern and rapped on it with her fist.

"Your attention, please," she said. "I am Councilor Belinda Greave, and on behalf of the city council, I welcome you all to Woeste, and I thank you for your response to our call."

Felix took one last look around at the competition. "Yeah. Yeah, okay," he said. "We got this. These people have nothing on us. We'll ignore Folstoy and focus on dazzling the other councilors. We got this."

"Councilor Traymon," Greave said. "Are these all the prospects?"

"They are, madam," Traymon replied.

"They most certainly are not, my good woman!" crowed a spritely man dressed in a mélange of fool's motley and a herald's formal livery. He strode into the dead center of the chamber, a red velvet shoulder cloak fluttering in his wake. He offered the council a deep bow and then raised a brass bugle to his lips and sounded a fanfare that rang off the stone walls. The tune acted as a summons, signaling the arrival of five new players to the unfolding game.

"You have got to be fucking kidding me," Felix spat.

"Now what?" Erika said.

"We're screwed is what."

With a resigned sigh, Derek said, "It's the Noble Blades."

FIVE
The Fine Art of Negotiation

They paraded in, spread out about the chamber, and struck poses so dynamic they would have made a portrait artist weep with joy.

The gaunt, pallid man in black robes cradled a gnarled wooden staff topped with a polished human skull, which he caressed with long, spindly fingers. Blood-red gems set into the eye sockets flickered as if lit from within by a candle flame. Two Sylvyns — an uncommon race rumored to be descended from faerie folk, characterized by slender, ram-like horns sprouting from their foreheads — stood back to back, mirroring each other. Both wore forest green acolytes' robes similar in style to Winifred's, but theirs were embroidered with stylized ivy tendrils and mysterious runes. The male half of the couple twiddled his fingers, producing a soft blue flame that danced and crackled merrily, like a campfire. With a musical laugh and a toss of her curly blond hair, the Sylvyn woman conjured a shimmering sphere of prismatic light in the palm of her hand. A northern bearded lynx, a species not quite large enough to be a proper big cat, settled in at her feet. A golden-skinned young woman wearing leather armor and a cocky smirk drew two matching rapiers and expertly windmilled them back and forth in a figure eight formation. The bard introduced them in turn as Vladimir Fullmoon, Master of the Dark Arts; Adam and Astra of the Great Green and their constant companion Furl; and Kelly Nightshadow, rogue extraordinaire. The bard — Mason Goldtones, by name — ceded center stage to an ebon-skinned dwarf dressed in golden plate armor and brandishing a warhammer as long as he was tall, which he planted on the floor like an explorer planting his flag of claim on a newly discovered land.

"And last but certainly not least, the strong and wise leader of the Noble Blades, the Hammer of Justice, the Living Avatar of the God Victor," Mason said, building to a nigh-orgasmic crescendo, "Darrus Stakar!"

Mason blew a shrill fanfare. As if on cue — which it was — Darrus raised his hammer overhead and let loose a bellow like a lion's roar. Kelly scraped her swords together, eliciting a steely *SHRING!* akin to a falcon's screech. The flames over Adam's fingers leapt to five times their height, and Astra's sphere burst into a spray of rainbow colors. Vladimir raised his staff and glowing crimson mist poured out of the skull's bejeweled eyes and swirled about his feet. And Furl, being a cat, sat there looking bored with the whole thing.

A near-perfect, awestruck silence fell upon the chamber — near-perfect, save for Winifred's appreciative applause.

"Stop it," Erika said, slapping Winifred's hands down. "What the hell was *that?*"

"A sign from the Gods we weren't meant to take

this job," Felix moped.

The other finalists shared this opinion. They slunk out of the chamber, heads bowed in defeat, until only the Noble Blades and our heroes remained.

"Seriously, who are these people?" Erika said.

"They're something of a legend in the adventuring community," Derek said. "They recovered the Crown of Yrgstall from the Crypt of Ahmo-Tyf, discovered the Lost City of Horth, slew Paartgrnang the Great Dragon..."

"They allegedly saved the world once, too," Felix said.

"Allegedly," Erika said.

"Things like that can be hard to prove," Derek conceded, "but everything else is stone-cold fact. They earned their reputation."

"So have we. And I didn't come all this way to give up to a bunch of pretentious goofs who know how to put on a flashy dog-and-pony show."

"We should see this through," Derek said, though his confidence in their success was no longer what it was.

"Well!" Greave said. "It seems that our decision has been made that much easier. Unless," she said, looking at Derek, "your party also wishes to withdraw from consideration?"

"No, councilor, we do not," Derek said, drawing a chuckle from Kelly Nightshadow.

"Very well, then. Let's proceed. Councilor Folstoy?"

"Councilor," Rheagan Folstoy said. "As you already know, a band of approximately twenty raiders attacked Woeste last month and stole from our city archives an iron mask belonging to Lord Ulysses Kilnmar, an item of little monetary value but rich in historical and sentimental value."

An irate snort caught Felix's attention. He followed the sound back to that same old man he saw bickering with Traymon, sitting in the public seating, his brow knit and his mouth bent in an unhappy scowl.

"One of our city outposts reported spotting the raiders emerging from the —" Folstoy paused, ever so briefly, upon spying Felix. He cleared his throat and continued, his mirthless smile taking on a wolfish edge. "Excuse me. One of our city outposts reported spotting the bandits emerging from the Monolith Forest, and members of our city guard pursued the raiders back to the edge of the forest."

"And why didn't your city guard pursue them *into* the forest?" Erika asked.

"Because the Monolith Forest is a cursed place," Councilor Dunstan Mock said. "Only the dead live among those trees. No living thing has ever gone into the Monolith Forest and come out again."

"Except for the raiders," David said.

"Um. Well, yes, I suppose that's —"

"And technically the dead don't *live* anywhere; they're *dead*."

This drew an appreciative laugh from Darrus. "Well observed, lad," he said, his words tinged with a faint lilt of indeterminate origin.

"Yes. Anyway —" Mock said.

"If your guard didn't follow the raiders past the edge of the forest, how do you know for sure they're hiding in the Gray Necropolis?" Erika said.

Mock's lips pressed into a tight line.

"We don't," Greave answered on Mock's behalf, "but there is only the one known path in or out of the necropolis. To exit by any other means would require blazing a new trail. I admit the forest's mystique might be a little — um, overstated, but it is a dangerous place. The raiders would be wiser to fortify their position within the necropolis in case anyone was brave enough to challenge the forest."

"What about the necropolis itself? What else is there?"

"Nothing. It's a dead city," Mock said as if speaking to a child.

"But you don't know that for a fact."

"It's an isolated, abandoned ruin. Places like that attract wild animals, Hruks, trolls," Derek said.

"Exactly. We have no idea what we could be walking into. If your people won't even go into the forest, much less the necropolis —"

"Young lady," Mock said indignantly. "I do not support this endeavor, not in the least —"

"You've been abundantly clear on that point," Greave said, mostly to herself.

" — but your line of inquiry is, frankly, disrespectful and unwarranted."

"Unwarranted? You're asking us to risk our lives," Erika countered. "I'll ask as many questions as I have to."

"Which is perfectly reasonable," Greave said. "Don't you agree, Dunstan?"

"I suppose," Mock grumbled.

"How's the over-under looking now?" Erika asked Felix on the sly.

"Pretty damn sketchy," Felix said.

"Seventy-five hundred," Darrus said.

"I'm sorry?" Greave said.

"The reward is now seventy-five hundred, for the added risk. As our contemporaries so astutely noted, there is no guarantee we'll find the raiders — therefore the mask — in the necropolis. If they are there to be found, I swear by my hammer Foecrusher —"

"Oh, Gods, he named his fucking warhammer," Felix muttered.

" — that the Noble Blades will find them, slay them, and recover that which is yours — for seventy-five hundred gold."

"One moment, please," Greave said before the seven men and women of the city council gathered into a tight circle. They returned to their lecterns after a minute or so of quiet discussion, and Greave announced, "Seven thousand five hundred gold for the successful recovery of the mask."

"And half that if we return without the mask, for our effort."

Greave looked to each of her fellow councilors, who nodded in return. "Agreed. Are there any further questions?"

"None," Darrus said. "For now."

"Very well. Now, as we are all well aware of the Noble Blades' reputation, let's hear from you," Greave said to Derek. "What have you to offer for credentials?"

Derek delivered his introductions as he did for Councilor Traymon, and the reaction to Erika's *curriculum vitae* drew similar reactions from the council — and, Derek noticed, from the Noble Blades.

"My. It seems we have an embarrassment of riches," Greave said. "Two most excellent choices before us — such a wonderful dilemma to have! I suspect our deliberations will take a while. I suggest you all take your ease at one of our local taverns and return in — let's say two hours?"

"Of course, Madam Councilor," Darrus said with a bow. "Come, my friends!"

The Noble Blades departed with as much pomp and circumstance with which they entered, complete with a jaunty recessional tune from Mason Goldtones' bugle.

"I'd ask how we could possibly follow that," Derek said, "except we have to actually follow that."

The quintet stopped at the first tavern they found, a small establishment two minutes' walk from city hall. As it was midday, the tavern was quiet and almost completely empty, and so the barkeep and the two servers present were happy to lavish extra attention on such a fine group of paying customers. They sat, and once the important business of ordering drinks and food had been dispensed with, Derek got down to the other important business of the moment.

"You going to tell us what the story is with you and that councilor?" he said to Felix.

"We have a history is all," he replied.

"I'll say. I saw the look he gave you," Erika said. "And you said no one in Woeste wanted to kill you."

"I thought he'd left town! After what happened —" Felix let out an exasperated sigh. "The last time I was in Woeste was for a job. Folstoy was the client."

"What was the job?"

"Nothing especially legal. Let's leave it at that. Anyway, Folstoy was so pleased with my performance he decided a bonus was in order, so he took me to the Pinceforth House." Felix folded his hands on the table and bowed his head. "Folstoy tended to get...aggressive with his companions. They had people who catered to those tastes, but she wasn't one of them."

"You mean Kat," Derek said.

Felix nodded. "Folstoy had a little too much to drink that night so he was worse than usual. I heard Kat screaming from down the hall. I ran into her room and pulled him off her. Unfortunately, I was a lot drunker than he was. He got in a lucky shot that put me on the floor. He kicked the shit out of me pretty good before Mavolo got involved."

"Kat said you did her a great service," Derek said, recalling his conversation of that morning. "Her and the Pinceforth House."

"Yeah, but that wasn't it. See, Folstoy wasn't a city councilor back then, but he had a lot of influence in town. When he threw his weight around, not too many folks were inclined to get in his way. When he was banned from the Pinceforth House, he vowed to run it into the ground by any means necessary. Giuliana isn't easily intimidated, but Folstoy had her seriously scared. She thought she was going to lose everything."

"What did you do?" Winifred asked.

Felix straightened up and put on a smile that fooled no one. "I didn't do a thing. Poor Folstoy had an accident. Fell down some stairs and broke his back. After that, he forgot all about pursuing his vendetta against Giuliana."

"He obviously hasn't forgotten about you," Erika said, unsure whether pride in or vexation toward the thief was in order.

"Doesn't matter. We lost this job the minute the Blades walked in," Felix lamented.

"I disagree," Derek said. "I think we have a good shot. Even the Blades were impressed with us."

"They're not the ones we need to impress."

With time to kill, the party lingered over their drinks and did their best to avoid agonizing over a decision that was well and truly out of their hands. With a half hour to go, they left the tavern and returned to city hall square, where they found Mason Goldtones standing before a sizable crowd, enthusiastically acting out one of his compatriots' many heroic adventures. The stars of the drama, the Noble Blades, kept a respectable distance from the performance lest they steal away the audience's attention.

"Ho, fellows!" Darrus called out as the companions tried to slip by unnoticed. He ambled up to them, his warhammer slung over one shoulder, his armor glowing under the midday sun. He craned his head to meet Derek's eyes. "You're a big 'un, and that's no lie."

"Everyone's a big 'un to you," Felix sassed.

"Nor is that!" Darrus laughed. "We never had a chance to properly meet. Darrus Stakar. You said your name was Strongarm?"

"Yes, sir, Derek Strongarm," Derek said, shaking the dwarf's hand.

"How funny. Stakar means 'strong arm' in old dwarvish. I'd say fate brought us both here, were I one to believe in fate — which I am not."

"Can't say I am either."

"Good for you. I just wanted to say, in all sincerity, I hope there'll be no hard feelings between us when the council hands down its decision."

"Don't you think you're being a little presumptuous?" Erika said. "The council could award the contract to us."

"We're the Noble Blades, lass. We haven't lost a job — or failed to complete a quest — in nearly ten years."

"There's a first time for everything."

Darrus grinned. "I suppose there is at that. Then let me say, may the best team win. Good day, gentlemen, ladies."

Felix resisted the urge to deliver a running kick to the departing dwarf's armored backside. "Arrogant bastard," he said.

"Let it go," Derek said. "There's nothing we can do now but wait."

And wait they did — in a foyer in city hall, away from Mason's one-man show — for a half hour that felt three times as long.

The two parties gathered again in the central chamber, each keeping a respectful distance from the other. The council members took their spots at their lecterns, their faces betraying nothing.

"Ladies, gentlemen, we have a proposition for you," Greave began. "We discussed your respective qualifications quite vigorously, and it is the consensus of this council that either of you would excel in executing this contract. Therefore, we propose a contest."

"A contest?" Derek said.

"Both parties depart for the Gray Necropolis in the morning. Whichever one returns with the mask will receive the full reward." Greave spread her hands. "What say you?"

"Ha! And I thought this adventure couldn't get

any more interesting!" Darrus boomed. "On behalf of the Noble Blades, we accept."

"Mr. Strongarm?"

"Could you give us a minute, please?"

Greave nodded her consent. A minute later, she received her answer.

"No," Derek said.

"Excuse me?" Greave said.

"Afraid of some healthy competition, are you?" Kelly taunted.

"Oh, come on. You can't possibly be that naïve," Felix said. "They're playing us. They're basically hiring both parties but offering to pay only one. They're getting twice the labor for half the cost."

"I think you mean twice the labor for the same cost," David said.

"Will you shut up? I'm trying to make a point."

"And you've made it, Mr. Lightfoot, but we're game nevertheless," Darrus said. "Your people versus mine, winners take all."

"Or, just a thought here, we could all go and split the reward fifty-fifty," Derek suggested.

Darrus chuckled. "And where would the fun be in that?"

"No deal, then," Derek said to the council. "You want both parties? Then pay both parties. Otherwise, pick one."

"Very well," Greave said. "We hereby award the contract to the Noble Blades."

To their credit, the Noble Blades did not openly exult in their triumph. They accepted the judgment with a humble thank-you bow to Greave and a respectful nod of acknowledgement to their now-former competition, and then followed Greave out of the chamber to finalize the details of the contract.

"Well, this was a huge waste of time," David said.

"Not now, David," Derek said.

"I know this isn't the outcome we'd hoped for," Winifred said, her sunny demeanor a little cloudier than usual, "but we should be proud of ourselves nevertheless. We gave the Noble Blades a run for their money."

"Please don't mention money," Felix said.

"How quickly fortunes can reverse, eh, Felix?" Folstoy said, rolling up to the group with the assistance of his attendant, Ilfreda — who, upon closer inspection, revealed herself to be an unusually burly elf of the Clan Lyth. A rapier hung at her hip.

"You're loving this, aren't you?"

"I take no particular pleasure in it, no." Folstoy absently ran a hand over his hair, which ran thin at the crest of his forehead. "I'm rather disappointed, to tell the truth."

"Horseshit you are."

"I am. I voted in favor of awarding you and your little band here the contract. I'm saddened you didn't get it. Truly."

Derek couldn't help but ask, "Why?"

"Because I knew you'd fail — miserably so."

"Oh, you devious son of a bitch," Felix said. "You didn't think we'd survive the job."

"I have no idea what you're talking about. I had every confidence you would recover the mask." Folstoy's smile vanished. "But, as we both know all too well, *accidents do happen.* Good day, Felix."

Folstoy gestured to Ilfreda, who dutifully pushed him out of the chamber.

"I don't know about the rest of you, but I feel a powerful need to get rip-roaring drunk," Felix said. "And maybe laid. But mostly drunk."

"Yeah," Derek sighed. "I can get behind that."

They trudged out, heads low, morale lower, and as they exited the council chamber, Felix cast a glance back as if to give the room itself his best evil eye, only to spot that same old man in the scholar's robes sitting there, fists clenched atop his thighs, his eyes narrowed to dark slits.

SIX
An Uncomfortable Evening with Unwanted Guests

Our dejected, demoralized heroes ate a somber dinner at the same tavern at which they ate lunch and then — lacking a better option and in dire need of comfort — returned to the Pinceforth House. Giuliana was delighted to see them again, but when she learned the circumstances of their return, she transformed into an aggrieved mother hen.

"Oh, the nerve of some people," she fumed. "Parading in as pretty as you please and stealing a job out from under you!"

"They earned the job fair and square," Derek said. The admission was bitter on his tongue.

"Earned it? Ha! They duped a bunch of ignorant bureaucrats with hoopla and hyperbole is what they did! There's no reason for all that showing off if they're so blessed wonderful. You mark my words," Giuliana said, thrusting a finger at Derek, "anyone who has to puff themselves up that much is hiding how bloody weak they are."

"Come on, Liana, no need to get yourself worked up," Felix said.

Giuliana harrumphed and shooed her guests out of the foyer with a sweeping gesture. "To the bar with you. Have a drink or five. It won't make your woes go away but it'll help you to ignore them for a spell."

"I just want to go to bed," David said.

"Come on then, my son, I'll see to it," Giuliana said, ushering David upstairs while the others heeded her sage advice and filed into the salon to begin the nightlong process of drowning their sorrows. Felisia rightfully intuited their day had not been a successful one and promised to keep the beer and liquor flowing steadily.

"These Noble Blades. They sound rather pretentious," she said, filling for Derek a large stein with barley wine.

"That's one word for them. We had this, man," Felix said, thumping a fist on the bar. "We had this in the bag until those sons of bitches showed up."

"Well, they did, so there's no point complaining about it," Erika said.

"You're awfully calm about this."

"That doesn't mean I'm not pissed off, but there's nothing to do about it."

Felix tossed back a shot glass filled to capacity with whiskey. It burned pleasantly in the back of his throat. "We could steal the job back."

"And how would we do that?"

"By finding the mask first. We head out now, haul ass to the necropolis, turn the place upside-down as fast as we can, and recover the mask before the Blades."

"But the city council doesn't have a contract with us," Winifred noted. "They'd be under no obligation to pay us."

"They would be if they wanted their trinket back."

"Or they could reclaim what is rightfully theirs, pay you nothing, and hold you liable for paying the Noble Blades the reward they were promised," Felisia said. "The law would not be on your side."

"Oh, sure, ruin a great theory with an ugly fact, why don't you?"

"Besides, it wouldn't be ethical or professional," Derek said. "Look, I'm not happy about how this played out either, and I'm not saying what the Blades did wasn't a little underhanded, but poaching a contract is *much* worse and you know it."

"Fine," Felix sneered.

"I think we should put this behind us and look toward the future," Winifred said. "This isn't a defeat, it's a setback, and we've certainly overcome those before."

"I hate it when I agree with you," Erika said.

"I know."

"Where's Dale? He does more than feet, right?"

"Oh, yeah," Felix said. "Man's hands are *magic*."

"Good, because my entire body is one big knot." Erika sucked down half her drink and held her glass out for a top-off before stalking off in search of her favorite masseur.

"And I believe I am going to turn in for the evening," Winifred said, excusing herself. "As enticing as good drink and good company sounds, a good night's sleep sounds better, under the circumstances."

"And what can we do for you to make your evening a little more pleasant?" Felisia asked the men.

"What would you like?"

"To never ever again see the Noble Blades' smug faces," Felix said.

"That, love, is the one thing I cannot provide," Giuliana said as she entered the salon, her lips fixed in a sour pucker. "Guess who just walked in looking to celebrate?"

"Oh, come on! Really?!" Felix shouted toward the ceiling trusting the Gods would hear his grievance through the many floors above him.

"I'm going to turn them away," Giuliana said. "I won't have the likes of them in my house."

"Please don't," Derek said.

"No, please do," Felix said.

"We appreciate the gesture, Giuliana, we do, but we don't want you turning away business on our account."

"Yes we do."

"No, we don't. She's already put herself out for us. Asking her to turn away paying customers would be a lousy way to thank her for her hospitality."

Felix released an exasperated hiss of a sigh. He waved Giuliana off, unable to speak. A second shot of whiskey did nothing to loosen his throat — or to help douse the angry fire burning in his chest at the sight of the Noble Blades sweeping in with their customary air of self-styled pageantry.

"Let the drink flow! Let love and laughter fill the air! Let merriment reign!" Mason Goldtones cried, punctuating each sentence with a chord from an antique lute. "For the Noble Blades have arrived!"

"And we get to listen to that horseshit all night," Felix said. "Thanks, Derek."

"Oh, and look who else is here," Kelly said, strutting up to the men. "I thought you said this was a top-notch establishment, Darrus, but it looks to me like they'll let *anyone* in."

"Here now, none of that," Darrus scolded. "If Madam Pinceforth calls these fine men guests, then they are undoubtedly people of quality."

"Not *high* quality —"

"Mind your tongue, Kelly," Darrus said, his buoyant demeanor clouding. "I won't have you picking fights, not tonight and not here. We are honored guests and shall behave as such. Understood?"

Kelly rolled her eyes but said nothing more.

"My apologies lady, gentlemen," Darrus said to the room. "It was neither my intent nor my desire to foul anyone's mood."

"Too late," Felix said, brushing past the dwarf.

"Leaving so soon? How sad," Astra of the Great Green said with a pout that caught Felix's attention and held it fast. Her features were at once angular yet delicate, her eyes dark yet bright, like those of a doe. "I thought us all friends here, yes? I think you a friend. My husband thinks you a friend. Furl thinks you a friend."

Felix glanced down to see the lynx snaking between his legs in a continuous figure eight, his purr loud and strong.

"Furl's a good judge of character, is he?" Felix said.

"He is."

"The night is young. Further friendships may yet be found," Adam said, smiling prettily. "Friendships, and perhaps more."

"You never know," Felix said, taking care not to step on Furl as he passed.

"That's right. Keep walking," Vladimir said in a coarse whisper.

"Vladimir, I suggest you follow Adam and Astra's sterling example and dedicate yourself to making friends rather than enemies," Darrus said. "This is a house of peace."

"Indeed it is. I'm Felisia Fairweather, the concierge," she said, emerging from behind the bar to give her new guests a proper welcome. "If there is anything you need of us, ask and I'll see to it."

"Miss Felisia," Darrus said, taking her hand and bowing. "If you'd do us the honor of pouring six glasses of your very best mead, that would be a fine start to the evening. Ah! Wait, I must correct myself; make it seven. I'd have our new friend here join us."

"Thank you, but I'll pass," Derek said, removing himself from the salon as politely as he could.

Derek retreated to the rear parlor to drink in peace — to drink, to fume over the cruel and unforeseen twists that had brought him and his friends to this low point, and to castigate himself for failing to find a solution to their plight. Felisia appeared periodically to replace his empty stein with a full one, but she never lingered. Too many duties to attend to, Derek reckoned; a full house demanded its concierge's full attention.

Halfway through his fourth drink, Darrus wandered in with a stein of his own. "Quite the house this is," he remarked, taking in the parlor. "Its reputation is well deserved."

"Mm-hm," Derek said, his gaze fixed on the

fireplace.

"I could say the same for you. Bringing the Reaper into dead Hesre? Fending off the Siege of Castle Somevil-Duur? Those are astounding feats."

"The city council didn't think so."

"Now now, don't sell yourself short, lad," Darrus said, taking the neighboring easy chair. "Greave told us the vote was quite close. Had one councilor gone another way, I'd be sitting here in lament and you'd be off to the Gray Necropolis."

Derek looked up. "One vote?"

"Amazing how one simple decision can so change the course of a man's life, eh? You came in second to the Noble Blades, and a damn close second at that. There's no shame to be found there." Darrus quaffed his beer. "Honestly, lad, I did you a favor."

"A favor?" Derek said, his heat rising suddenly. "How do you figure taking a paying job from us is doing me a favor?"

"I've been adventuring longer than you've been alive," Darrus said, not inaccurately; he'd marked his ninetieth year but three months earlier. "One of the reasons I've survived this long is because I've learned how to read situations and people, and I can tell by looking at you you're not meant for this life."

"I'm not."

"No." Darrus settled back in his seat. "Judging by your complexion and your accent, you're from southern Asaches, probably the Anstl region. That's largely agricultural land. Now consider that and your build, which suggests you've spent most of your life engaged in hard physical labor, I'd wager you grew up on a farm. And if I don't miss my guess, that discoloration on the back of your hands is from burning your-self. Perhaps while working the hammer and anvil, eh?"

Derek examined the back of his hand and learned that the old proverb did not hold true. He'd never before noticed the constellation of faded scars caused by stray sparks or a chunk of red-hot coal jumping unexpectedly out of the forge during his clumsier days of apprenticeship to his blacksmith father.

"And then there's that pretty face of yours. Not a scar upon it worth mentioning. Certainly nothing like these," the dwarf said, gesturing in the general vicinity of his face, which bore three old but deep scars. One of them rose out of the black wire of his beard and ended on the crest of his left cheek. Another crossed the plane of his wide, flat forehead. The third ran down the side of his face, near the base of his right ear, and partway down the side of his neck. "I grant you, your adventures are impressive, that's no lie, but you've been lucky — more than any one man has the right to be. You'd be wise to quit this life and go back to your farm before your luck runs out."

Derek, were he currently in a sound — which is to say, sober — state of mind, would never think to stand and pull up his shirt to expose a scar of his own, a scar that began at the rise of his left hipbone and traveled to his navel. It stood out against his skin as a pale line.

"Do you know what that is?" he demanded.

"That would be a wound inflicted by a sword," Darrus said. "A deep one at that."

"Close. This was caused by a Hruk chisel. Do you know how I got it?"

"I don't."

"That's right; you *don't.*" Derek bent over and snarled at Darrus, "You don't know a Godsdamned thing about me. You don't know who I am, you don't know what I've been through, and you damned sure are in no position to tell me how to live my life, you arrogant —!"

"Derek," Felisia said, appearing in the doorway, "let's leave this gentleman alone, shall we? Come."

She laid a hand on Derek's arm. His muscles were like columns of iron beneath her fingertips, hard and unyielding. He straightened and allowed Felisia to lead him away, upstairs, and into his bedroom.

"Oh, dammit," he groaned, burying his hands in his face. "I'm sorry. I'm sorry. I didn't mean to cause trouble."

"It's understandable. You've not had the best of days," Felisia said, closing the door. She took him by the arm again and guided him to the bed, where he fell back into the cloud of a quilt. She climbed in after him.

"Felisia, I don't — I'm not in the mood to —"

"Shh. Close your eyes."

He fought this, but the long day conspired with the multiple barley wines he'd quaffed to weigh his eyelids down. Felisia pressed against him and laid an arm across his chest.

"I feel like I let everyone down," Derek said.

"And how did you do that?"

"I don't know. They're my friends. I'm supposed to take care of them."

"Is that what they expect of you? Or is that what you expect of yourself?" Derek shrugged. "Are you a fatalist?"

"*Nooooo.* I don't believe in fate. I don't believe in destiny." He laughed. "I definitely don't believe in prophecies."

"Nor I, but I don't believe life is random, either. I believe the Gods sometimes put us where we need to be at a given time. Perhaps this is where you need to be. Perhaps you're meant to be elsewhere and losing this job is the universe nudging you in the right direction."

"I hope you're right."

Derek fell fast asleep as soon as he finished the sentence.

He awoke with the dawn still fully clothed; only his boots had been removed. Felisia was there next to him, also clothed. He carefully removed himself from under her arm and eased himself to the floor. It was a thoughtful but wasted effort.

"You're an early riser," Felisia said.

"Yeah," Derek said, adding under his breath, "most farmboys are."

"What?"

"Nothing. Do you mind if I go make myself some coffee?"

Felisia sat up and, with a musical purr, stretched out. "Give me a minute, I'll make some for you."

"No, it's okay, I can —"

"You're a guest of the Pinceforth House, and as long as you're a guest, it's my job to please you — whatever form that pleasure might take."

"You know what would please me?"

Felisia smiled. "What?"

"If you'd let me make coffee for you. It's the

very least I can do to thank you for — well, everything, but mostly for saving me from myself last night. And for the talk. I appreciate it. I know it's your job to be nice to me..."

"It is, but sometimes I'm nice to people because I sincerely like them." She got out of bed. "I don't care for coffee. Make it a cup of ginger tea and you have a deal."

Derek did her one better and made a simple breakfast of bacon and omelets to go with their beverages. They took their meals back to the main parlor and sat upon the table-slash-stage to eat.

"Will you be returning to Ambride today?" Felisia asked.

"I imagine so. I'll see what the others have to say once they're up, but there's nothing keeping us here. Unless you know anyone hiring adventurers?"

"Alas." Felisia picked up their plates and stopped Derek before he could voice a protest. "Fair is fair. You cooked, I'll clean. Ah, good morning, Mr. Stakar. How did you sleep?"

"Like a log, lass, like a log," said Darrus, his plate armor clanking dully.

"I'm heading back to the kitchen. Would you like me to bring you some coffee?"

"No, I'm right as is. We'll be moving out as soon as my mates are down."

"Then, on behalf of the Pinceforth House, I hope you enjoyed your stay and that we see you and your friends again someday."

Before departing, Felisia cast a quick glance at Derek. He made a point of focusing his attention at a random spot on the opposite wall.

Darrus laid his warhammer on the stage and folded his hands in front of him. "I owe you an apology, lad. You're right; I don't know your story. I have no right to pass judgment on you. I was rude, unforgivably so, but I am sorry nonetheless."

Derek withdrew his gaze from the wall. Darrus extended a hand sheathed in a golden gauntlet, which Derek took.

"Thank you," he said. Darrus nodded. "You're off already?"

"We have a deadline to meet. I told the council we'd return within six days, with or without the mask, and if we fail to do so, our reward is forfeit."

"Rather tight timeline, don't you think?"

Darrus shrugged. "A day to reach the Gray Necropolis, three days to search for the mask, we leave for the return trip the morning of the fifth day regardless of whether we find it — not that I plan on returning empty-handed."

"Yeah, well, life is what happens in between the plans you make," Derek warned.

"Ha. True enough."

"Good luck."

"Mr. Strongarm," Darrus said. "Mr. Lightfoot," he said, passing Felix on his way toward the foyer.

"Uh-huh," Felix rasped. "Tell me there's coffee," he said to Derek.

"Fresh pot in the kitchen."

Felix grunted and shambled away, just missing the rest of the Noble Blades as they paraded downstairs, bright-eyed, well rested, and dressed for duty. Kelly tossed Derek a smirk and a little goodbye wave.

"As always, my friends, I expect no less than

brilliance and perfection from the lot of you," Darrus said. "And now, onward — to adventure!"

"To adventure!" the Noble Blades cheered as one.

David was at the bottom of the main staircase when the Blades' rallying cry went up, and he reached the parlor in time to see the Blades depart, Mason Goldtones and his bugle serenade leading the way.

"They are always like that, aren't they?" David said, joining Derek.

"I think so."

"*Uckh.* Maybe we'll get lucky and they won't come back."

"Come on, David, don't talk like that. They're not bad people; they're just, um...a bit much."

"No, the shimmery gold curtains on my bed are *a bit much.*"

Felix returned with a beer stein full of hot black coffee. "So," he said, easing onto a couch, "something is definitely off about this job. I spent the night chatting with the Greens."

"Just chatting?" Derek questioned.

"Not *just,*" Felix admitted.

"Wait. With both of them?" David said.

"The night definitely took some unexpected turns. Gods, at one point I thought the damn cat was going to jump in. Anyway, I figured a couple of blow-hards like them might spill something interesting if I got them talking, and did they ever. They told me that all throughout their meeting with Councilor Greave, she said over and over the mask didn't have any mone-tary value, it was nothing but a historical curiosity — really hammered on that point."

"She oversold it," David said, remembering Felix's lessons in deception.

"Oh, yeah. And did you notice how quickly the council signed off on that pay raise the Blades demanded? They didn't even try to haggle."

"And if government officials are throwing money at a problem that casually..."

"Exactly. I'm telling you, Derek, this thing stinks."

"Okay, but what are we supposed to do about it? It's not our problem anymore."

"No," Felix said, sinking back in his seat. "I know this is going to sound crazy —"

"You want to look into it."

"Yeah, I do."

"That isn't crazy," David said, "that's stupid. What is there to look into?"

"The mask. There has to be more to it than historical significance."

"If there is, the council sure isn't going to admit it. So where else could we look?"

"We start where this all began," Felix said.

SEVEN
Among the Dusty Shelves and Stacks

Derek in good conscience could not agree to Felix's idea until after he consulted with Erika and Winifred. As he predicted, Winifred, ever the optimist, was happy to give anything a try if it stood to reverse their fortunes, while Erika echoed David's initial assessment, that remaining in Woeste to satisfy Felix's curiosity was foolish and a waste of time.

Outvoted and profoundly unhappy about it, Erika refused to join her friends in paying a visit to the archives — a building that, ironically, bore no historical character whatsoever. It was naught but a giant stone box, a warehouse for the storage of all things historical that did not even warrant a sign to identify its purpose — which caused some vexation among our heroes, who walked past it twice before venturing inside on a whim.

"This is an archives all right," David said, taking a generous whiff of the uniquely musty perfume of aged parchment and dust. The smell was not the only familiar element; the archives was Madam Roust's office writ large, but possessed of a marginally stronger sense of organization. High shelves filled to capacity with books and binders and odds and ends loomed over the quartet. Display cases of varying widths and heights and depths stood scattered about the open floor. Wooden crates and boxes sat pushed up against the walls, waiting to be opened and their contents to be examined and cataloged.

"This place is huge. I'm surprised the raiders could find anything in here," Derek commented, the remark sparking in Felix a most excellent question:

"How *did* they know where to look for the mask?"

"Let's ask her," Derek said, pointing out a woman in a plain dress emerging from a row of shelving, a thick tome held closed with a leather strap cradled in her arms.

"Oh!" she gasped, startled by her unexpected visitors. "Good morning. May I help you?"

"I hope so. My friends and I came to Woeste in response to the city council's call for adventurers."

"Ah," she said, indifferent. "You were hired to retrieve the mask?"

"We're assisting them," Felix said, jumping in. "They asked us to do a little research while they prepared for their expedition to the necropolis."

"Cedric's the man you want to talk to. He should be in the back," the woman said, nodding in that direction.

Cedric Unterfalt was indeed in the back of the building, sitting at a beaten old wooden desk behind a waist-high railing that encompassed his work area, creating a purely symbolic sense of isolation. He scribbled in a ledger, mumbling to himself, and paid no mind to the adventurers until Felix said to Derek, "He was at the call. I saw him arguing with Traymon outside city hall, and he was there throughout the presentation. He did not look happy."

"What was that?" Cedric said, looking up.

"Hi. Good morning," Derek said. "The woman up front said —"

"I know you," Cedric interjected. "From the meeting yesterday."

"Yes, sir." Derek made the introductions. "We were hoping to talk to you about the mask."

Cedric cocked his head and cast a suspicious eye at his visitors. "What about it?" He wiped the expression from his face and said with an affected neutrality, "Everything to be said about it has already been said. It's a historical curiosity, nothing more."

"Raiders don't storm the heart of a major city to steal a historical curiosity," Felix said, "and politicians definitely don't spend big money for the recovery of a historical curiosity. Come on, man, I know horseshit when I smell it."

"What business is it of yours?" Cedric said, growing defensive. "You weren't hired to find it."

"We're helping out the people who were," Felix said, repeating the lie effortlessly and convincingly, "and I think you wanted to help them, too, but the council obviously didn't share your concerns — or maybe I should say they didn't want you to share your concerns with the Noble Blades."

Cedric took the point of his dirty white beard between his thumb and forefinger and twisted it into a tangled spike. "They believed my concerns were unfounded," he said, suddenly intense, "that I was attempting to peddle myth and rumor as fact. I was trying to warn them."

"Of what?" Derek said.

Cedric rose and gestured for his guests to wait. He shuffled over to a bookcase filled almost to over-flowing with books and loose papers, plucked from out of the clutter a worn leather satchel, and brought it back to his desk.

"I came across this quite by accident," he began, wrestling a sheaf of papers from the satchel, "and while I must confess I've found nothing definitive, I have every reason to believe that mask might be exceptional-ly dangerous."

He motioned for his visitors to gather close. They surrounded the desk as he spread out select sheets of parchment, all of which bore sketches of a mask wrought of dark iron. Some of the renderings were crude and childlike, others meticulously detailed, but each depicted the mask as covering the wearer's face from forehead to chin, with open slits for the eyes and mouth.

"We've had the mask in our collection for years but I never thought much of it until I chanced upon an old journal, the author of which claimed to be a servant in the house of Lord Ulysses Kilnmar," Cedric said. "Lord Kilnmar acquired the mask through unknown means and began wearing it during meetings with his advisors and whenever he held court. The servant first thought it a simple bit of theater to intimidate others — such was Lord Kilnmar's style — but over time he be-came convinced the mask held some sort of innate power."

"What kind of power?" Winifred asked.

"That is where matters become frustratingly

muddy. Masks such as these were once common in certain circles, few of them reputable — cults, primarily. Later they became fashionable among certain despotic rulers such as Lord Kilnmar, who often liked to claim their masks held true power of a magical nature. I suspect in most cases they were empty boasts meant to inspire fear in their subjects and enemies, but I've found evidence that some of these masks may in fact be legitimate artifacts — scant evidence, I admit..."

"You believe Kilnmar's mask might have been a real artifact?" David said, his interest well and truly piqued.

"I've found nothing definitive one way or the other, but I couldn't in good conscience write it off as baseless nonsense."

"Someone obviously thought you were onto something," Felix said. "Who else knew about your theory?"

"It might be easier to quantify who *didn't* know. My colleagues were all aware of my findings, I personally mentioned it directly to several members of the city council who support the archives' work — it was never a secret, and you know how people talk."

"What about the mask itself?" David said. "What could it do?"

"I can't say with any certainty. The servant's journal mentioned occasions when Lord Kilnmar would instantly cow a defiant man with a look, or cause someone during a debate to surrender a position he previously held with steely conviction, or persuade anyone with a grudge or grievance to forget his purpose." Cedric passed a hand over his collection of illustrations. "These masks allegedly allowed the wearer to impose his will upon others of his choosing, manipulate emotions, even take possession of another's body."

"Is this all your research?"

"Everything I could find in our records, yes. If anything else exists that might shed light on this mystery, it's most likely in the hands of one of the academies." Cedric's expression hardened. "Blasted academics. Ever since my theory became public knowledge, I've had mages from one academy or another in here every bloody day demanding I hand over my notes. I swear, if I called my lunch magical one of them would swoop in, declare it his by right, and eat it right off my plate."

With nothing more to offer his visitors, Cedric put his papers away, returning them to their in-plain-sight hiding space among his personal library, and excused himself that he might attend to his day's duties.

Before returning to the Pinceforth House, the company stopped at the first tavern they found for lunch and made a round of inquiries about Woeste's academies — which, they learned, were numerous. The city boasted nine recognized academies, from the venerable Grande Acadamie Woeste to the upstart Knowledge Wellspring to the Hospitarium, which was dedicated exclusively to developing the healing arts and by all accounts the most open of the institutions. Its members gladly welcomed outsiders and rival academics, their interest in expanding and improving their craft taking precedence over personal pride.

"Sadly, I doubt they would have any useful information about the mask," Winifred said as they returned to the Pinceforth House. Mavolo offered a polite nod as they passed through the gatehouse. "It doesn't sound like anything they'd have an interest in."

"No, but if the Hospitarium is on good terms with the other academies, maybe they could open a few doors on our behalf," Derek said. "Couldn't hurt to ask."

"Maybe. I wouldn't get your hopes up," Felix said. "We're still talking about academics. Betcha the minute we mention the mask, they'll shut us out."

"Couldn't hurt to ask," Derek repeated.

Once inside, David surreptitiously tugged on Derek's sleeve and in a hush asked to speak to him in private. He followed the boy up to his room, where he shut the door and slipped the deadbolt into place.

"What's up?" Derek said.

"I have an idea. I could write to Madam Roust and ask if she might have any information about Kilnmar's mask."

"That's a great idea. Good thinking, buddy."

David nodded and looked away. "I have another idea," he said to the floor. "I think I can convince the local academies to help us."

"How?"

David hesitated. "By giving them an opportunity to examine something utterly unique in exchange for access to their records."

"We don't have anything like that."

His breath coming in short, shuddering pants, David pulled his backpack out of its hiding place in the bottom drawer of his nightstand and wrestled its contents out. With trembling hands, he peeled away its faded, ragged fabric wrapping and held it out to Derek, who recoiled as if he'd been presented with a venomous serpent.

"That's Habbatarr's book."

"I know," David said in a tiny voice.

"You said you got rid of it."

"I never said that," David said, aware of the fragility of that defense even as he offered it — and yet, Derek searched his memory and found nothing on which to base an honest rebuttal.

"Have you read it?"

"A little bit. I don't understand a lot of it. Some pages are written in strange languages, and some are complete gibberish."

The question snagged in Derek's throat. He feared the answer. "And the parts you do understand?"

"Some spells. A few potion formulas, but I don't know if they'd work. There was one page that was all about how to better focus magical energy to increase a spell's effectiveness," David said, brightening momentarily before shrinking back into himself.

A chill slithered around the base of Derek's spine as he recalled the holocaust David had unleashed on the invaders of Castle Somevil-Duur. He'd attributed the startling growth in his skill and power to practice or perhaps to a surge of adrenaline — something natural and benign, certainly not to the collection of dark and decidedly unnatural knowledge David now held in his hands.

"You told me it was my decision whether to keep it."

"I know it was," Derek said, "but I trusted you to —"

"What? To destroy it?" David said hotly. "That's what you wanted."

"I trusted you to be honest with me."

"...Oh."

"Yes, David, I did want you to destroy it. I think that book is too dangerous for you or anyone to have." He shrugged vaguely. "But I let you make the choice, and you made it."

"I'm sorry."

"Put it away."

David stuffed the book back into his pack. "I'm sorry," he whimpered again.

"I know you are, but an apology isn't enough, not for this. We need to be able to trust each other. We can't do that if you're keeping secrets from us."

"I know. I'm sorry."

"Then take responsibility for it. You go find Felix and Winifred and tell them everything. *Everything*. You understand?"

"Yessir." The color abruptly seeped out of his face. "Oh, Gods, are you going to make me tell Erika?"

"No, I'll tell her. I want to talk to her anyway. Much as I hate to admit it, using the book to get into the academies might be our best bet."

The sour taste of that statement lingered on Derek's tongue as he sought out Erika's room.

"Hey," he called, knocking. "You in there?"

"No," Erika said from within.

"Come on, I need to talk to you."

"Do I have to get out of bed?"

"I'd actually prefer it if you didn't."

Derek took her grunt as a summons. He warily approached the vaguely Erika Racewind-shaped lump under the covers. Only her head poked out.

"What?" she said.

"I definitely think there's more to this story than we thought," Derek said, relating the details of his morning.

"So? Not our problem."

"I know."

Erika sighed and cracked open an eye. "But you want to make it our problem."

"I want to try and figure out whether the Blades are in over their heads."

"Why? We sure as hell don't owe them anything."

"No, but if our positions were reversed, I'd want to know whether we were walking into a dangerous situation."

"It's called the Gray Necropolis. I think they know they're not going to a carnival."

"You know what I mean. Look, it's not as if we have any pressing business back in Ambride. I figure we can send David out with Winifred to do some poking around, the rest of us can look for work to keep us afloat —"

"Fine, whatever," Erika grumbled, burrowing back under the covers.

"Speaking of David."

"What did he do now?"

Derek steeled himself. "He still has Habbatarr's book."

"...He *what?*"

"Erika —"

"He *what?!*" she thundered, hurling away the covers and bounding to the floor. Derek automatically shielded his eyes behind his hand. Erika yanked it away. "He still has the book? He said he destroyed it!"

"Uh, no, he actually didn't," Derek said to a spot high on the wall behind Erika. "I said the same thing when he showed me the book, but when I thought about it —"

"Wait, he has it here? Did he bring that damned thing with him?"

"Yes, he did, but —"

"Where is he?"

"I already talked to him."

"I don't want to talk to him; I want to wring his neck for being so Godsdamned stupid!"

"Erika, calm down." Derek instinctively grabbed Erika by her bare shoulders and just as quickly jerking his hands away as though she were the surface of a hot stove. "And please, *please* get dressed. It's really hard for me to talk to you like this."

She threw on her pants and a shirt, cursing under her breath all the while. "There. I'm dressed," she declared. "Is it all right with you if I go kill David now?"

"Stop," Derek said, at last looking Erika in the eye. "I already talked to him and he feels terrible. He knows he disappointed us."

"Does that mean he's going to destroy the book?"

"No. Even if he wanted to destroy it, he can't. We need it," Derek said, presenting David's idea.

"Are you seriously proposing we let a bunch of paranoid, obsessive sorcerers get their hands on a book of dark magic?"

"I know it's a little risky, but —"

"It's not risky, Derek, it's stupid."

"I don't know if we have another option."

"No, we do have another option. We have a *fantastic* option: we pack up and go home. What?" she barked in response to a timid knock on her door.

David peered in, his eyes wide, red, and tear-stained. "Can I come in?" he said in a pathetic squeak.

"Why? So you can tell me you're sorry?"

"Yes?"

"Sorry for what? For lying to us? Or for holding onto that damned book after we told you to burn it? You know what, it doesn't matter. I don't want to hear it."

"Erika, come on," Derek said, but David had already withdrawn from the room. "Oh, good job."

"What, you're mad at *me*?"

"He was trying to make things right. The least you could have done was give him a chance."

"Why, so he can go and screw up again?"

"Yes. Because he's a child and that's what children do; they screw up. They make stupid mistakes. It's called growing up."

"This isn't stealing someone's horse for a joyride, Derek. His kind of stupid mistakes could get one of us killed."

"Says the woman who would have died from a poisoned arrow if David hadn't been there to take it out," Derek said, turning on his heel. "And let me remind you, he did that for someone who betrayed a lifetime of his trust. You owe him, Erika, maybe more than you could ever repay. The very least you could do is give him half a chance to atone for a mistake."

Derek left without giving Erika a chance to respond.

Not that she had a word to utter in her defense.

EIGHT
Gathering Intelligence

Not wishing to unnecessarily impose further upon Giuliana's generosity, Derek proposed leaving the Pinceforth House and finding cheap, temporary lodging in the city. Giuliana, however, would not hear of it and insisted on her guests remaining in her house as long as they needed. Derek, naturally, resisted her ongoing charity but eventually accepted a compromise in the form of interim residency in the cottage in the back of the property, which she held in reserve for private parties and the occasional long-term guest. There they would be able to live self-sufficiently and without interfering with Madam Pinceforth's business or straining her resources.

The cottage was what one might describe as cozy — which is to say, a tad too small to hold the quintet comfortably. There was a single upstairs bedroom with a single bed, and while the bed in question was large enough to easily accommodate three people sleeping abreast, the company could not arrive at a consensus as to which combination of three would generate the least discomfort for all involved. They settled on a rotating system wherein each night one of them would claim the bed and, per his or her discretion, share it with one of their fellows or hog it all to him- or herself.

In a small act of contrition, Erika asked David if he'd like to take the bed that night. With a pathetic look normally reserved for recently kicked puppies, he declined and slunk away to sequester himself in a small sitting room off the living room.

This is where Erika found him the following morning — on the floor, under the table, under a blanket, using his backpack as a pillow.

They ate breakfast at a nearby bakery that offered in addition to breads and pastries savory hot pies filled to capacity with eggs, bacon, sausage, and cheese. One pie could fill a man's belly and keep him satisfied to and past lunch. Derek ate four.

Four, plus the half a pie David was unable to finish. His appetite was not strong to begin with, but he forced himself to eat his fill in anticipation of the long day ahead. He nodded and grunted throughout Felix's dissertation on the best way to present himself to the academies and conduct negotiations, but otherwise he sat there in silence, his head bowed over his plate.

Derek asked Winifred, the most approachable among them, to accompany David, and together they set out into the heart of Woeste to begin their solicitations, beginning with the Grande Acadamie Woeste. As the city's oldest and largest academy, Derek reasoned it was most likely to boast the most comprehensive body of research on magical artifacts and would be the most eager to lay claim as the first academy in all Asaches to examine a book from the library of the legendary mad lich Habbatarr.

"Out of curiosity," Winifred said, "how are you going to convince anyone the book is legitimate?"

"That won't be a problem," is all David said in response.

The Grande Academie Woeste lived up to its name, at least on the outside. White marble pillars stood at attention like elite soldiers along the front façade, three to each side of a set of high double doors set within a marble arch. David pulled on them and found them sealed from within and then noticed a decorative gargoyle head carved into the stonework of the arch. A length of iron chain dangled from its wide-open mouth, which had the unfortunate effect of making the gargoyle appear as if it was vomiting iron links.

"Are you ready?" Winifred asked.

For a moment, the boy was silent. Then he straightened himself, set his jaw, and declared, "Yes."

He pulled experimentally on the chain. A bell sounded somewhere inside, deep and low.

The doors creaked open. A dark-skinned woman in rich red robes appeared, shadowed by a man clad in a mail hauberk and carrying a poleaxe about as tall as David. The woman, Adele Presse by name, passed her gaze over David before settling on Winifred.

"Yes?" she said to the elf, but it was David who replied.

"Good morning. My companions and I are in Woeste on the matter of the mask stolen from the archives," he said, taking care to speak clearly and precisely. "We understand that the Grande Academie is likely to have some information that might be relevant to our quest."

"The Grande Academie is not open to the public," Presse said with a weary note. This was far from the first time she'd uttered that exact phrase in that exact tone.

"I understand, but I have something I believe the Grande Academie would find very interesting, and I'm willing to let one of your people examine it at length in exchange for access to your records," David said, slipping off his backpack and bringing out the book. Winifred reflexively retreated a step.

"What is it? And if you say 'It's a book' I will clout you," Presse warned.

"My companions accompanied the late Lord Randolph Ograine into Hesre as his hand-picked bodyguards. This book," David said, holding it out, "was recovered from Habbatarr the lich-lord's personal library in Hesre."

"Ha!" Presse barked humorlessly. "What a tale! Boy, people turn up on our doorstep almost every week to present us with some spurious artifact. At least they have the decency to tell us a plausible story."

Unfazed, David found a select page in the book and held it up for Presse to read. She leaned in, her lips pursed in such a way as to suggest both a contemptuous sneer and a patronizing smirk, but the expression did not hold. As she read her features went slack, slowly, as if melting, and her skin took on an ashen cast.

"Oh," she gasped, blinking as though emerging from a trance. "Where did you get this?" she demanded.

"I told you," David said, "from Habbatarr's lair in Hesre."

"Get Mesztal," Presse said to her guard. "Now."

He ran off, his hauberk jingling.

"This...this is..." Presse said, rubbing the back of her hand across her lips. She never completed her thought.

Oren Mesztal, a lanky man with a pate scrubbed smooth by age and a short-cropped white beard that clung tenaciously to a few last threads of ginger, returned with the guard, and leveled a cool gaze at Presse's visitors.

"You have to see this," she said, waving a finger at David, who opened up the book for Mesztal's inspection. The aged scholar's eyes widened, and he made an impulsive grab for the book. David jerked it away and snapped it shut.

"What is that? Where did you get it?" Mesztal rasped, his throat suddenly bone dry.

"Maybe we should take this inside," David suggested.

The building's interior was strikingly similar to that of the Ambride academy, except the Grande Academie favored white marble over utilitarian granite, and thus did every chamber and hall seem bright and inviting (if a bit sterile). The same could not be said of the academics they passed. Few spared them a look, and those who did made the effort to scowl their displeasure at these unwelcome visitors to their hallowed halls.

Mesztal's office was considerably smaller than Madam Roust's and much tidier. Everything had its place, and things and places alike were clearly labeled by subject matter and alphabetized whenever appropriate. A stack of papers on the corner of Mesztal's antique desk looked like it had been assembled using a carpenter's level and square. He carefully picked up the stack, carried it to a wooden filing cabinet, slipped into the top drawer and then pointed commandingly at his now-barren desktop.

"I want to see that book," he said. "Now."

"And I'll be glad to show it to you as part of a fair trade," David said. "I'm looking for information that might be relevant to the theft of the mask of Lord Kilnmar."

Mesztal started, then chuckled humorlessly. "And what makes you think we'd have any such information? The mask is a historical curio. You'd be better served speaking to someone at the archives."

"We did, and they referred us to you. I'm told the mask is rumored to have magical properties."

"And a rumor is all it is," Mesztal said decisively.

"Then you have done some research into the mask?" Winifred said.

The academic's lips puckered. "Perhaps we could be of use to one another," he said. "Tell me about the book."

David repeated the story he told Presse. Mesztal probed and tested the tale, looking for an inconsistency that could reveal his guests as frauds, but did so half-heartedly. What little he'd glimpsed of the book's contents had been enough to convince him he was dealing with a genuine article.

Although he did not hold all the proverbial cards, David acted as if he did, as if he had nothing to lose by taking his discovery and walking away — just as Felix had advised. He gently demanded that he be allowed full access to everything the academy had in its possession regarding the mask of Lord Kilnmar itself and on (real or alleged) magical masks in general, and in return Mesztal would be allowed to peruse Habbatarr's book under Winifred's strict supervision. Neither would be allowed to take notes in the interest of keeping their respective secrets as confidential as possible. When Mesztal insisted that no other academy in Woeste be allowed access to the book, David refused. When Mesztal pressed the issue, David calmly put the book back in his backpack and slung it over his shoulder. Mesztal relented before David reached his office door.

And so for the next several hours, there in the office, Mesztal pored over the book, his expression locked in a wide-eyed gawp of perverse fascination, while David read through the academy's considerable body of knowledge regarding artifact masks and, to a lesser degree, the mask of Lord Kilnmar, which remained an enigma even to the learned men and women of the Grande Academie Woeste. Oh, there were theories aplenty, and to the academics' credit, they were all quite sound, but as is often the case with historians, opinions were sharply divided as to the mask's precise origins. Each researcher presented ample evidence to support his or her preferred hypothesis whilst simultaneously dismantling opposing cases, and every argument, whether pro or con, was compelling in its own right — which meant that no one theory stood out in David's mind as the most likely.

David and Winifred left in the afternoon, over Mesztal's vehement protests. He'd examined but a few pages thoroughly and there was so much more to see, but David held fast to the letter of their bargain. However, he did promise to return should Mesztal discover any new information — not that he expected to ever make good on that vow.

"I think Mesztal showed me everything he had," David said once the academy was well behind him. "If he'd had anything else, he would have given it to me just so he could've spent more time with the book."

"It worries me he had as much time with it as he did," Winifred said. "It worries me that we're going to let others read it."

"It isn't dangerous." Winifred raised an eyebrow. "It isn't. I've read it a bunch of times. Yeah, there's some scary stuff in there, but nothing dangerous."

"If you say so."

"Winifred?"

"Yes?"

"Are you angry with me?"

"Why would I be angry with you?"

"Because I still have the book."

"Ah. That," Winifred said, her smile slipping ever so slightly. "No, David, I am not angry with you."

"You're not?"

"No. But I am disappointed."

David winced as though punched in the gut. "Derek said it was my decision whether to keep it," he argued miserably.

"It was, and I stand by letting you make the choice, even if I don't agree with it — but that isn't why I'm disappointed. You promised me you would tell the others you kept the book. I never thought to ask if you had. I assumed you'd make good on your promise."

"I was going to. Honestly, I was going to."

"But?"

"I got scared. I knew how everyone felt about me having it in the first place."

"Then why did you keep it?"

"I wasn't going to. I wasn't," he insisted, "but I got curious and started reading it. When I realized there was actually some practical knowledge in there, I decided to study it so I could —"

The boy shuffled to a stop.

"So you could what?" Winifred prodded gently.

"Be useful. I thought if I could actually *do* something I wouldn't be this dead weight you carried around because you felt bad for me. I know that's the only reason you haven't sent me away."

"Oh, David, that isn't true," Winifred said, kneeling down. "We all care about you, very much. We would never reject you."

"My father did," David said, the words scraping against one another.

And with that, a floodgate he had held shut for months through constant distraction, through denial, through sheer force of will finally burst open, and he fell weeping into Winifred's arms, purging all his deferred anguish in a torrent of great wracking sobs. He shuddered violently with each hiccupping gulp of air, and Winifred feared the boy might pass out right there on the sidewalk as passers-by, curious about the cause of the spectacle but not overly so, dedicated themselves to passing by. It's just some boy having a tantrum, they told themselves. There's no reason to get involved.

There's no reason to care.

The Pinceforth House was oddly quiet. True, the

start of its normal business hours was still some time away, but Winifred had expected to see at least Madam Pinceforth at her desk in the foyer, dutifully updating her ledgers.

Winifred, her arm across David's slumped shoulders, navigated through the house, through a rear sunroom, and stepped out onto a spacious back porch shaded by a heavy canvas awning. This is where she found if not the entirety of the Pinceforth House's hosting staff then at least a solid majority, lounging in chaises and sitting in small clusters, sipping drinks and snacking on fruit and gazing out over the back lawn toward a newly fallen tree — or more specifically, toward a shirtless Derek as he worked to hack the crown of said tree to pieces. He swung an axe in a slow, steady rhythm, muscles founded on heredity and honed through a lifetime of labor glistening with the sweat of an honest day's work. He paused to push a sodden lock of hair out of his eyes and survey his progress, a satisfied smile on his lips.

"Oh my," Felisia purred. "I could watch this all day."

"We have been watching it all day, dear," Madam Pinceforth noted. "Oh, hello, Winifred, David."

"Giuliana," Winifred said. "What's this?"

"Derek insisted on doing something to repay me for your lodging. That tree began rotting out last summer so I told him he could take it down for me."

"And what a divine show it's been," a host by the name of Barrimore Offsit said, his eyes flitting back and forth between Derek and a sketchbook splayed open upon his lap. An entire page had been dedicated to a lovingly detailed charcoal portrait of Derek that was suitable for inclusion in a so-called "copper naughty" — short, cheap erotic adventures that cared not a whit for the finer points of storytelling such as plot or character. As long as the tales included gratuitous carnal activity and colorful euphemisms for the participants' genitalia, readers were generally content.

"I take it then they had no luck finding work?" Winifred said.

"No. I hope your day was more productive." Giuliana said, directing the remark toward David, who did not answer.

"I believe we're off to a good start," Winifred said on his behalf.

"I should...um," David said, gesturing vaguely before trudging off toward the cottage.

"Is he all right?" Giuliana asked.

"I don't know," Winifred said. "Where are Felix and Erika?"

"In the kitchen, I believe."

Winifred spun on her heel and returned to the house, tearing through the halls at a clip until she reached the kitchen, where she found Felix and Erika leaning against a counter and enjoying steaming mugs of tea.

"We need to talk," Winifred said.

"Hello to you, too," Felix said.

"What's your problem?" Erika said, instantly struck by the fact that, for once, Winifred was without the slightest hint of a smile.

"David," she said. "The poor boy is absolutely terrified we're going to abandon him."

"Where would he get a stupid idea like that?"

"From you."

"Me? What did I do?"

"You aren't very affectionate toward him."

"I'm not affectionate toward anybody," Erika noted.

"*What?* The devil you say," Felix said.

"Neither are you," Winifred said, rounding on him. "You're rather mean to him, as a matter of fact. He thinks you hate him. Even after all we've been through together, he's convinced you'd cut him loose in a heartbeat to save yourself."

"What? I would *never* do that to the kid."

"Neither would I," Erika said, bristling. "He knows I would never —"

"Betray his trust? You conspired with his father to sacrifice him to Habbatarr," Winifred said. "He hasn't completely trusted you since Hesre, and you've done precious little to repair that damage."

"Oh, for — first Derek throws Hesre in my face, now you. How long am I going to have to live that down?" Erika said, throwing her arms up. Tea sloshed onto the floor.

"Oh, no," Winifred said, raising a reprimanding finger. "You do not get to have hurt feelings, Erika Racewind, not over this. You have sins to atone for, and it's well past time you did your penance."

With that, Winifred marched away, leaving two pairs of ears burning in her wake.

"I want you to remember this moment the next time you bitch about how relentlessly cheerful she is," Felix said to Erika.

"Once, when I was little, my grandmother told me she was disappointed in me. That," Erika said, jabbing a finger at the point in space where Winifred had recently stood, "made me feel almost as shitty."

"We should go talk to the kid."

"I suppose."

"But later. After he's cooled down."

"Sure," Erika agreed. "Later."

Now, to their credit, Felix and Erika did make honest efforts to speak to David. Felix approached the boy that night during dinner but was rebuffed. David said he needed to write down everything he'd learned at the Grande Academie before it slipped from his memory and couldn't spare time to talk. He then took some soup and some bread and retreated to the sitting room, which is where Erika found him the next morning, slumped over in his chair and fast asleep. When she woke him, David immediately shooed her away so he could finish his work in peace.

And so it went for the next several days. Each morning Winifred and David would visit one of the academies and, using the invaluable currency that was Habbatarr's book, buy their way inside. David would then methodically peruse every single book and scroll and scrap of parchment that might contain relevant information about the mask of Lord Kilnmar, and then hurry back to the cottage to transcribe his thoughts in private. Any disturbance, no matter how small or benign, was met with an impatient glare and a curt request to "Make it quick, I have work to do," and he'd spend whatever brief audience he deigned to grant rapping an anxious tattoo on the floor with the heel of his foot.

Erika stopped bothering him after the second day. Felix persisted for two days past that before giving up.

The routine varied only once, when a messenger appeared at the Pinceforth House's front gate one evening, carrying a thick envelope that he insisted on delivering directly to its intended recipient as per the explicit instructions of its sender, one Madam E. Roust. David took the parcel's contents, a sheaf of handwritten notes, into his makeshift office and did not emerge again until morning, when it was time to head out and solicit the next academy.

"Where's he off to today?" Erika asked Derek one morning as they partook of their morning coffee out on the cottage's small front porch.

"The Hospitarium, I think?"

"The Hospitarium? Wasn't that the last academy on his list?"

"I believe so, yeah."

"Gods, have we really been here for nine days?" Derek started. "What?"

"The Noble Blades left for the necropolis nine days ago."

"So?"

"They should have come back *three* days ago," Derek said. "The Noble Blades are missing."

NINE
The Going Price for a Mission of Mercy

"Darrus told me he'd planned for two days of travel, one day each way, and three to explore the necropolis," Derek said.

"That doesn't mean they're missing, Derek, it means they're late," Erika said. "Plans change."

"Sometimes for reasons completely beyond anyone's control. Something could have happened to them."

"I feel like I've been asking this question a lot lately, but what are we supposed to do about it? If something did happen to them, it's not our problem. They knew the risks."

"Did they? I think we've established they didn't get the whole story before they took the job. Gods know what sort of mess they walked into."

"Ohhh, for −" Erika sighed. "You want to go after them, don't you?"

"Well..."

"No. Absolutely not. I am done wasting our time, Derek, you hear me? Done. We came here to earn some money and we haven't made a single goldie."

"She has a point," Felix said, stepping out onto the porch with a yawn and a stretch that did more harm than good. His lower back seized up, a protest against a third consecutive night sleeping on the floor of the kitchen with no more padding than his well-traveled bedroll.

"Funny to hear you say that, considering you're the reason we stuck around in the first place."

"Guilty as charged, but now we have an opportunity to make it literally pay off."

"How? You think we can talk the city council into funding a rescue mission?" Derek said.

"No, but I do think they could be talked into giving us the Blades' contract. As I recall, they promised results within six days. They haven't delivered. I'm assuming the council still wants their stupid mask back."

"All the other adventurers are long gone. That makes us the only game in town," Erika said, picking up on Felix's train of thought. "It's worth a shot."

"One problem: David," Derek said in a half-whisper. "He's been running himself ragged researching the mask. I don't know if he's up for a job like this."

"Then we leave him here and let him rest up," Felix said.

"I agree," Erika said. "He won't be any good to us or himself if he's not in top form."

"Sure, you go tell David we're leaving him behind," Derek said. "I bet that'll go over real well."

"Come on, man, that isn't what we meant and you know it," Felix said.

"I do, but he doesn't. All he'll see are the only people he has left in the world taking off without him. We can't do that to him."

"And bringing him with us before he's ready puts us all at risk," Erika said.

"Let's take this one step at a time. It's a moot point if the council doesn't want to hire us."

"Yeah. All right," Felix said, heading back inside. "Let's go get dressed to impress."

At Derek's suggestion, Winifred remained behind so David wouldn't wake up to an empty cottage — not that they expected the boy to rouse of his own volition, but better safe than sorry, they reasoned.

En route to city hall, Derek, Felix, and Erika discussed several possible sales pitches and debated how far they should push their luck when it came to the delicate matter of negotiating a price. They were still hammering out the details when Councilor Greave welcomed them into her private office.

"I'd call your presence here fortuitous," Greave said, taking a seat behind a small writing desk, "but I suspect this visit is no accident."

"It isn't. I spoke to Darrus the morning of his departure," Derek said. "I know they were working on a deadline, and that if they missed their deadline they'd forfeit their pay. Considering they stood to collect a decent reward even if they failed to recover the mask — "

"One could assume ill fortune has befallen them. Yes, that's the council's belief as well. We've been debating whether to put out a second call, but seeing as you're here..." She ended the thought with an expansive sweep of her hand. "I will of course need the full council to approve a new contract, but I believe my colleagues — well, *most* of my colleagues would be willing to honor the original agreement of five thousand for the mask's return."

"I believe the contract was for seventy-five hundred."

"That was the price we negotiated with the Noble Blades."

"In compensation for the added risk," Felix pointed out.

"And considering the Noble Blades have disappeared, I'd argue their concerns were well-warranted," Erika added.

"We could probably make a sound case for ten, but we're reasonable people."

"I could make a sound case for hiring another team of adventurers," Greave said.

"Could you? We know what the job's worth. Try to hire someone else, we'll make sure they know what it's worth too. Besides," Felix said disarmingly, "all the other adventurers are gone. You'd have to put out another call and wait for the response — that'll take a couple of weeks. We're right here and ready to go."

Greave leaned back in her chair, fingers tented, eyes narrowed in thought. "Fifty-five hundred, and you have one week to return with the mask. Miss the deadline or return empty-handed? You get nothing."

Derek and Erika stepped back to give Felix room to work.

"Seventy-five hundred if we succeed, half that if we don't, no deadline," he countered.

"Six thousand for success, two if you come back empty, the deadline stays."

"Seventy-five hundred if we succeed, half if we don't, no deadline."

Greave laughed humorlessly. "You don't seem

to understand how negotiations work, Mr. Lightfoot."

"You don't seem to understand how adventuring works, councilor. You're asking us to hike through a cursed forest to search a dead city crawling with Gods-know-what to look for an item literally no larger than my head that might not even be there anymore because none of your own people have the balls to even attempt it. You resorted to hiring adventurers for a reason. Seventy-five hundred if we succeed, half if we don't, no deadline."

"Six thousand," Greave said. "Three if you come back without the mask. No deadline."

Felix checked with Derek and Erika. They both nodded.

"Done deal," Felix said.

"Not quite," Greave said. "I still need the council's approval."

Which she received in another close vote in closed session. Mock led a minority opposition, arguing that the operation was a waste of time and money and, more benevolently, risked further loss of life. If the Noble Blades could not complete the mission, what hope had a group of nobodies?

(His word, not mine.)

Greave, however, had more faith in our heroes and made a persuasive argument in favor of a second contract, noting that the first, slightly more lucrative contract had not been paid out. Folstoy was especially vocal in his support for this proposal, and to an outside observer who knew nothing of the sordid history between him and Felix, his parting wish that the party should realize nothing but success and return home safe and sound would convey as utterly sincere.

With time on their side, Derek, Felix, and Erica left city hall and made the short trip over to the archives, where they questioned Cedric Unterfalt about the Gray Necropolis. He shared his considerable knowledge with them gladly and allowed them to make a copy of the only known map of the dead city, with the caveat that he could not vouch for its accuracy, having never stepped inside the necropolis himself — though not for lack of desire, he noted. Over the years, he had filed multiple requests with the council to lead an expedition into the Gray Necropolis to rediscover its lost secrets and dispel the many myths that had sprung up around it, but a fear of the blighted land passed down from generation to generation always won out over academic curiosity.

After that, they hit several local merchants for necessary supplies — food that would keep for days on the road, clean water, assorted sundries — and returned to the cottage to make their travel plans.

"Where's David?" Derek asked, peeking into the empty sitting room.

"Upstairs, sleeping," Winifred said. "He's still exhausted, the poor thing."

"We have to make a decision," Erika said to Derek.

Winifred arched an eyebrow. "About?"

"The city council hired us to find the mask," Derek said, though his tone was more appropriate for bad news than for good. "We have to decide whether David is up for going with us."

"I don't think he is," Felix said. "The kid's wiped himself out playing junior historian."

"I agree," Erika said. "I think he should stay here

and rest."

"I think David deserves to speak for himself," Winifred said.

"This isn't about just him. He's part of this group, which means his decisions affect the rest of us."

"No, Winifred's right," Derek said. "David should get a say. All we can do is lay it all out for him and trust him to make the right choice, for himself and for the group."

"The last time we trusted him to make the right choice, he held onto a book of dark magic we all wanted him to burn," Erika said, "and he kept it a secret from us."

"And he admitted he made a mistake," Derek reminded her. "Besides, as much as I hate to admit it, the book proved valuable. David never would have been able to access the academies' records if —"

"Oh, please," Erika sneered. "That was a complete waste of time. We haven't learned anything valuable."

"You don't know that. David's still working."

"Then let him stay here and do his work, and we can go do ours. Everyone wins."

"Erika..."

"Will you people shut up?!" David squealed from the foot of the stairs. "I'm trying to sleep!"

"Oh, David, we're sorry," Winifred said. "You go back to bed. We'll continue our conversation outside."

"No, hold on. We might as well do this now." Derek beckoned to the boy. He shambled over, rubbing the sleep from his red-ringed eyes. "We have some news. We just got back from meeting with the city council. They've hired us to recover the mask."

"They have? What about the Noble Blades?"

"The Blades never returned from the Gray Necropolis."

"They didn't? Are they okay?"

"I think it's a given they're not," Felix said, "considering they *never returned.*"

"Felix," Derek chided. "Here's the thing, David: we think it might be a good idea if you stay here."

With that, David was instantly and complete awake. "Did I do something wrong?" he said, an apology pouring out of him without the benefit of knowing what his latest offense might be.

"Easy, buddy, it's okay, you didn't do anything. In fact, you've maybe done too much." David cocked his head quizzically. "You've been pushing yourself really hard. You're exhausted to the point of collapse."

"We picked up enough provisions for two weeks," Erika said. "That's two weeks of constant movement, of sleeping on the ground, of staying on our toes and watching each other's backs."

"If you're not at a hundred percent, you put yourself and the rest of us in danger," Derek said.

"I don't want to be left behind," David said immediately.

"I know you don't, but if you're —"

"What if you don't come back?"

"I promise you we're coming back."

"The Noble Blades didn't," David shot back. "Don't promise me you'll come back because you can't, you can't make that promise because you, you can't keep it! I don't want — I'm not staying behind!"

"David, listen to me. Listen to me," Derek said.

He lowered himself to a knee and took the frantic boy by the shoulders. "We're not going to make you do anything; this is your decision. If you don't want to stay behind, say so and that's that. We can hold off a day or two and give you time to rest up and then we'll all go together, okay? *We will not leave you behind.*"

David, unable to speak anymore, not without losing what little composure he had left, simply nodded.

"All right. Then you have to make me a promise: no more work, okay? You go to bed and stay there. Get some sleep. The rest of us will plan out the mission, and we'll see how you're doing in the morning. Agreed?"

"Okay," David croaked, his throat tight and raw.

Derek let him go. He paused at the base of the stairs, fixing Derek with a look, before returning to the bedroom.

"He's not up for it," Erika said, but Derek let her proceed no further.

"We'll see," he said. "Let's get to work."

They worked out on the porch throughout the afternoon and into the evening, poring over Felix's impressively detailed reproduction of Cedric's map of the Gray Necropolis to plot a best course of action, and they shared with Winifred what they'd learned about the dead city, which was this:

Once upon a time, Woeste-Star, then the true capital of Woeste, was where the city-state's wealthy and powerful lived in seclusion from the common folk. The Monolith Forest served as a natural, impenetrable protective barrier, its trees too massive to be felled and too hardy to succumb easily to fire, its single access road too narrow to allow the passage of siege engines, and any army attempting to march down this corridor would be slowed to a crawl, thus granting the city guard ample time to prepare to fend off the incursion.

In the end it was not invasion that brought Woeste-Star to ruin but cruel, mysterious, implacable nature in the form of a contagion known as the Gray Rot — so called because the first symptom was a strange bleaching of the skin that rendered the victim the sickly pallid gray of a woodland mushroom, and the culmination was a rapid decomposition of the flesh that briefly turned the afflicted into a living horror before reducing him to a corpse. The contagion, the origin of which was never discerned, swept through the city like a wildfire, consuming the entire populace within a matter of days. When the Gray Rot first struck, the city guard quarantined Woeste-Star as a preventive measure to keep the disease contained. Anyone who tried to leave, even if they had yet to manifest symptoms, was struck down by archers stationed around the city at the edge of the forest. Their bodies were burned where they fell.

City guards remained outside the walls for six months to ensure no one escaped to spread the blight — far longer than necessary; it only took three weeks to transform Woeste-Star into a blighted land. In layman's terms, a necropolis generally refers to an expansively large and elaborate cemetery populated by extravagant tombs and monuments, but in the case of Woeste-Star — the Gray Necropolis — it had truly become a dead city.

Although similar afflictions were known to medical scholars, nothing matched the Gray Rot in terms of its virulence or how cruelly it afflicted its victims. Woeste's new lord, hastily chosen in the wake of Lady Laika Grandorse's gruesome demise, declared the former Woeste-Star indefinitely off-limits to ensure no one could accidently rediscover the Gray Rot and bring it into Woeste proper.

That new lord, it should be noted, was none other than Ulysses Kilnmar.

Over time, the specific and quite sensible reason behind the quarantine was forgotten and replaced with rumors, myths, and folktales parents told their children to keep them in line. On occasion someone in city government would propose reclaiming the lost city, but more recent rejections were based not in fear but in a sense of fiscal restraint; the cost of rehabilitating a long-abandoned city to make it once again fit for human habitation was considered too great, and the Gray Necropolis should be left alone to return to the earth.

"Considering someone is using the necropolis as a base of operations, I think it's safe to say the Gray Rot isn't an issue anymore," Derek said.

"That's something, I suppose," Erika said, frowning at Felix's map. "I'm not confident of our chances of finding the mask."

"Such a pessimist," Winifred commented.

"I always hate to agree with Erika, but I'm with her," Felix said. "Even if the necropolis is totally abandoned, which I doubt, the place is huge. There are too many places to hide something as small as a mask."

"That's assuming it's still there," Erika said. "If we don't run into the raiders, I say we take that as a sign they've left and taken the mask with them, turn around, come back, and collect the half reward."

"I can live with that."

"I can't," Derek said. "We were hired to find the mask and we should make every reasonable effort to do so."

"Let me save you further debate." The quartet looked up to see Kat approaching, leading in a frowning Councilor Mock, who said, "I'm afraid that we must negate our contract with you. Your services are no longer required."

"What? Why?" Erika demanded.

"Because the Noble Blades have returned." Mock added soberly, "Well, most of them."

TEN
Under the Influence

As the only two with any sense of genuine concern for the Noble Blades, Derek and Winifred returned to city hall with Mock, who explained that the Blades had returned a half hour ago and reported directly to the council, which then dispatched Mock to the Pinceforth House in the hope of catching our heroes before they departed on what was now a non-existent quest.

"They found the mask?" Derek asked.

"No," Mock said with an odd inflection. "They're rather insistent there is no mask to be found. They claimed they searched high and low and all they found was a long-abandoned camp, presumably belonging to the raiders."

"You sound like you don't believe them."

"Do I?" Mock shrugged. "I have no reason to doubt them. They're the Noble Blades; their reputation is beyond reproach. Besides, if they were of a mind to deceive us, why return *after* the deadline for forfeiting their reward?"

It was sensible argument, Derek thought. The

Noble Blades could have easily camped out in the forest for a few days, come back, claimed to have found nothing, collected a partial but still generous reward, and departed, leaving the council none the wiser — and yet, the note of skepticism in Mock's voice remained.

"You said *most* of them had returned," Winifred said. "There were casualties?"

"Unfortunately. Their bard — Mason, was it? And that strange cat who followed the Sylvyns around."

"Oh, no," Winifred whimpered, tearing up immediately. "What happened?"

"We're not sure. Stakar said something about an ambush in the forest, things coming out of the woods and attacking them as they approached the necropolis. He wasn't very clear about it, but the poor man appears to be in a state of shock. Perhaps you could speak with them?" Mock said to Derek. "You know, adventurer to adventurer?"

"I can try," was the best Derek could promise.

The Noble Blades were still in conference with the full council when they arrived, though informally so; the councilors were down on the main floor instead of behind their lecterns, chatting with the remaining members of the ill-fated expedition. Derek spotted Darrus near the stage, speaking with Greave and Folstoy, and went straight over.

"Mr. Strongarm," Greave said.

"Councilor," he replied. He gave Folstoy a nod out of courtesy and then said to Darrus, "Councilor Mock told me what happened. Darrus, I'm so sorry about Mason and Furl."

Darrus stared up at him for a moment, utterly blank. "Mr. Strongarm," he said flatly. He blinked, nodded, and said, "Your sympathy is appreciated."

"Mr. Stakar was just telling us what happened," Greave said.

"Creatures, the likes of which we've never seen before, burst forth from the depths of the Monolith Forest and assailed us," Darrus said. "We barely escaped with our lives. Except for Mason and Furl, of course."

"I'm so sorry," Derek said again. "I know what it's like to lose comrades."

Darrus nodded mechanically. "Your sympathy is appreciated."

"Mr. Strongarm, if we could speak in private?" Greave said before leading Derek away to a quiet corner. "I do apologize, but under the circumstances I may have no choice but to nullify your contract."

"You think the mask is long gone?" Derek asked.

Greave hesitated. "In the interest of full disclosure, that is not the consensus of the council as a whole. Some of us believe the trauma suffered by the Noble Blades may have affected their diligence — perfectly understandable, of course — and it would be worth the time and expense to send a second party out to make absolutely certain the mask is beyond our reach."

"But others disagree."

"Yes. Councilor Mock maintains the Noble Blades could have returned right away but they did not. Despite their losses, they carried on and carried out their mission. They willingly forfeited their reward in the hope of finding the mask and giving their companions' deaths meaning. Dunstan believes their account and he does not wish to send more people out to die for a lost cause."

The loss of such a generous payday stung, but Derek could respect Mock's reasoning. Some people had no reservations about ordering others to march headlong into the jaws of death; he could not begrudge those who balked at accepting that burden. Before departing, he informed Greave he and his friends planned to remain in town for another day or two before returning to Ambride, in case the council decided to authorize a second expedition.

"Do you think they will?" Winifred asked as they left the council chamber.

"You never know," Derek said, though in truth he regarded a change of heart as unlikely.

"Those poor people. I spoke to Adam and Astra. They were absolutely desolate."

"Darrus seemed to be taking it hard, too."

"Seemed to be?"

"I mean he was. He lost people under his command. You don't shrug off something like that," Derek said, refusing to let his mind wander across the years to revisit a past he'd worked so hard to leave there.

Winifred took Derek's hand, and she held it all the way back to the Pinceforth House, and she did not let it go until they broke into a sprint, spurred into motion by a startled yelp from somewhere within the cottage.

Derek drew his longsword and threw open the front door just as Erika leapt into the common room from the back of the cottage, her wicked dagger drawn and poised to strike.

"No! Get back!" Felix cried, frantically waving them off. The animal perched atop the back of the couch growled a low growl, its fur puffed out to twice its normal thickness, its stub of a tail twitching in warning. "It's okay, guys. It's okay."

"David, stay back," Erika said as he came thundering down the stairs, rudely roused from a deep sleep by the tumult. "What the hell is that thing doing here?"

"Damned if I know."

"No, seriously, what's Furl doing here?" Derek demanded. At hearing his name, Furl relaxed, if slightly, but he kept his bright green eyes fixed on Derek.

"I don't understand," Winifred said.

"Join the club," Felix said. "Derek, you're scaring him. Maybe you should put the sword down."

Derek kept his blade at the ready. "Felix, Furl's supposed to be dead."

"He's what?"

"We just spoke to the Noble Blades," Winifred said. "They told us Furl was killed, along with Mason."

Furl let out a series of chirrups, like the chattering of a house cat vexed by birds playing outside his window, just out of reach.

"I think Furl disagrees," Felix said, to which Furl replied with a low sound that resembled in passing a feline meow. "Come on, guys, put the hardware away."

Reluctantly, Derek and Erika sheathed their weapons.

"This doesn't make sense," Winifred said. "Why would the Blades claim Furl was dead?"

"And why would he come to us?" Erika said.

"I don't think he came to *us*; I think he came to find Felix," Derek said, which drew another meow.

"Why me?"

"You did spend a night rolling around with his masters," Erika said. "Maybe he trusts you."

Furl leapt down from the couch and confirmed Erika's theory by twining about Felix's legs, his purr like the rumble of distant thunder.

"That's it, isn't it?" Derek posed to the cat.

"Derek, it's not going to answer you," David said. "It's a dumb animal."

"No, he's not. He knows something. We just have to figure out what."

"Maybe he didn't come here so much because he trusts Felix but because he *doesn't* trust the Greens," Erika said.

Furl settled on his haunches and gave another meow.

"They obviously lied about Furl," Derek said, turning to Winifred, "but you said they were distraught."

"I didn't say they were distraught, I said they were desolate," Winifred said. "It was like they were deep in a state of shock."

"That was how Darrus was, too. He seemed dazed, like he was barely aware of where he was."

"Like he wasn't himself?" David said.

"Yeah. What're you thinking, buddy?"

David skirted past Erika and ducked into the sitting room-cum-office to grab his notes, which had grown in thickness to rival that of a manuscript for a pretentious historical drama.

"I have a theory about the mask of Lord Kilnmar," he began. "There was this warlord in the time before the wardens' court, Krizik Corrigon, who ruled several of the western territories. He commanded one of the biggest armies in the history of Asaches and his warriors were absolute fanatics. Some even worshipped him as the living embodiment of the God Victor. He wore this great iron helm, a gift from an ally, and after his death, it became this sacred totem. His followers believed Corrigon had imbued the helm with his very will, and whoever wore it would have the power to command his army. Not surprisingly, every last one of his generals believed they were Corrigon's rightful heir and deserved to wear what they came to call the Helm of Dominion. Infighting broke out, the army fractured, and the helm was lost to the ages. I think the mask of Lord Kilnmar might be the visor from the Helm of Dominion."

"Where'd you find all this?" Erika said.

"At the archives. At the academies. Madam Roust had some information. None of it made sense on its own, but the more I learned the more I realized everyone had one or two pieces of a larger puzzle."

"Which you put together," Derek said, duly impressed.

With a modest shrug, David said, "If the academies weren't so stubborn about sharing information they would have figured it out years ago."

"What does the Helm of Dominion do, exactly?" Erika pressed.

"According to legend, whoever wore the helm could bend anyone to his will, make them say or do anything they were commanded. The mask probably has that same power."

"Oh, boy," Derek said. "Everyone, gear up. We need to go have a talk with the Noble Blades."

***

They prepared in haste and in likewise fashion returned to city hall, where they found the Blades still in conference with the council — or rather, a portion thereof; Mock, Traymon, and Delilah Scheere looked up with a shared start as the companions strode into their chamber. The Noble Blades, however, barely registered their entrance.

"Mr. Strongarm," Mock said. "Didn't expect to see you again so soon."

"Councilor, please forgive the intrusion, but could we speak to you?" Derek said as pleasantly as possible. "In private?"

"Is something wrong?"

"No, but it is important we speak to you right away. It's about the mask."

"What about it?"

"We have some information. With all due respect to our contemporaries here," Felix said, gesturing toward the Noble Blades, "we'd rather not say anything in front of them."

"The mask is gone," Darrus said. "We looked for it. We couldn't find it."

"Councilors?" Derek gently prodded.

"Ladies, gentlemen," Mock said to the Blades, "if you'd kindly step outside for a minute?"

"The mask is gone," Darrus said again.

"We looked for it," Kelly said. "We couldn't find it."

"Yeah, so you've said," Felix said. "You want to make yourselves scarce so we can — "

"The mask is gone," Vladimir said.

"We looked for it," Adam said.

"We couldn't find it," Astra said.

"The mask is gone," Darrus repeated, this time with greater volume but without a drop of passion.

"We looked for it," Kelly said.

"We couldn't find it," Vladimir said.

"Councilors," Derek said, taking the hilt of his sword in-hand. "You need to leave. Right now."

They did as told, fleeing in all directions. The Noble Blades made no effort to stop them.

"Darrus, why did you tell us Furl was dead?" Derek asked.

"Furl is dead. He was killed during the ambush," Darrus replied. "We were ambushed in the Monolith Forest."

"What ambushed you?"

"Creatures. We've never seen their like before."

"Describe them," Erika said.

"...We've never seen their like before."

"Describe them."

Darrus's face cracked, flaring ever so briefly with an expression that could have been one of rage or of anguish — or of pain.

"Creatures," he hissed through clenched teeth. "We've never seen their like before."

"Darrus, listen to me," Derek said. He took his hand off his sword and held it up in a gesture of peace. "You're not yourself. None of you are. We're here to help, okay? We don't want to fight you."

"The mask is gone," Kelly said.

"Creatures," Vladimir said.

"He was killed in the ambush," Adam said.

"We looked for it," Astra said.

"Ah, shit," Felix muttered as the Noble Blades recited the same snippets over and over, like bit part stage actors rehearsing their handful of lines to perfection. "I remember the last time we heard people talking like that."

"They're not zombies," Derek said. "They're under the influence of the mask."

"The mask is gone!" Vladimir said.

"The mask is gone!" Astra cried.

"THE MASK IS GONE!" Darrus bellowed.

Darrus led the charge, roaring incoherently, his warhammer Foecrusher raised high. Kelly drew her rapiers and followed in Darrus's path. To his right, the Greens conjured spheres of crackling energy. To his left, Vladimir drew in power from some otherworldly source. Glowing smoke materialized out of thin air and entered the skull atop his staff, as if the totem were inhaling the malevolent spellstuff through its eternally clenched teeth.

"Don't hurt them!" Derek said an instant before Darrus's warhammer fell. It was a crude strike, easily evaded, but it landed with enough force to crack the stone floor. This convinced Derek that ignoring his own advice might be a wise course of action, and he retaliated with a piledriver of a punch to the back of the dwarf's skull. Darrus sprawled face-first onto the cool granite.

Erika, who never intended to follow the order in the first place, drew her weapons and deflected Kelly's twin rapiers as they pierced the air en route to piercing her gut. Erika responded by slapping the flat of her sica across Kelly's head, staggering her. A stiff kick to the groin doubled her over. A pommel strike to the crown of her skull knocked her down.

Winifred sprinted toward Vladimir, her quarter-staff cocked. The necromancer held her gaze as she crossed the chamber in a few strides but did not hasten to release whatever spell he was preparing. Indeed, he was still chanting under his breath, uttering an incantation in a language considered by most scholars to be dead and gone, when Winifred swung her staff into his midsection. He let out an explosive bark of pain that caused his spell to misfire. Dark spellstuff spilled out of his staff and splashed to the floor like water before transforming back into a luminescent fog that swirled about Winifred's feet, contrarily hot and cold at the same time. She brought the tip of her staff around and, with a snap, rapped Vladimir's tailbone. He went rigid and, without so much as a grunt of pain, fell to his knees.

The Greens, talkative sorts that they were, had divulged a great deal to Felix during their shared evening, including the curious fact that their magic had, over time, become synchronized. They were perfectly capable of casting discrete spells, but when they intertwined their castings, their power increased dramatically. However, this also meant that all it took to foul both in the midst of a "harmony casting" was to disrupt one, so Felix nocked an arrow and took careful aim at Adam. He barely flinched as the arrowhead skimmed off the meat of his thigh, opening a gash that bled freely, but it did the job. His globe of roiling magical energy flickered, crackled, and then popped like a soap bubble. Astra's did likewise, and yet she thrust her hands toward Felix as if bringing her casting to its natural conclusion.

All of these things happened at once, in a burst of mayhem that was as brief as it was violent, and in the silence that followed, the companions looked to one another with baffled expressions that mirrored the same unspoken sentiment: how did they manage to defeat the famed Noble Blades so quickly?

"The mask," Darrus grunted as he struggled to rise.

"The mask," Vladimir groaned.

"The mask!" Astra screeched, a thread of lightning leaping from her outstretched fingers. The bolt sliced the air between Felix and Erika, forcing them to dive for cover. Several more followed, thrown with reckless abandon, without concern whether an ally was caught within the crossfire. Derek and Winifred threw themselves atop their respective opponents, pressing them back to the floor.

It was by pure chance a bolt found a target in David, but chance is not what saved him from a horrible death. The dancing white lance skimmed off a dome of invisible force, as did a second, a third.

"*Pe'vetus!*" David cried, coupling his incantation with a gesture: he thrust out his hands as if in presentation and a focused gust of hurricane wind tore across the chamber, striking Astra with battering ram force and launching her off her feet. She tumbled through the air and crash-landed among the stone benches.

David turned, his attention drawn by a flash of motion in the corner of his vision. Kelly staggered toward him, lurching like a drunkard, and swiped with her rapiers. Felix grasped the lad by the belt and pulled him out of harm's way, then threw himself clear as Kelly turned her swords on him. The blades whistled through the air where, a split-second before, Felix's neck had been.

As she drew back for another attack, Erika pounced, driving a fist into Kelly's face. A second punch caused her to drop her rapiers. Erika wrapped an arm around her throat and squeezed, cutting off her air. Almost immediately she sank to her knees, as limp as a rag doll.

"The mask," Adam slurred. Magic sputtered and sparked about his fingers as he tried to muster a fresh offensive. Winifred put an end to that by rapping her staff across the back of his head. He crumpled to the floor, teetering on the edge of unconsciousness, blood staining his pale blonde hair with pink.

"The mask. The mask. The mask," Darrus droned on, his low monotone standing in stark contrast to his desperate flailing. Despite his superior size and weight, Derek could not keep Darrus pinned for more than a second or two before the deceptively powerful dwarf wriggled free.

"Little help over here?" Derek called out.

"Let him up," Erika said. Derek got off Darrus, who jumped to his feet, ready to resume the fight. Erika returned him to the floor with a vicious kick to the head. He flopped onto his back, his gaze distant and unfocused.

"That wasn't what I meant," Derek said.

"You're welcome," Erika said. She glanced around. The Nobles Blades, injured and wounded though they were, stubbornly fought to rise again and start the melee anew, and at her feet, Darrus's lips continued to work, forming the same two words over and over: *the mask...the mask...*

144

"That is fucking creepy," Felix said.

"We have to do something," Winifred said. "We have to help them."

"Can you do anything?" Derek asked.

"I don't think so. I've been trained to heal the body. Maladies of the mind require different magics, different techniques."

"This isn't a malady," David reminded his friends. "They're under the influence of the mask."

"The mask!" the Noble Blades moaned as one.

"I repeat: fucking *creepy*," Felix said.

"Can you do anything?" Derek posed to David. "This is dark magic, right? Was there maybe something in Habbatarr's book that could undo this?"

"All I learned from the book was how to strengthen my magic, a breaking spell, a light spell I can't quite figure out," he said. "I didn't see anything about negating dark magic. Not on the pages I could read, anyway."

Darrus, his hand trembling, reached for Derek's ankle. "The mask," he hissed.

"That's it. That's how we free them," Derek said. "We have to recover the mask of Lord Kilnmar."

ACT TWO
In Which our Heroes Journey into Darkness
of the Literal and Metaphorical Varieties

ELEVEN
Through the Forest, Deep and Dark

The Noble Blades continued to resist as our heroes trussed them up using coils of hempen rope appropriated from the Blades' own packs, but their will to fight had largely vanished, and it was with minimal difficulty that the companions led their captives to the nearest city guard's post for safekeeping. There they were placed in one of the larger cells near the back of the holding area. Once inside, their aggression subsided further, and they took to shambling aimlessly around the cell, making no effort to test the door or make a grab for their captors. Nevertheless, at Erika's recommendation, a guard ran over to the nearby sanitarium and borrowed three thick leather half-masks normally employed to prevent patients from spitting at or attempting to bite their caretakers. These were secured around Vladimir and the Greens' faces, effectively negating their ability to work magic.

Once the Noble Blades were secure and strict instructions had been left with the guards as to their care, the companions returned to city hall to share with the full council their working theory: the mask of Lord

Kilnmar was in all likelihood part of the Helm of Dominion; the Noble Blades had run afoul of whoever now possessed the mask and had fallen under his thrall; and that person had sent the Blades back to Woeste to report their failure and, hopefully, put an end to any effort to recover the lost artifact.

"If that's so and the Noble Blades are under the influence of the mask, how then would you resist its power?" Greave inquired.

"Unlike the Blades, we're aware of what the mask can do," Derek said, "so we can make sure to avoid any direct confrontation with whoever has it."

"If only the Blades had known what the mask was capable of," Erika said with a hint of an accusation that went unnoticed by Greave and her colleagues.

"If only," Greave lamented. "But you believe retrieving the mask is the key to freeing the Noble Blades from its influence?"

"It's our best bet," Derek said.

"Then may the Gods be with you in your quest."

As soon as the companions parted company with the councilors, Felix said, "Serious question here: how *are* we going to avoid getting — er, dominated?"

"Like I said, we avoid directly confronting whoever has the mask," Derek said.

"And if that doesn't work out? Our Plan As have a bad habit of blowing up in our faces, you know."

"Don't allow the mask to affect you," David said.

"Oh, *that's* useful," Felix drawled.

"I'm serious. Look, magic that directly affects a living being is tricky, even when it's beneficial. Winifred can't completely heal a wound just like that," David said with a snap of his fingers for emphasis. "It takes time and concentration."

"That's true," Winifred said. "Healing magic can go awry rather easily if the practitioner loses focus — or if the patient resists."

"You're saying all we have to do is refuse to let the mask overcome us and we're safe?" Erika said. "It can't be that simple."

"It might be. The mask is basically casting a spell, and there are a lot of ways to confound that kind of invasive magic, especially if we know what we're up against," David said. "A strong will might be enough to protect us."

"I'd call Darrus strong-willed. He succumbed to the mask's power."

"He might have been caught off-guard."

"Or he's not as strong-willed as we think he is," Felix said.

"I don't know," Derek said. "Darrus wasn't himself during that fight. None of the Blades were. We shouldn't have been able to take them down as easily as we did. I think they were fighting the mask's influence."

"Possibly," David said. "Or maybe the spell was wearing off. Or maybe it loses power over distance. Or maybe —"

"Maybes don't help us at all," Erika said.

"No," Derek agreed, "but at least we have some idea what to expect."

"Besides, if we wanted safe jobs, we'd all quit and go raise sheep or something," Felix added.

"Point taken," Erika said. "Let's get back to the cottage and rest up. We're going to have a long day ahead of us."

Derek roused his friends at dawn amidst the expected degree of complaining but atoned by preparing a meat-heavy breakfast to lend them the strength they needed to tackle the first leg of their journey: the Monolith Forest. None of them anticipated clearing the forest before nightfall, but they agreed they'd be wise to make the most out of what daylight they had.

Furl, who'd spent the night sleeping contentedly at Felix's feet, joined them at the breakfast table as if to declare his intent to join in the mission. Felix tried to dissuade Furl from following them, but this was a short argument. One can only debate a cat for so long.

Mavolo met them at the front gate with their horses, which he'd personally prepared for what would be for them a short trip. Kat and Felisia were there as well to bid them farewell and wish them good luck. The latter sentiment Felisia imparted on Derek with a lengthy kiss, which he reckoned would provide him with a store of luck that would hold him through his immediate quest and several more besides.

The taste of Felisia's lips lingered on Derek's until they had cleared central Woeste and were passing through the city-state's outer agricultural belt, a miles-wide ring of undeveloped land thinly populated by ranches and farms — with an emphasis on *thinly*; the belt was mostly open plains the cattle and sheep ranchers shared for grazing purposes, dotted here and there with wheat fields still several weeks away from having their winter plantings harvested, cornfields that had just undergone their spring planting, and the occasional rice paddy or cranberry bog. Derek was tempted to slow his pace and soak in an atmosphere he found comfortingly familiar and sorely missed, but his sweet nostalgia took a hard turn toward the bitter, and the ensuing fit of wistfulness lent haste to his pace.

All the better, really, as the companions would have to make the majority of the journey on foot. They were warned that horses dared not approach the Monolith Forest much less enter it, and as they crested a steep hill, their mounts put the truth to the rumor. They stamped and whinnied in protest, quailing at the prospect of traversing what the locals insisted were cursed woods.

Upon beholding the next leg of their quest, Derek could understand why the good people of Woeste believed in cursed woods.

The Monolith Forest began abruptly, its perimeter as clearly defined as the curtain wall of a great castle. Trees taller and straighter than any of the company had ever before seen thrust toward the sky before exploding in expansive crowns of deep emerald green. The road they'd followed to this point continued into the forest and faded away, consumed by the deepening shadows within. A humble guard post, a cottage with an attached watchtower, stood halfway between the hill's peak and the edge of the forest. A large stable sat off to the side of this outpost, and the sound of many horses champing and stomping anxiously drifted out to greet the party as they approached. They secured their horses to a hitching post outside the stables and crossed to the outpost, intending to state their business to the two guards stationed there — neither of whom was especially interested in said business. Their express duty was to sound an alarm should anyone — or anything

— unknown to them emerge from the forest, and as far as they were concerned, the adventurers were now a known quantity and no longer alarm-worthy. The senior guard, a grizzled woman by the name of Agatha Don Contess, offered the quintet one word of advice before shooing them on:

"There's only one road through the Monolith Forest. Stay on it."

"Right," Derek said. "See you in a few days."

Agatha shrugged a shoulder. "We'll see."

As soon as they crossed into the forest, the high sun abandoned them. Winifred shivered, but the sharp drop in temperature had nothing to do with this. She gazed skyward, but there was no sky to behold, only pinpoints of light scattered about a ceiling of near-black, as if the forest were cast in perpetual night. She gazed about, expecting to see some degree of undergrowth — bushes, ferns, natural flower beds, tufts of grass — but the forest floor in all directions was a solid carpet of dead leaves from autumns past.

"There's nothing alive in here," she said, straining to detect the faintest indication of a living thing scampering or scurrying anywhere within these primeval woods.

"I have no problem with that," Erika said. "That means there's nothing waiting to attack us."

Nevertheless, Felix and Erika paused to string their longbows and take stock of their quivers, then fell into an hourglass formation, with Felix, Furl, and Winifred taking point, Derek and Erika watching the rear, and David in the center.

For many long hours, they marched, always scanning the trees for a flash of motion or a telltale rustle of leaves.

For many long hours, they saw nothing and heard nothing.

When the sun finally slipped below the horizon, the Monolith Forest disappeared into an uncompromising darkness the likes of which Derek and Felix had seen only in caves and subterranean ruins.

"*Iscu'nera,*" David said, a disembodied voice in the void. A whitish-blue energy flickered dimly over his hand like static electricity across a woolen blanket. "*Iscu'nera.* Oh, come on, you stupid spell, work."

"What are you trying to do?" Erika said.

"I'm trying to dispel the darkness. It's one of the spells in the book but it doesn't want to work."

"Hold on," Derek said. He fumbled blindly through his pack until he located a travel torch, a simple length of wood wrapped at one end in pitch-soaked cloth. After locating David by touch, accidentally jabbing him in the eye in the process, he had the boy ignite the torch. The light and the warmth it brought were meager but welcome. The companions huddled around the torch to coax some feeling back into their frigid fingers.

"We have to make a decision," Derek said. "Do we press on or do we camp for the night? Personally, neither option is thrilling me."

"No," Winifred agreed. "Either way, our fire risks drawing attention to ourselves."

"You said there was nothing alive here," David pointed out.

"I said there was nothing *alive.*"

"We need to rest," Erika said, "but I'm not sure whether we'd be able to scrounge up enough wood for a decent fire."

"Which would require someone stepping off the road," Felix said, eyeing the darkness lurking at the edge of the torchlight with deep distrust.

Once they'd arrived at a consensus that camping for the night was preferable — if marginally — to forging ahead, Felix and Erika stepped off the road to find serviceable fuel for a proper fire. Equipped with a torch of their own, they remained tethered to Derek by a length of rope, and they made sure to always remain within sight of their fellows. Firewood was scarce — bone dry, perfect for a campfire, but scarce. The trees, a species known as the towering whitewood, began their life cycle by developing what would one day become their crown, which would grow and widen as the trunk launched skyward, straight as an arrow. Being among the hardiest of the hardwoods, towering whitewoods resisted most blights and parasites and thus shed branches rarely, almost always due to a lightning strike shearing off part of a tree's crown.

Felix and Erika returned with such a branch, a limb as long as Derek was tall and as thick around as his wrist. He took it apart with a machete he carried for such purposes — no warrior worth his salt would ever subject his sword to such an insulting task — and in the center of the road constructed a pyramid of the pieces, which he then set alight with his torch. They hunkered around the meager campfire, woolen blankets draped over their shoulders to pool and trap as much body heat as possible. Furl contributed what he could, sprawling across Felix's lap and overflowing into Erika's.

"Fire's not very big," David observed.

"Necessary evil, buddy," Derek said. "We were lucky to find this much wood so we have to make it last all night."

"Same goes for our food," Erika said. "We can't count on finding any game here or in the necropolis."

"Great," David griped.

"No one made you come."

"Erika," Winifred said, a chastisement.

"What do we do about...um. You know," David said.

"You have to go?" Derek asked.

"...Yes."

"Normal routine, I'd say."

"We should go in pairs," Erika said.

"I can't go if someone's watching me," David said.

"I didn't say we'd watch each other."

"I'd rather go alone."

"That's not safe."

"I'll just go behind that tree right there," David said, pointing at the closest silhouette. "I'll take a torch, I'll tie the rope around my waist...I'll be fine."

Grudgingly, Derek handed David the small shovel he carried for the purpose of digging latrines, then one end of his coil of rough hempen rope, which David looped around his midsection. Derek tugged on the tether, testing it, and let the rope uncoil in his hands as David stepped off the road and behind a tree.

"How far away from the necropolis do you think we are?" Winifred said.

"If we set out right at dawn, we should make it there before midday," Derek estimated. He gave the tether an experimental tug, feeling for the weight on the other end. "If we press on, we could reach the city center a few hours after that. I say we find someplace secure to spend the night, get some sleep, and start searching first thing the next morning. It'll be safer if we stick to working during the daytime."

The rope went slack in Derek's grasp a split-second before David shattered the silent night with his shriek. Derek leapt to his feet as David hurtled onto the path in a frenzy, his unbuttoned pants yanked up almost to his chest. He skidded to a stop behind his compatriots, gibbering incoherently and pointing back toward the woods with a trembling finger.

It would be inaccurate to say that the thing that emerged from the forest glowed, for that would suggest it was a source of illumination or phosphorescence. No, this vision was simply an absence of darkness — a reverse void in the shape of a person, a shape lacking in any detail that might reveal who it had been in life. It drifted up to the edge of the road — its legs dissipated before arriving at the feet — and settled there.

"It's all right, David," Derek said. "It's just a specter. It's harmless."

"It's — what — it — I —" David babbled. "Where did it come from?"

"They're souls who got lost on their way to the next world, some say."

"Kat said people sometimes come into the forest to kill themselves," Felix said. "I can understand how they'd get lost in here."

"The poor things," Winifred said.

"More," David moaned. "More of them."

A second specter emerged from the gloom, its face a mournful mask with two dark, soulless pits for eyes. Furl crouched low, a rumble sounding deep in his throat, as a third followed, then a fourth. David squeaked and frantically slapped Derek on the back. He turned to see three more slipping in behind them, as silent as the grave.

"What do they want?" David whimpered.

"They don't want anything," Felix said. "They're ghosts."

"We've encountered specters before," Derek said. "They have no awareness of the world around them. They don't even know we're here."

"Then why are they all staring right at us?" Winifred said.

"They're not staring at *us*," Erika said.

And that was true; the specters, now ten in number, standing on either side of the road yet refusing to cross onto it, were not staring at them as a collective.

They were all staring at David.

TWELVE
Welcome to the Gray Necropolis

The specters remained unwelcome company throughout the night, their empty, staring eyes fixed on David, who spent more time cowering under his blanket than sleeping under it.

The otherworldly visitors vanished with the rising sun — which is not to say the sun penetrated the forest canopy any more this day than it did the previous. The Monolith Forest stubbornly remained immersed in shadow and gloom as the company rose, ate a sparse breakfast of jerked meat and dried fruit, and resumed their hike toward the Gray Necropolis — although they did so at a smarter pace than the day before. True to Derek's word, the specters caused the intruders to their woods no harm, nor made any obvious attempts to do so, but the companions concurred that it would be in their best interests to remove themselves from the forest with all due haste.

It was late morning when they emerged onto an expanse of flat, level ground overgrown with high grass the color of straw, an arid plain separating the forest from the outer wall of the Gray Necropolis.

Derek, curious, grabbed a handful of grass. The tall blades crunched in his grip and snapped in two with the tiniest tug.

They followed the road toward the main gate — or rather, toward twin stone pillars that once anchored the main gate. Iron hinges caked with rust the color of dried blood were all that remained of whatever once stood here to keep unwanted visitors outside Woeste-Star. The perimeter wall, however, had survived the punishment of time and the elements quite admirably. Derek scanned the wall for cracks, holes, fissures, any telltale signs of degradation, but found few, and those he did detect were relatively minor. The wall might not have been on par with the great curtain wall of Castle Somevil-Duur, but it had been built strong and sturdy. If one were to take the time to scrape off the skin of sickly green moss creeping up its face, the casual observer might never realize Woeste-Star had been abandoned for several generations.

However, that illusion would not have held past the gate, as our heroes discovered upon entering the city itself. A structure to their immediate left, a small guardhouse, had long ago collapsed in on itself and now sat in a sad heap of rotting gray timber. A nearby row of townhouses was ready to follow suit. The façade of the center home had partially peeled away from the underlying framework to form a precarious canopy of planks covered in flaking, chalky blue paint — a cresting wave on the verge of crashing down into the cobblestone street below. The stone buildings within view had endured better but had not completely defied degradation. Cracks like jagged fingers reaching up from the ground split the foundation of one squat cube of a structure, which a weather worn inscription in a cornerstone identified as a constable's outpost.

"This is cheery," Felix said.

"Okay, people, first things first," Erika said. "We need to establish our base camp, someplace secluded and defensible."

Felix shrugged off his pack and dug out his map. "See that?" he said, pointing out a distant tower rising up against the backdrop of the midday sky. "That's the central watchtower, and that's attached to the city guard headquarters." He indicated the headquarters on his map, in the center of the necropolis. "It's strategically located, it'd give us a clear view of the whole city..."

"Which means there's every chance the raiders have already claimed it."

"If they're still here."

"Only one way to find out," Derek said.

They ducked behind the outpost and charted a course to the barracks that kept them always out of view, behind a building or in an alleyway, in the event the raiders had indeed commandeered the tower and taken the precaution of posting lookouts. Felix spent a few minutes staring at the map, committing their zigzagging path to memory, then tucked it back in his pack. He led the procession through the dead city, checking each stretch of road ahead and signaling to his companions once he'd confirmed a clear path. They moved cautiously at all times — slowly, quietly, rushing only whenever forced to momentarily expose themselves to the great tower and any eyes that might be looking down on them.

A straight and true course would have cost them an hour of precious daylight. Their somewhat circuitous route and their deliberate pace more than doubled that.

The last bit of their route was the riskiest, for it left them no choice but to expose themselves fully. The barracks itself, which resembled a castle keep in miniature, was surrounded by a wide ring of dead, sunbleached grass — a training field for the city guard, Derek reckoned. Once they left the shelter of the surrounding city, they'd be out in the open for a minute or so at a sprint — more than enough time for an eagle-eyed lookout to spot them and sound an alarm. To shrink that window of opportunity, they circled around to the barracks' southeastern face, to a set of high, wide barn doors. One door hung on its hinges, if barely.

"That's not a good sign," Derek said, peeking out from behind their final blind, a block of small shops sitting in the growing shadow of the barracks.

"What's not a good sign?" David asked. Derek pointed to the other door, which had at some point fallen off — and been picked back up and set leaning against the adjacent wall. "Oh."

"Shit," Erika spat.

"Now what?"

"We came all this way," Felix said. "Might as well see it through."

He peered up at the tower, dark and looming against the afternoon sun. He slipped out onto the street and stood there for a moment, braced for a claxon at best, a rain of arrows at worst. Neither greeted him. He allowed himself a tiny sigh of relief before stalking toward the barracks, toward the black hole in its face where a door once hung, dead grass crunching beneath his feet. In the perfect silence of the Gray Necropolis, each footstep was as good as a thunderclap.

Erika nocked an arrow and stepped out into the street. Furl crouched at her feet, the fur along his spine prickling, his tail stub twitching.

At last, Felix reached the doorway. He peered inside but sunlight refused to enter the space beyond more than a few feet. One, two, three steps and he was gone, consumed by shadow.

Erika drew a breath, and with it her bow.

Felix sprinted back into the light, his face ashen. The hulking beast that followed at a gallop, a mass of thick, ropey muscles covered in a sheath of leathery skin, was as tall at the apex of its arching spine as Felix was at the head and twice as long as that, not counting the whip-like tail that added another three feet. Its build and the jagged tusks thrusting from its jutting lower jaw hinted at its shared ancestry with wild boars, but at some point in the species' development, the gnashtooth took a turn toward the hideous to become the monster it is today — a monster with equally powerful tastes for carrion and living flesh alike.

A monster that always hunts in packs.

Three more gnashtooths crashed headlong through the barracks door in hot pursuit of a hot meal in the form of Felix Lightfoot. Erika loosed an arrow. The barbed arrowhead bit deep into the lead gnashtooth's eye socket but failed to find the animal's tiny brain. The thing reared back, whipping its head about in a mindless frenzy.

Erika held her ground as Felix blew past, as the gnashtooths hurtled toward her, gummy strands of spittle dangling from their hungry maws. She launched arrow after arrow, all of them finding their targets but none of them striking a lethal blow. A second gnashtooth faltered, furiously snorting and sniffing because of the arrow sticking out from a cavernous nostril. The third barreled face first into the ground, hobbled by a shaft in the crook of its foreleg. The fourth, the largest of the pack, held its course, straight and true, heedless of the oncoming arrows.

"Hold fire!" Derek shouted. Erika froze in mid-draw, against her better judgment; the giant gnashtooth, stubborn and strong, was coming straight at her, head bowed, tusks like twin lances ready to gore her through the belly.

And then David stepped forward and uttered a word of arcane power. Erika's skin prickled from the heat as a twisting column of flame leapt from his outstretched hand and landed upon the desiccated field, setting it ablaze, and at last, the relentless gnashtooth relented, rearing up on stumpy hind legs and letting out a guttural squeal as the flames licked its body.

The beast's panic was short-lived; the tinderbox of a field ignited instantly but exhausted its fuel almost as quickly. As an attack, it was negligible — but as a distraction, it sufficed. Derek charged in and brought his longsword down on the gnashtooth with all of his considerable might, intent on cleaving through the monster's skull.

The impact reverberated up Derek's arms. Hot blood spattered across his face.

The gnashtooth backed away, wagging its head in bewilderment. A waterfall of gore spilled from a ragged fissure crossing the crown of its now exposed skull. Erika dashed in before it could recover and rammed her sica through its eye socket, sinking the blade up to the hilt. The beast recoiled, ripping the weapon out of her hand. It thrashed and bucked and spun and, with a gurgling squeal, crashed onto its side.

The loss of their pack leader jolted the remaining gnashtooths out of their respective stupors. The hobbled gnashtooth lurched forward, unable to bring its drunken lope up to a full gallop. Winifred dashed by on its lame side, whooping and hooting to draw its attention. The monster pivoted to follow. Derek capitalized and, aiming for its trunk-like neck rather than its skull, sank the point of his longsword deep. The gnashtooth squealed and flailed away, vivid crimson blood fountaining from the wound. It collapsed, shuddered, and fell still.

"Derek, behind you!" Winifred cried.

He whirled and instinctively threw a sweeping slash at an enemy that had not quite arrived yet. The half-blind gnashtooth hurtled toward him, its head cocked to keep his prey within its limited field of vision. Derek tensed, preparing to leap clear.

"*Corin'es!*"

A violent spasm contorted the gnashtooth's body, and it screamed a disturbingly human scream. Bones snapped and splintered. Its spine twisted into a spiral, and its skull imploded with a wet bass pop. Blood and liquefied brain matter spurted out its ears, its nose, its mouth. Its mass, suddenly reduced to the consistency of bread dough, crashed to the ground and pooled out into a barely coherent blob, like a jellyfish washed up upon the shore to die a slow death under the merciless sun.

The color drained out of David's face as he beheld his gruesome handiwork, and he promptly fell to his hands and knees and vomited up his meager breakfast.

Erika strode over, her sica dripping with the blood of the fourth and final gnashtooth. "What the hell was that?" she demanded. "What did you do to it?"

"A spell. From the book," David panted. He spit several times, but the thick, bitter film coating his mouth remained. "A spell to break your enemy."

"You broke it, all right," Felix said. "Gods."

Winifred experimentally poked the pulverized gnashtooth's mass with her staff. It yielded as easily as a full wineskin.

"Ew."

"Be disgusted later," Erika said. "We have to clear the area."

"Why?"

"Because we've compromised this location."

"By killing a bunch of wild...whatever these things are?" Felix said.

"They're not wild. Look," Erika said, pointing with her sword to the puddle of gnashtooth — or rather, at the worn leather harness looped around its shoulders and over its withers. "They're on the others, too. They belong to someone."

"Someone who'll eventually notice their pets have been slaughtered," Derek said.

"And might be on their way here right now to investigate the ruckus we just raised."

"Well, shit," Felix said. He gazed up at the barracks, checked the position of the sun, and once he'd oriented himself, motioned for his companions to follow. "I know where we can go. Come on."

***

As Woeste's former capital, Woeste-Star possessed all the amenities of a seat of power, including a stately stone meetinghouse where residents once gathered to discuss the pressing issues of the day, present their concerns to a designated representative of the sitting warden, and on rare occasion voice their appeals to the warden directly.

The company started on the ground floor, in a great hall much like a church in its arrangement, complete with deliberately uncomfortable bench seating for the common folk. The basement provided storage space, though whatever was once stored here was long gone; only barren shelves and empty cabinets remained. It also housed a small jail for the constabulary, the offices for which occupied the entirety of the top floor, which was accessible by two narrow stairwells and a severely rusted iron ladder bolted to the inside of a bell tower, the shaft of which began in the basement and ended two stories above the peaked roof, providing a makeshift lookout post. Their sweep of the building turned up no evidence of current or recent use, by man or by beast.

It wasn't a perfect option, Erika declared, but it would work well enough as a defensible base camp.

Working quickly to avail themselves of the remaining daylight, the companions tossed every chair and table and desk down into the stairwells, choking them off from below but leaving the paths to the roof open. Once that task was finished, Erika climbed up to the belfry to take a look around, leaving the others to set up camp for the night.

Felix unceremoniously dumped his pack on the floor, kicking up a cloud of dust. "Done. Camp's set up. Let's eat."

"I'm with you," Derek said, a hunger he was previously unaware of making its presence known by way of a burbling growl in his belly. "What'll you have, David? Some jerky? Granola?"

"Not hungry," David mumbled.

"You should eat anyway. You need to keep up your strength," Winifred advised.

Derek proffered a piece of jerky. David took it and gnawed on it listlessly.

"You okay, buddy?" Derek asked. David shrugged. "You're bothered by what you did to that creature, aren't you?"

"I didn't know the spell would do that," David said, the gruesome crunch of the gnashtooth's every bone shattering at once echoing in his mind. "I know it was just an animal and it was trying to kill us, but I didn't mean to do that to it."

"Never regret taking out something's that trying to kill you, kid," Felix said through a mouthful of dried apricots.

Derek offered a contrary opinion. "It's okay to feel bad. Killing anything, even an animal, isn't something to celebrate or take pride in. You did what you had to do, but that doesn't mean you have to be okay with it."

"You're okay with it," David said. "You don't get upset when you kill someone."

"No. But it does bother me that it doesn't bother me."

"I don't understand."

Derek, with a thin, melancholy smile, said, "I hope you never do."

Night came as a surprise, falling sooner than anyone expected. Feeble moonlight peeked through the narrow slit windows, doing precious little to counter the darkness. Hesitant to light a full campfire and possibly draw attention to their hideout, Derek and Winifred huddled around David as he held a small but potent magical fire in his cupped hands.

"You're getting very good, David," Winifred remarked. "Your control is excellent."

"Thanks," David said. "It isn't the book."

"What?"

"My control. I've been practicing. I didn't learn it from the book."

Winifred, desperate to believe him but unable to find that much faith within herself, simply nodded.

"Move over," Erika said, squeezing into the circle to warm her hands.

"Have you seen anything?" Winifred asked.

"No, but our vantage point isn't that great. The bell tower's fine for guarding the perimeter but that's about it. I'm considering sneaking back to the barracks to take a look around from the watchtower."

"Felix already had that idea," Derek said. Erika glanced about, only now marking the thief's absence, and scowled. "Don't worry, Furl went with him."

"Oh, well, if the cat went with him...you didn't think to run it by me first?"

"You were in the bell tower. Besides, it's Felix. He won't get caught."

"Do you remember what happened the last time

we were in a dead city and you insisted Felix wouldn't get caught?"

"To be fair, he wouldn't have gotten caught if I hadn't made so much noise," David said.

"And don't think I've forgotten that, either."

David clapped his hands together, snuffing out the fire, and stalked off to a dark corner.

"Oh, come on," Erika griped.

"Erika," Winifred said. "You've said enough."

"Godsdammit," Erika spat. "I'm going back to the belfry."

"Don't go yet," Felix said, a disembodied voice in the darkness. "You're going to want to hear this."

THIRTEEN
Stalkers in the Night

Felix stood at the mouth of the alleyway for several minutes, silent and still, watching and listening. The gnashtooths lay where they fell, mountainous silhouettes in the night, and already they'd begun to emit the sickly sweet tang of putrefaction.

"What do you think?" Felix whispered to Furl. "As good as it's going to get?"

The lynx glanced up at Felix, his eyes gleaming green under the half moon, and then slunk toward the barracks, as low to the ground as a serpent. Felix followed, his footsteps as light and as soundless as his feline companion's — right up until they reached the edge of the training ground, where the delicate crunch of charred grass threatened to betray their position. Felix eased across the field, pausing at erratic intervals to break up the rhythm of his footfalls, while Furl proceeded at a steady, deliberate pace.

They reached the yawning entrance together and slipped inside.

The air here was thick and moist, like midday in high summer, and the stench, one part dung heap and one part slaughterhouse, made Felix's eyes water. These creatures, he mused, clearly did not observe the old axiom of *Don't shit where you eat.*

Felix gave himself a minute or two to adjust to the new environment, to let himself go nose-blind to the fetor and let his eyes adjust to the deeper darkness, before venturing farther — and even then, his surroundings insisted on remaining vague shapes devoid of telling detail. He tested each step before committing to it, feeling the ground ahead with a toe and without exception finding said ground to be disturbingly moist and spongy.

"Don't suppose you have a light on you?" he asked Furl.

"*Murr,*" Furl replied.

"Didn't think so."

He'd left his full pack behind at the meeting-house in the interest of traveling light but had brought with him a handful of potentially useful supplies, including some flint and steel and a small tin filled with pitch-soaked excelsior. He used the former to light the latter, and the latter to light a stub of a candle. He cupped his hand over the tiny flame and moved deeper into the makeshift pigpen.

A looming silhouette separated itself from the gloom. Felix moved his hand, and the flame revealed the hulk of an old carriage, something akin to a Moste Grande but less elegant in its lines and absent of adornment. It was a utilitarian vehicle, plain yet practical — and incomplete, he realized as he cast his pale light down where the wheels should have been; the front and back axles rested on a cradle of carefully stacked timbers. The wheels themselves sat in a pile nearby, next to a wooden toolbox, atop which lay a pair of leather work gloves.

A repair job, interrupted by the plague and never resumed. A slice of daily life in Woeste-Star, forever frozen in time.

Something just beyond the carriage caught Felix's candlelight, glinting warmly, flickering like a will-o'-the-wisp, beckoning to him.

Against his better judgment, Felix heeded the call.

According to Cedric Unterfalt, when the Gray Rot struck, the residents of Woeste-Star were confined to the city to prevent the disease from spreading to the world beyond. Hundreds upon hundreds of people died within Woeste-Star's walls and countless more outside them as they made a desperate, doomed effort to escape — and yet, they'd not found a single body anywhere, not so much as a finger bone. Now Felix had a corpse before him, but it was not the mere discovery of the remains that startled him, but the condition. This was not a body that had dropped more than a century ago to be stripped of its flesh by decay. No, this sorry individual met a more recent demise — and a violent one at that, one that snapped bones into splinters and reduced the skull to fragments.

Felix knelt and reached for the object that had caught his attention: an ostentatious gold brooch clinging to a scrap of deep red velvet. He held it close to his face to make out the intricate character engraved on the broach: a stylized musical note. Furl sat at Felix's feet and confirmed his deduction with a low, mournful whine.

"I'm sorry, boy," Felix said, stroking the cat's

head. He nuzzled close.

And then he stiffened into an arch, his fur puffing out from the base of his neck down to his bobtail. Felix followed Furl's gaze back toward the entrance. He listened for a moment and heard nothing, but then spied the unmistakable glow of distant torchlight. He snuffed out his candle and dashed deep into the carriage house, where he and Furl pressed against the far wall, trusting their concealment to the shadows.

For several taut minutes, the only sound was the anxious wheeze of Furl's breath.

Felix identified the outburst of expletives by their tone rather than by their content. A susurrus of an exchange followed — two voices engaged in a heated discussion. Felix shrank to the ground, putting up his hood and throwing his cloak over himself and Furl, willing himself to appear as a discarded horse blanket or some random pile of detritus as the murmur coalesced into intelligible language.

Two figures stepped into view. The silhouette on the left raised his torch. The light refused to penetrate the carriage house beyond a few yards.

"What do we do?" one of them asked. His companion said nothing. "*What do we do?*"

After a further pause, the other man said, "We have to report this."

"He'll be livid."

"He'll be livid we didn't come out and check on the gnashtooths earlier like we were supposed to. Whoever did this..." He left the thought unfinished. "Come on."

Felix pressed his lips together, refusing to release a sigh of relief.

"What do you think?" he whispered. Furl replied with a staccato series of agitated chirps. "Yeah. Me too."

"Please tell me you don't honestly believe Furl talks to you," Erika said.

"He's a *cat*, Erika," Felix said.

"*Mrrwr*," Furl grumbled.

"Well, you are. Anyway, we followed them halfway across the city, to what I think used to be a common house of worship back in the day. It was lit up inside like a solstice festival. I didn't want to risk a closer look but I think it's safe to say I found where our raiders are hiding out."

"Can you find your way back?" Erika asked.

"No problem."

"Good." Erika grabbed her bow and threw her quiver over her shoulder. "Let's go, people."

"What, now?" Derek said.

"We need to run reconnaissance. Better to do it under the cover of night."

"Mm. Good point."

"David, you stay here. We'll be back in —"

"What? No!" David cried. "I don't want to stay here all by myself!"

"We'll leave Furl with you," Erika said. The lynx narrowed his eyes at her, as if in accusation.

"But I want to come with you."

"No. This is a stealth mission. You'd risk exposing us."

"I can keep quiet!"

"What, you mean like you are now?" Felix said.

"I'm sorry, buddy, but Erika's right," Derek said.

"There's a lot more to sneaking around than simply being quiet. If you don't know what you're doing, you'd put us all at risk. You hold down the fort, we'll be back before you know it."

"Don't leave me behind," David said, his breath coming in labored wheezes. "Please."

"The answer is *no*, David," Erika snapped. "You're staying here, end of —"

"Erika," Winifred said, leveling a hard stare at her elven sister.

"I'll be right down," Erika said. She waited until her companions had descended the bell tower ladder. "David. Are you scared we won't come back?"

Tears rimmed his eyes. He nodded.

"Listen to me. This is a simple recon run, in and out. When we're done, we'll come back for you, we'll figure things out, and we'll finish this job together. Okay?"

"You can't promise that."

"You're right; I can't." Erika took a knee and laid a hand on David's shoulder. "But I will promise you this: we're not — *I* am not going to abandon you. I did that to you once and it was the worst mistake I've ever made in my life. I'm never going to do that again. I swear to you, *I will not abandon you*."

A tear rolled down David's cheek. He threw his arms around Erika's neck and squeezed tight.

"Oh, you had to ruin it," she sighed. She indulged David for a minute or two and then, with effort, pried his arms loose. "No flame, no noise. Got it?"

David nodded.

"We'll be back in an hour. If anyone who isn't us tries to come up here? You know what to do."

She left then, left David standing there in the darkness, in the silence.

And despite her solemn vow, David wondered if he would in fact ever see his former guardian again.

David pulled his blanket tight around his shoulders and repressed a shiver. The days were appropriate for the leading edge of summer, bright and sunny and warm, but the nights remained stubbornly indebted to the spring and would remain so for some time yet. Typically, summer did not fully assert itself until —

Until around my birthday, he realized. He was a summer child in the truest sense, born on solstice day, now less than a month away. He'd turn sixteen then — another step toward manhood, another step toward assuming his rightful role as high lord of all Asaches. He should have spent his day following his father around as he met with his advisers and reviewed the ledgers detailing the economy of an entire continent. He should presently be sitting in his father's study, in front of a warm fire, learning from him the finer points of administration and diplomacy in anticipation of the day when he would ascend to high lord.

But that was another life — and a lie of a life at that. Sitting at the head of the wardens' court was never part of his destiny; that future belonged to his brother Alexander. Always had.

What future, then, belonged to Randolph David Ograine?

Furl surveyed the boy, his narrowed eyes reflecting the meager light of a candle stub David had lit in defiance of Erika's orders, after his imagination had conjured one too many imaginary threats lurking in the darkness, waiting to pounce on him and feast on his innards. He reached out to stroke Furl's head, seeking a moment of comfort and companionship, but the lynx recoiled and backed away, a low hiss slipping out.

"What? I was just trying to be friendly." Furl hissed again. "*What?* Did I do something to you?"

Furl answered with a sneer that exposed a needlelike canine.

"*Pfft.* Why am I talking to you? It's not like you can understand me."

"*Mrrurr.*"

David cocked an eyebrow. "You...*can't* understand me. Right?"

"*Rurr.*"

With no one around to cast judgment on him, David decided to indulge his curiosity. "If you can understand me, meow twice." Furl replied with two short chirps. "Okay. So what's the deal? Why don't you like me? Was it because I called you a dumb animal?"

"*Murr.*"

"I'm sorry." He reached out, offering a conciliatory pet, but Furl wanted nothing to do with it; he again hissed and moved out of David's reach. "*What?!* I said I was sorry, you stupid cat!"

"*Mraah!*"

"Fuck you, then!" David hugged his knees to his chest. "Be that way. I don't care. Stupid cat."

Furl, his fur prickling, skittered toward David. He flailed away with a yelp, certain he'd pushed the lynx to the breaking point and was about to suffer the beast's wrath, but Furl pivoted and fell into a crouch, his eyes fixed on — something. Something in the dark, something David could not see — but oh, he could hear it, shuffling toward him, feet scraping on the cold stone floor. He raised a trembling hand and prepared to utter the incantation that would reduce the intruder to pulp — if it indeed was an intruder and not another illusory phantom brought about by anxiety and isolation. Any such doubt was dispelled when a vague silhouette materialized in the murk, its shape solidifying as it shambled toward the candlelight.

Corin'es. David mouthed the word of power over and over, felt the energy build within him. *Corin'es. Corin'es.*

His shriek prevented him from uttering the incantation, and that was all that saved Erika Racewind from dying a most grisly death by pulverization. She lurched into the candle's paltry halo, her eyes wide and wild, her face a mask of drying blood. She took a stuttering step and crashed to her knees, knocking over the candle and plunging the room back into the void.

"Erika!" David scrambled toward her on all fours. "What happened? Are you okay? Where are the others? Are you hurt?"

Erika seized him by the shirt. "Quiet. Need. To be. Quiet," she grunted. "Listen. *Listen.*"

"Okay, I'm lis— Furl, would you shut up?" David said in the general direction of Furl's disembodied, distressed whine.

"Go." She pulled David close. "Need. To go."

"What? What about the others? Where are Derek and Winifred and —"

"Need to. Go. Now," Erika said, her urgency bordering on panic.

"All right, we'll go. Can you get up? Are you hurt?"

"David…"

"Hold on, I can't see a thing," he said, resting one hand on Erika's shoulder and with the other patting the floor around him in search of the dead candle. Furl hissed a cobra's hiss as Erika's fingers slipped up around David's throat, almost of their own volition.

"You. Need. To go. NOW."

"Okay, okay!" He raised his free hand and, expecting another failure but nonetheless hopeful, said, "*Iscu'nera.*"

Erika's entire body went rigid and she screamed through clenched teeth. David yelped and kicked away, and the sudden frenzy sent Furl bolting into the farthest corner to growl and spit from a safe distance.

"David," Erika panted. "What — what did you do?"

"I don't know! I'm sorry!"

"No. Again."

"What?"

"Do it again. *Hurry.*"

He crawled toward the sound of Erika's breathing, heavy and guttural, and found her hands. Her grip was that of a drowning woman clinging to her rescuer, desperate and terrified — two words David would never normally associate with his erstwhile guardian, and that is why, despite the many questions swirling about in his head, he did not hesitate to repeat his incantation:

"*Iscu'nera.*"

Erika convulsed again. Her fingernails bit into David's palms hard enough to draw blood. He cried out but did not pull away — not that he could. Magical energy popped and flashed across her body, like heat lightning flickering soundlessly across summer storm clouds, and then she fell limp. A gurgling rasp escaped her lips like a death rattle.

"Erika?" He shook her, gently at first and with increasing alarm the longer she went without responding. "Erika? Erika!"

"I'm okay," she said at last. Furl crept up to her, gave her an experimental sniff, and then sat at her shoulder as if to confirm her claim. "What was that spell?"

"It's a — well, I *thought* it was a light spell."

Grunting, wincing, Erika propped herself up on her elbows. "That isn't how you described it before."

She was right, he realized; it wasn't. "The book described it as a spell to dispel darkness."

"Dispel darkness," she echoed, and she nodded. "Yeah. Okay. Good. We're going to need that."

"Why? What happened?"

Erika's lips curled away from her teeth to form a rueful snarl. "We found the mask," she said.

That was not all they found, she explained...

FOURTEEN
The Master of Puppets

There are many gods and many faiths throughout Ne'lan, some of them so old as to be nearly forgotten, so diminished in their presence in the world that
their collective congregations could be tallied on one's
fingers — but still they endure, for deities are stubborn
things. Even today, ancient god-monsters who feature
prominently in dusty myths foretelling of global apoca-
lypse exist — theologically speaking — alongside the
more contemporary pantheon of abstract concepts such
as love, strength, hope, and good fortune given human
form.

Oh, there are the occasional conflicts among the
extremely devout, for devotion shall always bring out
the worst in some people as easily as it brings out the
best in others, but as a rule, the faithful regard their
own chosen path as one among many that all lead to
the same ultimate truth. Why quibble over the journey
when everyone arrives at the same destination?

Common temples arose out of that belief, offering pilgrims and parishioners from all faiths a place to
gather, worship as they saw fit, and freely share their

spiritual perspectives with others that each might learn from the other. The Woeste-Star common temple was an especially impressive example that embraced a baroque aesthetic over simple lines and modest adornment — a telling reflection of the citizenry's true character. Ornamental turrets stood at the corners, each one topped with a quartet of highly detailed stone grotesques oriented toward the cardinal points of the compass. A row of a dozen Ionic columns dominated the façade, rising up beneath a frieze engraved with a tableau depicting *The Song of Marthus,* an epic poem in which the titular mythic hero survives a series of punishing trials that test his many human flaws, tearing him down and rebuilding him one piece at a time until he emerges reborn as a true champion of all mankind.

While none of them could say so with absolute certainty, the company suspected that the bizarre figures standing in the temple's sweeping front courtyard, lined up like soldiers for inspection, were not part of the original décor. They were shaped like people in a general sense, though the proportions were inconsistent from form to form and their outlines were crooked, uneven. Moonlight shone through their silhouettes much the way light might shine through the weave of a crude wicker basket.

"What are those things?" Derek said in a whisper. He squinted, as if willing his eyes to penetrate the night and reveal a telling detail. "Statues?"

"They're irrelevant is what they are," Erika said. "Felix, circle around to the left. I'll meet you in the rear. Derek, Winifred, stay out of sight and keep watch."

With that, Erika and Felix slipped out from their hiding spot inside a public stable that once accommodated visitors to the temple. Erika ducked into alleys and behind abandoned carriages and into recessed building entrances, dashing from blind to blind until there were no more and she had to make that final sprint across a stretch of open courtyard to reach the temple itself. She braced herself, glanced about, listened, and when she was as convinced as she could be there were no witnesses, she went.

She reached the temple and flattened against the cold stone, willing herself to become one with the shadows. No alarms sounded, no cries of warning rose up, but she did not permit herself a sigh of relief — not yet. She'd accomplished but one small goal; many more chances to be discovered lay ahead.

She crept along the outer wall, catlike in her movement, and paused under a tall, narrow window, the lower lip of which was barely within reach. A warm, flickering light leaked through the slit but did not stray beyond the opening, as though the glow itself was imprisoned within. Erika grasped the edge, pulled herself up, and peered inside. Fresh torches, recently lit, sat in iron sconces set into the walls at regular intervals. These sconces were the only original features remaining within the temple; it was otherwise devoid of seating or reliquaries or shrines or any of the trappings one might expect to see.

More notably, it was devoid of any presences, human or otherwise.

She checked each window she encountered as she made her circuit, and each window revealed only more of the same.

Upon reaching their agreed-upon rendezvous point at the rear of the temple, Felix reported similar findings — or, rather, a lack thereof. The temple, as far as either of them could discern, was for the nonce vacant.

"Where do you think everyone is?" Felix asked.

"Hunting for us is my guess," Erika said.

"How bold are you feeling?"

"You want to go in and look around, don't you?"

"Why not? If the mask is somewhere inside and we have half a chance to snag it and get the hell out of here tonight, I say we take it."

"If."

"We won't know if we don't take a peek, will we?"

Erika searched for a sound reason to dispute Felix's logic, mostly because she hated agreeing with the thief about anything, but came up empty.

"In and out," she said. "No unnecessary risks."

"Works for me."

Having found no rear entrances or viable alternate points of entry — all the windows were too narrow for either of them to squeeze through — they circled back around to the front, pausing at the corner of the grand structure long enough to determine they were still alone, still unobserved, before stealing inside.

Presented with two wide stairways, one leading up to the main temple and one leading down into mystery, they chose to go down.

Felix lit a candle stub to light their way through the lower level, the purpose of which immediately became clear. The candlelight revealed a simple cot, a wooden frame with a heavy canvas hammock, near the entrance. A tightly rolled wool blanket served as a pillow, and a second blanket sat in a pile at the foot of the cot, spilling over the edge and onto a canvas backpack. Similar arrangements occupied much of the level, with cots butted up along either wall and in a haphazard row up the center, leaving two wide paths stretching the length of the temple.

"This isn't a raiders' camp," Felix said. "Too organized."

Erika grunted in agreement.

Toward the back of the floor, a canvas sheet hung suspended by a length of rope secured to opposing torch sconces. Erika pulled back the sheet to reveal a small private area incrementally more elaborate than those that occupied the main floor. The cot was larger, sturdier, the blanket heavier and thicker, and instead of a pack a small wooden chest sat at its foot. A small clerk's desk such as one might find in a moneylender's office stood against the back wall.

"Keep an eye out," Felix said, kneeling before the chest. He set the candle on the floor and dug his lockpicks out of their home in his belt pouch. He took a moment to examine the lock, shiny and new, before selecting his tools and setting to work gently probing its innards, feeling for the delicate tumblers and nudging them into place.

"Shit," Erika said. "Felix, kill the light!"

He blew out the candle but continued his work undaunted; picking locks was a tactile art, not a visual one. Erika peered through a gap in the curtains. A man and a woman in leather armor, both wearing swords at their hips, came down the stairs, the warm light of a brass oil lamp leading the way.

Erika wrapped a hand around the hilt of her

dagger. Felix froze, fearful that the tiny *click-click* of his picks in action might be enough to betray their presence.

The pair stopped in front of a bunk near the end of the row, close enough that Erika could have reached out with her sword and touched them. The woman knelt and retrieved a longbow and a leather quiver full of arrows from beneath the bunk. She strung the bow in silence, slung the quiver over her shoulder, and followed her lamp-toting companion back toward the stairs. Erika waited until the telltale glow faded away and darkness fully reclaimed the barracks, and for several minutes after that, before breaking her silence.

"Finish up," she whispered.

"On it," Felix said.

A few gentle pokes and prods succeeded in popping the lock. Felix slipped it free of its hasp, lifted the lid, and cautiously probed the chest's interior with his pick to find something soft and yielding within — a cushion, hiding beneath a length of heavy cotton fabric.

"Godsdammit," he cursed.

"Nothing?"

"Nothing. Complete waste of time."

Not entirely, Erika thought, but what they'd learned did not warrant pushing their luck any further. "Let's get the hell out of here."

Felix packed up his tools and followed Erika back toward the stairs. They paused at the base of the stairway, watching and listening. A gentle murmur drifted down from the temple proper — voices, soft but numerous, the drone of guarded conversation. Erika held up a hand, a silent command to hold position, then pointed to the ceiling. Felix nodded and drew one of his sabers. He slipped by and took the steps at a crawl, hunched low, ready to retreat back into the shadows at the first hint of approaching footsteps.

He crept up onto the landing and froze, almost as if daring someone to spot him and sound an alarm.

As confident as he could be he'd made it this far unobserved, Felix softly snapped his fingers twice. Erika joined him on the landing, and they braced themselves for their final dash to freedom.

Felix peeked outside. His heart briefly leapt at the sight of several figures populating the courtyard — the strange statues they'd spotted earlier, he realized. He motioned to Erika, an all-clear signal, and together they sprinted down the temple stairs. They split off after reaching the courtyard and ducked behind the nearest statues, intending to make their retreat in a series of cautious bursts that took advantage of the generous cover the misshapen figures provided.

Felix, glancing back to confirm whether they'd made a clean getaway, caught a flash of pale moonlight gleaming off his statue. He stepped back to behold the figure in all its macabre glory — and in that terrible moment learned the answer to the question that had been sitting in the back of his brain since their arrival. The city's entire populace, struck down so swiftly by the Gray Rot and left to die where they fell, never to receive the dignity of a proper funeral — *so what happened to all the bodies?*

The horror before him was a grotesque mockery of the human form composed entirely of bone — hundreds, perhaps thousands of bones large and small, buffed by the sun and the elements to an ivory finish and held together by thick strips of leather and clots of dark, rubbery pitch. A crooked column of multiple rib-cages comprised its core. One arm ended in a jagged mace studded with teeth. The other sprouted claws of repurposed ribs. Several individual skulls bound into a crude sphere by leather cording served as the thing's head, and cloudy red gems had been inserted into two of the many available sockets to approximate eyes. It was a nightmare made real by some demented sculptor, a demon from the nether realms set loose upon the earth.

Felix choked on a gasp when the construct's compound head twisted to turn its lifeless gemstone eyes on him.

It moved with preternatural speed. Felix dove clear, narrowly avoided a sweep of its rib-claws, and nimbly rolled back up to his feet — and right into the path of a second golem as it windmilled an arm ending in a spiked fist of leather-wrapped rib bones. Felix scrambled out of the way with inches to spare.

As if in response to a silent call to arms, the rest of the unnatural army roused from its unnatural slumber. A pair of golems converged on Erika, flanking her. She ducked beneath a wild swipe and, as she dropped to a knee, pulled her sica and fluidly turned the draw into her first strike, targeting what passed as the thing's knee joint. The tip of her blade severed a web of leather pretending to be a network of muscles and tendons. The golem took a step, and the limb failed. Erika skittered out of its way as it sprawled onto the ground. She capitalized on the moment and drove her sica through the other knee, then wrenched the blade as if pulling a lever to slice through the leathern pseudo-musculature. The construct, mindless and unfeeling, pushed itself upright and renewed its advance, clumsily waddling toward Erika on its stumps.

Derek proved more effective in halting its assault. With the momentum of a full sprint behind his swing, his longsword easily shattered the golem's head of heads into fragments. Its gemstone eyes caught the moonlight as they tumbled through the air, glinting like droplets of blood. The remaining mass fell inert, again becoming a monstrous but harmless statue.

The other golems, as if enraged by their ally's defeat, grew more aggressive. Their attacks became frenzied, reckless. While Derek and Erika chose to meet their foes head-on, focusing their attacks on the golems' few proven vulnerable spots, Felix and Winifred used their superior agility to weave through the lumbering hulks and draw their attacks into one another, and on this the golems obliged, battering each other as easily as they'd smite their fleshy prey.

Unfortunately for our heroes, the quintet of raiders that charged forth from the temple, drawn out by the unmistakable din of pitched battle, were not so careless. They spread out along the perimeter of the fight, taking care not to stray too close to the rampaging golems — or their targets, for that matter — and dedicated themselves to corralling the intruders so the bone sentinels could carry out the lethal task for which they were created.

Winifred, opting to challenge this strategy, slipped past a pair of golems, who obligingly ran one another through with their skeletal fists, and brought her quarterstaff down on a raider's shoulder. He screamed and collapsed to his knees, a sensation simultaneously freezing and burning racing down his now useless arm. Winifred raised her staff again to deliver a second incapacitating blow.

"STOP!"

The command, deep and resonant, overcame the cacophony of shouts and cracking bone. The golems froze in mid-motion, falling perfectly still — and so too, to their alarm and dismay, did our heroes, though theirs was not a perfect stillness. Derek's arms, locked in mid-swing, trembled with potential energy aching for release. Erika fought to turn toward the sound of the voice, but the air felt as though it had thickened to the consistency of tar.

A figure draped in a dark purple robe swept into view, backed by a veritable army. The raiders spread out to thoroughly surround the battlefield while the stranger who commanded them wove between the frozen golems as silently as a specter drifting through the trees of the Monolith Forest.

"Drop your weapons," he said. "All of you. Drop your weapons."

Winifred was the first to comply, her fingers uncurling of their own volition — or were they? — and letting her staff fall to the ground at her feet.

The stranger approached Felix and brazenly stood in front of him, easily within reach, as if daring the thief to ram his sabers through his gut — and Felix wanted to do just that, so very badly, but all he could do was glance up at the man and behold the engraved iron mask covering his face.

"Drop your weapons," he said again.

The sabers fell from Felix's grasp.

The stranger drifted toward Derek and repeated his command. Derek's grip on his sword slackened.

Somehow, he held on — for the moment, but that moment was slipping away.

"Erika," he grunted.

"Damn you," the masked man snarled, "I said drop your weapon! Do it! *Do it!*"

With the stranger's focus turned completely onto Derek, the fog enshrouding Erika's mind lifted ever so slightly — but it was enough. She hurled her dagger, a true act of desperation; the heavy, curved blade was ill-suited for such use; even had her hand been steady and sure, the chances of it striking true were slim.

Steel met iron. The dagger pinged off the ancient mask, staggering the stranger. As he fell to a knee, his raiders drew their weapons and came at her, howling for her blood.

"Erika," Derek said. His longsword hit the ground with a thud. "Run."

FIFTEEN
Unmasked

"You ran?" David said, incredulous at the very notion of Erika Racewind fleeing a fight.

"I had to."

"But you left Derek and Winifred and Felix behind."

"I had to," Erika snapped. "It took everything to resist the mask's power as much as I did. When he spoke, it was —" She fumbled for a way to describe it, the experience of someone else's will supplanting her own, compelling her to obey, and came up short. "The last thing I heard him say was, 'Come back,' and it was like his voice got stuck in my head. All I wanted to do was turn around. It almost hurt to disobey."

"Is that why the others didn't escape too? Or do you —" His throat tightened. "Do you think they're — ?"

"If they wanted us dead, they would have just killed us," Erika said, mostly for the sake of keeping David calm.

"We're going to rescue them, right?"

Erika's lips pressed into a thin, bloodless line.

"That depends on you."

"Me?"

"I have an idea. You won't like it."

"I'll do whatever you need me to."

"I need you to trust me. More than anything, I need you to trust me."

"Of course I trust you."

That declaration, heartfelt and earnest, kindled a warmth in Erika's chest that, for a moment, caused her stoic façade to slip. She allowed the tiniest of smiles and then reasserted herself. Sentiment would have to wait; they had friends to save.

"Listen carefully. This is what we're going to do," she said.

David stumbled. He threw out his hands instinctively, but bound together as they were, their use in breaking his fall was negligible. He let out a yelp of pain that was as real as his tumble, as real as the black eye Erika had inflicted upon him to enhance the theater of their deception.

"Don't move!" someone shouted. Erika grasped David by the shirt and jerked him back up onto his feet. He blinked away tears and beheld a trio of raiders running across the temple courtyard, swords drawn. Their capture wasn't unexpected — indeed, it was critical to Erika's plan — but he cowered nevertheless. He'd seen enough action in his short life to know enemies could be frustratingly uncooperative when it came to adhering to a plan. Erika, however, did not flinch in the slightest when one of the raiders raised the tip of his sword to her throat. Her expression remained utterly blank.

The woman holding the weapon gave David a cold, mirthless smile. "Who are you, boy?"

"Please don't hurt me," he said. Again, sincerity lent credibility to his performance.

"Ohh, sorry, little man. That's not my call to make." She leaned in. "Unless you give me any trouble. Then it will be my decision."

The raiders herded their captives across the courtyard, past what remained of the bone golem army. The battle had reduced their numbers by a third — by half if one included among the casualties constructs that had been deprived of a limb or two yet remained stubbornly functional — but they did not need the force of numbers to chill young David to his core. Erika's description did not do the macabre things their deserved justice.

At sword point, Erika and David climbed the stairs leading to the temple. Their captors called out, and a wall of raiders, more than a dozen strong, parted in the middle like stage curtains opening to reveal the evening's player — the man in the dark robes — and his unwilling company of Derek, Felix, and Winifred. They stood among the cultists — the word popped into David's head; it felt like the most apt description — chillingly still and dead-eyed. The only discernible sign of life was a distinct tension in Derek's face manifesting as a twitching at the corner of his lip. David impulsively moved toward him, only to be rudely jerked back by one of his captors, the woman who threatened to discipline him should he misbehave.

The masked man turned, his robes flaring, and immediately his eyes fell upon David. Perhaps it was a trick of the light, the flickering torches playing on the iron face in such as a way as to create the illusion of movement, but David swore he saw the mask's brow crease in a moment of bewilderment.

"Hello again, my young friend," the man said.

David started. *Again?*

"My friends!" the man boomed, spreading his arms. "If any doubt lingered among you whether we were on a righteous path, behold! The Gods have delivered to us he who possesses nothing less than a grimoire of great, dark knowledge scribed by our lord himself!" He pointed to a spot on the floor — a summons. "Come here, boy."

David did not move. Again, he was certain the mask responded as would a human face, its eyeholes narrowing into an irritated squint.

"Come here," the man repeated.

Erika, unseen by the cultists, tapped David's foot with her own. He steeled himself and left her side. An eternity later, he stepped within arm's reach of the masked man, who seized a handful of David's shirt and held him fast.

"Where is Habbatarr's book?" the man said. "Do you have it here? Is it hidden? Tell me."

David clenched his teeth, biting down on the question jumping into his brain: *How does he know about the book?*

"Answer me, boy. Where is the book?"

David shook his head. Now that he was so close to his mysterious host, close enough to smell his breath, he could clearly see that the mask was a solid piece of iron, utterly incapable of expression. The face behind it, however, was quite animate — and growing quite angry.

"I said tell me where it is."

"No," David replied in a whisper.

"Tell me where the book is," the man demanded. *"Tell me."*

His commands were more than verbal assaults — so much more. They had the power of the mask of Lord Kilnmar behind them, a power so great that it reduced David's friends to puppets, and yet that same power slid off him as easily as water beads off a duck's feathery coat.

"No." A laugh slipped out. "No."

The cultists murmured among themselves, a curious and nervous buzz.

"Tell me!" The masked man seized David by the head and glared at him with wild, maniacal eyes. "I command you to TELL ME!"

And David, grinning, said simply, "Go to hell."

The man roared and threw David away. He then leveled a commanding finger at Felix. "You. Draw your saber and hold it to her throat."

Felix hesitated but a moment before doing as ordered, placing the edge of his saber in the crook where Winifred's jaw and neck met.

"NO! Don't hurt her!" David pleaded. "Please don't hurt her. I'll tell you."

"A wise decision," the masked man said. "Now: where is the book?"

David drew a slow breath. He took a moment or two to study his tormenter, to fix in his mind the man's features, and then he closed his eyes so that he would not have to witness what came next.

"Corin'es."

What escaped the masked man was less a

scream and more a violent retching noise, a strangled squeal backed by a chorus of snapping and cracking. Something warm and wet spattered across David's face.

And then he opened his eyes to an explosion of chaos in mid-detonation. Two cultists fell dying, their bellies sliced open, as Erika skewered a third. A handful more converged on her, cattle stampeding blindly to their slaughter, while others, their faces drained of all color, stood frozen in horror over the broken heap that was their leader. David sprayed a plume of flame across this loose line of cultists trapped in mid-stupor, driving some back, igniting others.

He then bolted toward his mesmerized friends, his hands outstretched. With one, he seized Felix by the wrist and pulled his blade away from Winifred's slender throat; with the other, he latched onto Winifred's forearm. He uttered his incantation, a combination of blind terror and pure desperation and sheer force of will lending him the strength he needed to hold on as Felix and Winifred thrashed like wild horses bucking off an unwanted rider. It was not until their paroxysms ceased and they went limp in his grasp that he released them.

"Winifred? Felix?" he said. "Are you —?"

Felix, teeth bared like a ravening wolf, lunged at him, blade poised for a strike, and for a heart-stopping instant, David feared his magic had failed him — but the thief knocked him aside, and as he spun he caught sight of his friend's true target: a cultist — the very one who'd practically dared David to defy her — coming in for a sneak attack. Felix rammed his saber home, punching the blade through her breastplate. He gave the saber a vicious twist before jerking it free.

"Winifred, watch my back!" David said, dashing up to Derek in order to free him from the masked man's thrall — or rather, what remained of it; he wore the slack, dull expression of a man awakening from a deep sleep, and he seemed distantly aware of the mayhem around him even as David cast the purging spell. His reaction to the cleansing magic was less violent than that of his compatriots, and his recovery was almost instantaneous. He plunged headlong into the melee, and within minutes, every last raider lay upon the floor of the Woeste-Star common temple, dead or soon to be. None of their number had exercised discretion and fled into the night. The thought never occurred to them. They had sworn a sacred oath and each and every man and woman honored that oath, until the last, even when it became clear theirs was a losing battle. Such is the nature of the fanatic.

"Find me someone who isn't dead yet," Erika said. "I want answers."

"Good luck with that," Felix said, taking in the carnage strewn at their feet. "We were pretty thorough."

As if in defiance of the thief's assessment, a groan rose up, wet and gurgling.

"Here," Winifred said, kneeling at the prostrate form of the man in the mask of Lord Kilnmar. The company gathered around and marveled at the perverse miracle; David's spell had broken nearly every bone in the man's body, yet he tenaciously clung to life — or perhaps, Death was taking her time in claiming this particular tainted soul.

"David, take the mask," Erika said.

"Uh-uh. You take it," David said. "I don't want to touch it."

"I think you're the only one who should touch it."

There was a question in David's frown, but he did as told. The iron mask was warm to the touch, unnaturally so, and it was with some dismay David realized there was nothing holding it onto the man's face — no cord or attached skullcap of any kind.

"I know him," David said.

"You do?" Derek said.

David looked again. The dying man's face had been skewed out of true by the breaking spell and was ballooning like an overripe plum, rendering him almost unrecognizable, but the bald head and the tidy white beard with its hints of fading red jumped out in David's memory. He could not recall that the fellow's name was Oren Mesztal, but he did remember, "We spoke to him at the Grande Academie. I let him study Habbatarr's book."

"That book is ours," Mesztal rattled. He coughed up red foam and bared blood stained teeth. "It belongs to the Deathless Legion."

David gasped reflexively, and Mesztal's grin hardened into a self-satisfied rictus.

Erika knelt down, sparing the time to pat Mesztal down in search of her dagger, which she found tucked in the belt beneath his robe, claimed as a prize. "Tell us everything," she said, pressing the tip of her blade into the soft underside of Mesztal's jaw.

He wheezed — a feeble laugh. "Or what? You'll kill me?"

"Or I leave you here to die, slowly and painfully.

Tell us what you know and I'll put you out of your misery."

"My only misery is knowing that bastard child has my lord's book. *It belongs to us,*" Mesztal wheezed.

Erika smirked. "That bastard child is Randolph Ograine. Take a good look at him. Take a good look at the Reaper himself. Take a good look at the boy who killed your lord." Her smirk became a savage grin. "How's that for misery?"

Erika Racewind was scrupulous about keeping her blades razor sharp. Oren Mesztal never felt it enter.

"Oh, nice," Felix said. "He definitely won't tell us anything now."

"He wasn't going to talk." Erika wiped her weapons on Mesztal's robe before sheathing them. "We had everything to gain and he had nothing to lose."

She sat, a sudden enervation overtaking her. Like a contagion, the exhaustion hit Derek, Felix, and Winifred in turn, draining them of the will to move.

"Gods, I feel like I could sleep for a month," Derek said.

"That might be an aftereffect of the mask's influence," David said, in that moment remembering that he still had the mask in question in his hands. He gazed down at it, and a chill coiled around his spine. The mask seemed to be gazing back at him.

"We need to melt that Godsdamned thing to slag right fucking now," Felix said.

"Find me a workable forge and I'll take care of it," Derek said. "Unless this is one of those deals where we have to throw it into a volcano or smash it on the anvil it was forged on."

He looked to David, who shrugged. "No idea."

"I agree we should destroy it, but not here," Erika said. "We need to get out of the necropolis as soon as possible."

"You think there might be more of these, um...raiders?" Winifred said. The word, inexplicably, felt all wrong now.

"Cultists," David said.

"Cultists. You think there might be more of them?"

"My gut says no," Erika said, glancing down at Mesztal, "but why take that chance?"

"Besides, we got what we came for," Derek noted.

"Exactly. I say we hunker down for the night and head out at dawn."

With no better idea presenting itself, our heroes left the temple, taking great care to give the bone golems the widest possible berth, and wended their way back to their extemporaneous base of operations. Furl greeted Felix with a level of enthusiasm not normally seen in cats — which is to say any — and curled up in the cradle of his body when he laid down to sleep. Winifred followed presently, and Erika was exceptionally grateful when Derek offered to take first watch. She nodded off as soon as she finished stretching out on the floor.

"If you want to get some rest, I can keep an eye on things," David said.

"I'll let you know," Derek said. "You did good tonight, buddy."

"I did?"

"Oh, yeah. I don't know how you were able to shrug off the mask's power like you did — "

Neither did David. He kept this admission to himself.

" — but I'm glad for it. Think it's safe to say you saved us all."

"Oh."

"You sound surprised."

"I'm not used to being the one doing the saving." David's shrug went unseen in the darkness. "I'm not used to being useful."

"What're you talking about? You've been useful plenty of times. You're the one who took out an entire room full of raiders back at Castle Somevil-Duur. That really turned the tide for us. And you're the one who killed Habbatarr."

"Huh," David grunted, but the mention of his late nemesis overrode any sense of personal pride he might have otherwise enjoyed. "That man said he was part of the Deathless Legion."

"Yeah," Derek said, although the last time he'd heard that name, it was attached to a cadre of reanimated warriors under the command of Adolphus Drakemore, a necromancer who claimed fealty to the lich-lord of Hesre. "We always knew Habbatarr had followers..."

"But I thought the cult died out with Habbatarr."

"So did I. Apparently not."

"But why? He's dead — I mean *dead* dead. What's the point of worshipping him anymore? It doesn't make any sense."

"Not to us, no, but we're not insane. Whatever the cult is up to, it probably makes perfect sense to them."

"So what do we do?"

"For starters, we make damn sure that mask doesn't fall back into the Deathless Legion's hands," Derek said, recalling David's tale about the mask's alleged origins. "I think it's safe to say we know now who gave it to Lord Kilnmar."

"Maybe." David shrugged. "Doesn't matter, really. The Deathless Legion *believes* Habbatarr created it."

"Yeah, and that's our problem; we're fighting belief. Fighting people is relatively easy, but faith, good or bad, is a lot harder to kill. Destroying the mask is the only way I can think of to get the cult off our backs."

"Do we need to destroy it, though? I mean, what if we gave it to someone we could trust, like Madam Roust? She could keep it hidden. Maybe we could study it, figure out if there's a way we could use it against the cult? I mean, shouldn't we explore all our options? It could be useful to us."

He said *we*. He said *us*.

All Derek heard was *I* and *me*.

"Do you really think that's the smart move?"

David laid a hand on his pack, the one holding the mask, and pulled it toward himself protectively.

"Just a suggestion," he said.

"I think the wisest course of action is to melt it down as soon as we get the chance," Derek said. "It's too dangerous for anyone to hold onto."

Especially, he thought, anyone who seemed to be completely immune to its dark power.

SIXTEEN
All Stands Revealed

Exhaustion claimed Derek more quickly than he'd anticipated. He nodded off soon after his conversation with David, leaving the boy to hold a lonely vigil.

When Derek failed to automatically rise at first light, David made every effort to rouse him, but the enervation that had fallen upon the company held fast and strong. He shook his friends, gently slapped their faces, yelled and stomped on the floor, turned to one of his less frequently used spells to sprinkle rain down on their heads, but to no avail; they never once stirred. All he accomplished was to agitate Furl, who paced an anxious circle around the quintet, yowling all the while.

Spent, David sat on the floor intending to catch his breath and think the problem through. He closed his eyes, took a breath...

And when he opened them, half the day had passed, as evidenced by the bright midday sun streaming through the window slits. In a panic, he screamed Derek's name and gave him a violent shake, and at last he awakened, if only technically; it took him several more minutes to shrug off the fog that follows a long, deep sleep.

It was early afternoon by the time the company fully roused themselves. They hastily gathered up their belongings and began their return journey, knowing full well they would again have to make camp in the impenetrable darkness of the Monolith Forest. Working on the optimistic assumption they would rise in a timelier manner the following morning, Derek estimated they'd still have a half a day's worth of travel ahead of them before reaching Woeste — but that projection also assumed they would cross half the forest before nightfall, which they did not. Their pace at the outset was at best languid, by late afternoon had ground to a trudge, and when night finally arrived to plunge the forest into solid darkness, they could barely muster a brisk shamble. Felix effectively made the decision to camp for the night when he shuffled to a stop, sat down, and slipped into a light doze sitting up. Winifred followed, and then Derek, and then David. Erika fought off sleep for as long as she could before succumbing, and she slumped onto the ground without waking anyone to take over watch duty.

A ring of specters kept the companions company throughout the night.

And in the morning, Derek returned to his habit of being the first to wake. He sat up, immediately alert and aware — the first of several good signs. His friends all awoke with minimal encouragement and showed no signs of the torpor that had weighed upon them so greatly the previous day. Eager to make up for lost time, they took the first leg of the day's travels at a vigorous clip, pausing but once to rest and take lunch.

The end of their path appeared several hours later in the form of a distant pinpoint of daylight, like the first star of the evening hanging low and all alone in the night sky. That faintest tease of pending freedom reinvigorated our heroes, and they jogged, then ran, then sprinted toward the break in the trees. Furl was the first of them to escape the Monolith Forest's smothering gloom, and he spun and leapt with delight upon reaching open ground.

The lynx's exuberant chattering acted as an alarm that summoned forth Agatha Don Contess. She flung open the guardhouse's rear door and strode out, hand upon her sword hilt. She eased into a ready stance as Derek, hands raised in a gesture of peace, crossed the no man's land separating the forest from the guardhouse.

"It's okay. We're okay," he said. Don Contess nevertheless remained primed. "We found the mask."

She started. "You what?"

"We found the mask of Lord Kilnmar."

"You — you —?" Don Contess stammered. Her expression hardened and she said, "Show me."

A second guard appeared at Don Contess's side, his sword drawn but down, as David removed the mask from his backpack and held it aloft. Don Contess said something to her subordinate, soft and low, never taking her eyes off David's prize.

"Let me see it," she said, gesturing at the boy to step forward. Erika stuck an arm out, barring him from doing so. Don Contess frowned. "How do I know that's the real mask?"

"What, you think we just happened to find another creepy iron mask back there?" Felix said, jerking a thumb in the general direction of the Gray Necropolis. "Come on."

"Look, let us get our horses and then we'll be out of your hair, okay?" Derek said.

Don Contess made a sour face. "Lar, you ride ahead to let the council know their mercenaries are back."

"Adventurers for hire," Felix corrected.

"I care." Don Contess dismissed her underling with a sharp nod. Lar nodded in return and ran off toward the stables.

"I don't suppose we could get a hand prepping our horses," Derek said.

"I'm not a groom. You know where the stables are," Don Contess said, ending their discourse there. She turned on her heel and disappeared back into the guardhouse.

"Bitch," Felix said. "I have half a mind to drag her ass back out and make her help us."

"Let's not," Derek said. "The council's going to be pissed at us enough when we refuse to hand over the mask."

"Shit. Right," Felix muttered, and the collective mood turned glum; by refusing to relinquish the object of their quest, they realized, they would almost certainly have to forfeit their bounty.

"Considering how dangerous it is, I think it's a fair tradeoff," Winifred said in a half-hearted attempt to cheer her friends. "We can't risk letting the mask fall into the wrong hands again."

"Yeah," Derek said, sighing. "Home stretch, people. Let's see this through."

***

The horizon was soaked in the rich, deep purple of dusk by the time the company reached the edge of the city proper. The evening promised to be warm and pleasant, the kind of evening that would lend itself nicely to several hours of heavy pity drinking on a tavern patio.

City hall was dark when they arrived, save for hints of lamplight glowing behind the windows of the domed council chamber. A trio of guards gathered around the rear entrance regarded the party with cool disinterest as they approached.

"The council is expecting you," one guard said to them. He instructed one of his mates to tend to the horses, and then he ushered the party inside.

The full council was there within, and they greeted their hirelings with a myriad of expressions — some glad, some neutral, some displeased, all of them subdued. The contingent of city guards ringing the edge of the main floor, if they had opinions one way or the other, kept them to themselves.

Greave stepped forward, smiling, shadowed by Mock, who was not. "I do hope our friends are in a right state of mind?" Greave inquired.

"We are," Derek said. "Speaking of which, how are the Blades doing?"

"They're still not themselves. They continue to wander about their cell in a fog."

Derek nodded.

"To business," Greave said. "You've recovered the mask?"

"We have, yes, but..."

Her smile slipped. "But?"

"We can't give it to you."

"You what?" Mock snapped.

"Councilor Mock, we're sorry, but we've seen for ourselves how dangerous the mask is, and we can't in good conscience —"

"Your conscience is irrelevant," Greave said. She reasserted her gentle smile. "We will keep the mask safe. Its power will never again be abused."

"And we're going to see to that personally," Erika said.

"That isn't your decision to make," Mock said. "The mask is ours. It belongs to us — to the city," he said as if issuing a correction.

"Quite so," Greave agreed. "Now, please hand over the mask."

"Give it here," Mock said, and he held out a demanding hand. "Now."

"Dunstan," Greave said, a gentle reprimand. "I'll take the mask, Mr. Strongarm."

"Give it to me."

"Dunstan, I have this under control, please let me —"

"Give it to me!" Mock repeated.

"Derek," Erika said.

Something in her voice caused Derek to make a casual scan of the room. Traymon and Scheere, backed by a quartet of guards, had drifted to one side of the chamber, near Mock. Another group of guards responded to a small tilt of Greave's head, circling past her, Folstoy, and fellow Councilors Lemuel Stripling and Jann Mittle to place themselves between the company and the rear exit.

"Let's not make this harder than it needs to be," Greave said with waning patience. "Give me the mask and we can all —"

"No! The mask is mine! MINE!" a red-faced Mock roared. He pumped a fist, a spastic gesture, and a heartbeat later, every sword in the chamber was out of its scabbard and trained on our heroes. "The mask is mine by divine right, and I shall use its power to restore my dark lord to glory! I swear to all the Gods, *Habbatarr will rise again!*"

"What?!" Greave squealed.

"Oh, you poor unsuspecting fool," Mock said with a manic titter. He pulled up his sleeve to reveal on his inner forearm a brand, inflicted long ago, depicting a skeletal hand. "You never knew, did you? That I and my followers were working our master's will right under your noses!"

Greave blinked at Mock, shook her head, sputtered, and then wrestled off a leather bracer and displaying her forearm — and the identical brand thereupon. Their respective factions — Folstoy, Mittle, and Stripling on Greave's side, Traymon and Scheere on Mock's — followed suit and revealed the telltale brands upon their inner arms.

"What?" Mock said. "You're all —?"

"Loyal to the Deathless Legion? Oh, yes," Greave said, a laugh slipping out. "Oh, my dear Dunstan. It appears we've both been a little too effective in keeping our secrets, haven't we?"

"Indeed — but now that we've made clear where everyone stands..." Mock said, turning his gaze on who now stood revealed as a mutual enemy.

"Hm, yes. It does simplify matters, doesn't it?"

"It does. What say we simplify them further?"

"An excellent idea."

The councilors raised their hands, mirroring one another in gesture and in intent, which was to signal their respective minions to move in and slaughter the heroes who dared to oppose them. Unfortunately for them, they had become so engrossed in their dialog that they failed to notice the companions quietly planning their response — a response that opened with David releasing a brief blast of arcane fire to momentarily blind and drive back the encroaching cultists. To do more would be to risk turning the chamber into an indiscriminate funeral pyre for friend and foe alike.

Derek and Erika led the charge toward the chamber's rear exit and cut down the trio of guards barring their exit. Their escape path clear, our heroes fled into the night — with no less than an entire city standing between them and freedom.

ACT THREE
In Which Our Heroes Find Themselves Surrounded, Outnumbered, Hunted, and Generally Inconvenienced

SEVENTEEN
A Tale of Two Cults

"Get them, you idiots!" Mock roared at his followers. "Kill them! Kill them and recover the mask!"

"You heard him," Greave said to her minions. "Go after them!"

Their respective lackeys hesitated a moment longer, as if expecting this surprising new alliance to fall apart as quickly as it formed, and then did as bade. They stepped past their fallen comrades and poured out of the chamber before scattering in all directions to begin the hunt.

"It's not enough," Folstoy said. "We need to send the full city guard after them."

"And the militia," Scheere added. "They can seal off the borders to ensure —"

"And tell them what, exactly?" Traymon said. "Not everyone within the guard are true believers, and we've barely begun to spread the gospel within the militia."

Greave, unconcerned, said, "We tell them the truth: that the adventurers we hired to retrieve the mask reneged on their contract."

"They threatened us and slew three of our brave city guards before making good on their escape," Mock said, seamlessly continuing Greave's train of thought.

Folstoy nodded approvingly. "Sound the alarm," he told Ilfreda, who obediently dashed off to ring city hall's great bronze bell for the first time in many years.

"How nice that we're at last of one mind," Greave said with a smile.

"Agreed," Mock said, "and in the interest of cementing our harmonious new relationship, I'd like to extend a sincere apology."

"What for?"

"For unwittingly putting us at cross purposes. You see, I was the one who orchestrated the theft of the mask. I began plotting soon after that twit Unterfalt shared his little discovery with the council."

"A discovery, I recall, you dismissed out of hand as nonsense," Greave said, and a small gasp of realization escaped her lips. "Ah. A ruse to throw off future suspicion?"

"Quite so. I arranged for some of my followers to conduct a raid on the archives and take the mask to the Gray Necropolis. I thought sure no one would be brave enough to follow — and then you suggested hiring adventurers to recover the mask."

Greave nodded, recalling the meeting at which she put forth her proposal and Mock's restrained but heartfelt objections. "I'll give credit where it's due," she said. "That your people were able to subjugate the Noble Blades themselves is beyond impressive."

"The power of the mask," Mock said, his mood shifting, "although Mesztal was supposed to help protect it, not use it himself."

"Mesztal?" Traymon interjected. "I know him. He's with the Grande Academie."

"He is — their foremost expert on necromancy, in fact. It didn't take much to turn him into a disciple. The promise of further knowledge was too great a temptation."

"And where is your man now? Dead?"

Mock shrugged mildly, though he suspected that was the case.

The first tolling of city hall's great bell shook the building to its foundation. The air itself thickened from the sound and carried with it an electric tingle that prickled the conspirators' flesh beneath their ceremonial garb of office.

"Once we recover the mask, we'll need to come to an agreement on what to do with it," Greave said.

"You mean we'll need to agree on which of us claims it," Mock said. "I nominate myself."

Greave gave him a thin smile. "Of course you do."

"Perhaps it would be wisest to let a neutral third party hold onto it," Traymon said — but to his ire, his suggestion went unacknowledged.

"I can offer you something of commensurate value," Mock said. "That boy, the young sorcerer? He has a book of dark knowledge scribed by our lord's own hand."

Greave started. "He has *what?*"

"Yes. Mesztal examined the book himself. He was only allowed to read a few pages but he was absolutely certain it was authentic. Think about it, Belinda; you and I in possession of not one but two artifacts touched by Habbatarr. We would become hierophants among the Deathless Legion. The power we'd command —"

"Would be second only to Habbatarr himself. Ohh, the glory he would bestow upon us," Greave said, the corners of her lips twitching — and then her expression turned suddenly cold and iron. "We have to find that boy. We have to recover the book."

"We will," Mock declared. "Fate brought him to us. He won't escape. If we have to raze this entire city to the ground, we will find him."

"This way!" Felix said, cutting a sharp left into a narrow alleyway.

"Do you know where we're going?" Derek asked.

"Away from the people who want to kill us."

"Oh, brilliant plan," David drawled.

"If you have a better one, kid, let's hear it," Felix said, his words drowned out by the sound of a mighty bell tolling nearby.

"Shit," Erika said. "Don't think that's a viable option anymore. Wait, stop. Felix, here."

She pointed out a corroded padlock securing a thin wooden door. Felix understood immediately and took out his lockpicks. A deft poke and prod sprang the lock, which he pocketed before entering the shop — Madam Schaft's Fineries, a boutique specializing in high-end women's formalwear. Felix crept up to the front of the shop and peered out through the bow window, using for a blind a frilly and grossly overpriced party gown hanging on a wooden dress form.

"All clear," he reported.

"That won't last long," Erika said. "Our best hope was to get out of Woeste before the city guard had a chance to mobilize in force. Now they'll be moving to get ahead of us and set up blockades on every road leading out of the city."

"That doesn't mean we're trapped," Derek said.

"No, but it does make getting out of here a lot tougher," Felix said. "We can use the alleys to get through the city center, but after that we'll have to cross a lot of open ground, no matter which direction we go."

"You know the city better than we do. Is there a path of least resistance?"

"I don't know it that well," Felix admitted, "but I don't think any one way is better than any other, really."

"Except for the one that takes us back toward the Gray Necropolis," David said.

"Yeah." Felix grinned. "Yyyyeahhhh..."

"Oh, you can't be serious."

"No, he may be on to something," Erika said. "The Gray Necropolis is for all intents and purposes a dead end. It would be a waste of manpower to post a heavy guard along that road."

"Right. Because it's a *dead end*," David pointed out. "As in, if we go that way, we'd be trapped in the necropolis."

"Not if we punch our way through the forest on the other side," Derek said. "It would be slow going, sure, but we could do it."

Winifred raised a hand. "I would like to point out, while that might lead *us* to freedom, we'd be leaving a lot of innocent people behind."

"We can't possibly take the entire city with us,"

Erika said, "and that's assuming there's anyone in Woeste who *isn't* part of the Deathless Legion."

"I think the lovely people back at the Pinceforth House might take offense at that accusation."

"Oh, shit!" Felix spat, his curse overlapping an identical one slipping out of David's mouth.

"We have to go back," he said.

"Hell yes we do," Felix agreed. "There's no way I'm leaving Kat and the others to —"

"I left the book back at the house."

"You what?!"

"Shh!" Erika hissed.

"I asked Madam Pinceforth to hold onto it until we got back," David said. "What was I supposed to do? Bring it with me?"

"No, you made the right call," Derek said.

"The hell he did," Felix said.

"Argue about it later," Erika said, "after we get the hell out of Woeste."

"Erika, we can't leave Kat and Liana and the others here."

"Or the book," David said.

"We also can't fight the entire city guard," Erika countered.

"No," Derek said, an idea forming. "Not by ourselves."

EIGHTEEN
Ten against the World

City guard James Tolke made a noise that was something of a sigh mingled with a bored yawn and flipped to the next page in his book, a swashbuckling adventure novel by Alain Porcus, whose vivid prose injected life and energy into even the most mundane of events. It was oft remarked Porcus could craft a dinner scene between two monks observing vows of silence that was every bit as thrilling as the epic sea battles for which he was famed, but his rip-roaring storytelling style was woefully inadequate to keep Tolke's mind awake and alert. It had been a solid hour by his reckoning since the alarm bell tolled and his fellow guards poured out of the station, leaving him to mind the proverbial store — a burden typically foisted on the rookies like him — and he'd heard nothing since. And so, duty bound, there he stood, leaning on the front desk, reading his book, wishing for something exciting or at least interesting to happen.

The station door opened with a tiny, mouse-like squeak. James Tolke looked up from his book, and the old saying *Be careful what you wish for* popped into his head.

On instinct, he reached for his sword, but his hand froze when the white-skinned elven woman spoke, her voice low but commanding. That she had an arrow nocked and drawn lent further authority to her order.

"Don't do it," Erika said. "Don't move. Don't call for help."

Tolke raised his hands, slowly, and eased out from behind the front desk. Derek stepped forward and relieved Tolke of his weapon.

"Are you alone?" Derek asked.

"Yes," Tolke said. "I mean, there are no other guards here, just a few prisoners."

"Good. Take us to them."

"Hold on," Erika said. "Check his arm."

"Right." Derek pulled up Tolke's sleeves. Neither arm was marred by the brand. "We don't want to hurt you, so don't give us any trouble. Felix, Winifred, keep watch up here."

"On it," Felix said, taking position by the front door.

Tolke led Derek, Erika, and David toward the back of the station, across a cluttered main floor that conveyed no sense of professional organization such as one might expect from a city guard. Desks sat scattered about like dice on the ground in a game of Kings and Commoners, and upon those desks lay weapons and armor that should have been stored away in the armory — including, he noticed, a distinct warhammer and pieces of golden plate armor sized for a dwarf.

The door separating the main floor from the jail was a ponderous thing, a plain and solid iron slab set into the stone wall. It stood slightly ajar, the hasp for its padlock empty. Tolke pushed it open and said, "They're right in here," at which point Derek seized him by the shirt and jerked him back.

"You told us you were alone," Erika said.

"We are."

"Uh-huh," Derek said, drawing his sword.

The holding area beyond was well lit, illuminated by several lanterns — simple tin boxes with polished interiors that reflected and magnified the fat pillar candles within — that hung from iron hooks placed well out of reach of the cells. At the back of the room, several silhouettes shuffled about in a large cell.

"We know you're in there," Derek called out. "Drop your weapon on the floor and come out where I can see you."

Silence — silence, save the whispery scuff of many pairs of boots dragging across the stone floor.

"See?" Tolke said. "I'm alone."

Derek locked eyes with Tolke, briefly, but long enough to take his measure and decide he wasn't dumb enough to leave a jail door unlocked — merely dumb enough to think he could disguise a warning as a casual declaration.

"Do not have time for this," Erika said, marching into the holding area, her bowstring tight. Right away, she spotted the guard pressed into a corner, hoping the shadows would conceal her presence. "I see you. Step out. Slowly."

She did as told, hands raised.

"Over here."

"Sorry, Maisie," Tolke said, entering the holding area at the point of Derek's sword.

"You tried," Maisie said.

"I'll say it again," Derek said. "We don't want any trouble."

"You're sure going about it the wrong way."

"Yeah, well. Go on," Derek said to David. "Erika and I will hold them here."

David located the Noble Blades, and his heart sank. They were as when he last saw them: languidly milling about their cell like zoo animals whose captivity had thoroughly crushed their wills. Furl appeared at David's side and let out a low, plaintive yowl. Astra of the Great Green paused, turned a vacant gaze toward the animal, and then returned to her pacing.

"It's okay, Furl," David said. "I'll fix them."

He reached through the bars and snared Darrus's wrist as he shambled by. The dwarf made one listless effort to pull free. David tightened his grip and uttered his incantation. Arcane power surged into the warrior, and a scream caught in his throat. He twitched, then flailed, then thrashed free of David's grasp and careened into Vladimir Fullmoon, who in turn crashed into the Greens who then knocked Kelly Nightshadow to the floor. The Noble Blades collapsed into a heap of bodies with nary a cry or a grunt.

"Mr. Stakar?" David said. "Mr. Stakar?"

Darrus sprang upright with a shrill gasp, like that of a man tasting air after nearly drowning. He looked around, wild-eyed, panting, pale.

"Mr. Stakar?"

"David?" Darrus croaked.

"Derek! Erika! I think he's okay!"

"Take care of the rest of them," Derek said, tossing over Maisie's keys. "Hurry."

"You came to help them?" Tolke said. "Why didn't you just say so?"

"Because we didn't know if we could trust you."

"Still don't," Erika said.

"Don't take it personally. She doesn't trust much of anyone."

"Certainly not around here."

"What the hell does that mean?" Tolke said.

Derek and Erika exchanged looks.

"Check her," she said, training her arrow on Maisie. Derek pulled one sleeve up, then the other. Her skin was clean and unscarred.

"I know this is going to sound unbelievable, but a cult has infiltrated your city," Derek said.

"A cult?" Tolke said.

"The entire city council and Gods know how many of your city guard are Habbatarr worshippers."

"You're right; that is unbelievable," Maisie said.

"Habbatarr?" Tolke said. "I thought he was dead."

"Technically, he always was. Point is, we found them out and they're not too happy about it." Derek sheathed his sword. He gestured to Erika, who, reluctantly, relaxed her draw and returned the arrow to its quiver. "We don't want to have to fight our way out of Woeste."

"Seeing as you're grossly outnumbered," Maisie began.

"Some of you are good people who I'd rather not hurt, but I can't stop and ask every guard I encounter if he's a cultist. If we're pushed into a corner, we'll have no choice but to come out swinging."

"I don't take kindly to threats."

"It's not a threat; it's a statement of fact," Erika said. "You don't want to lose people? Then you convince your comrades to stand down."

"How?" Tolke asked.

"Derek?" David said. Behind him stood the Noble Blades, at last free of the mask's lingering influence, though it would be inaccurate to say they'd completely recovered from the experience. The Blades all wore pinched, pained expressions most common among those suffering from severe hangovers.

"Darrus? Are you good to travel?" Derek said.

"If needs be," the dwarf said.

"Needs be. David, take them out of here and help them find their equipment. Make it fast."

"Right," David said, leading the Blades away.

"Look, I understand you might not be able to call your people off, but if you could at least direct them away from the south roads, we'd appreciate it. All we need is a clear path out of the city."

"I can't make any promises," Tolke said.

Derek nodded.

"We have to go," Erika said.

"Right." Derek paused in the doorway. "The cultists have a brand on their inner forearm, a sigil that looks like a skeletal hand. If you see anyone with that brand, you can't trust them."

Tolke stood there for a moment, listening to the stampede of footsteps as it faded into the distance, and with a furrowed brow turned to Maisie. The question on his lips, an inquiry about the brand he'd glimpsed once, the one on Maisie's right shoulder blade, was replaced by a small bark of pain as Maisie sank her longsword deep into his belly. He staggered back, a wet heat spreading down his legs. The world spun wildly, and he collapsed to the floor.

Maisie calmly wiped her sword clean with a rag, which she then pocketed for later disposal — not that anyone would think to search her, she reasoned; not after she told her comrades how those mercenaries the city council hired stormed the station and cut down poor, brave, foolish Tolke as he tried to stop them from freeing their friends the Noble Blades.

That, Sergeant Maisie Karlsbade thought, should suitably motivate the many non-believers within the city guard to exercise a little extreme prejudice.

The next leg of the adventurers' flight for freedom did not last long, no more than a few minutes before the Noble Blades' pace dwindled to a languorous jog.

"Darrus," Derek said.

"I know. I know," Darrus panted, suddenly aware of how empty his belly was. It gurgled at him angrily. "Food. We need food."

At Derek's behest, Felix broke into a darkened warehouse so the Blades could rest a while and partake of the largely untouched store of provisions from our heroes' packs.

"Far from a full-course turkey dinner," Darrus said upon finishing his fourth piece of jerky, "but it serves."

"Did you not eat at all while you were under the mask's influence?" Winifred asked.

"My belly says no. My mind, however, cannot confirm that. I barely remember anything after encountering the man in the mask." Darrus frowned deeply.

"Truth be told, I don't know how much of what I do remember is real. I recall...a fight? With you?"

"That one's real," Derek said, recounting the melee that followed the Noble Blades' return from the Gray Necropolis. "You came after us pretty hard."

"Ahh, lad, I'm so sorry."

"It's okay. It wasn't your fault."

"The hell it wasn't," Darrus rumbled. "This entire debacle is my fault because I was such a damn arrogant fool."

"What happened?" Erika said.

Darrus sat on a wooden crate and prefaced his tale with a heavy sigh.

"We got to the Necropolis easily enough and spent a day or two nosing around, getting the lay of the land," he said. "Wasn't much of anything to see — nothing but long-abandoned homes and buildings at every turn. And then we encountered those terrible creatures with the great tusks..."

"Yeah, we ran into them too," Felix said, adding as if in apology, "I, uh...I found Mason."

"One of those fucking animals dragged him off," Kelly said.

"We gave chase but the bastard beast eluded us," Darrus said, shaking his head. "We went on the hunt, but we were so blind with rage, so hellbent on avenging Mason, we walked right into a pit of vipers nesting in an abandoned temple. Walked in like damned bloody amateurs!"

"You didn't know what the mask was capable of," Winifred said. "We didn't know ourselves until David did a little research."

Darrus turned a curious eye toward David, who

explained, "It was the faceplate of the Helm of Domin-ion, a magical artifact enchanted ages ago by Habbatarr."

"The lich lord of Hesre?" Darrus said.

"And figurehead leader of the cult that's set up shop here in Woeste," Derek said, summarizing the state of affairs for the Blades.

"So what's the plan for taking these sons of bitches down?" Kelly said.

"The plan is to get out of here," Erika said. "There's no way we can take on the entire city guard by ourselves — especially not in your condition."

"We can handle ourselves just fine," Kelly protested.

"No, we can't," Darrus said.

"Darrus —"

"No, Kelly. We overestimated our capabilities once already and look what it's cost us. Miss Racewind is right; the first order of business is to escape with our lives."

"The first order of business is to evacuate every-one from the Pinceforth House," Felix corrected.

"You want us to go out of our way to clear out a whorehouse?" Kelly sneered.

"Call it a whorehouse again and I'll kick your teeth in," Felix snapped.

"Easy, partner," Derek said, resting a hand on Felix's shoulder — not to comfort him, but so it would be easier to restrain him should he lunge for Kelly.

"Derek, Folstoy knows those people are my friends. He's not above going after them if he can't get to me. I'm not leaving them behind."

"And I don't intend to. I told the guards back at

the station we were heading south. With luck, they'll concentrate their people on the south roads and leave the west roads open."

"Bit of a gamble, lad," Darrus remarked. "If they suspect a ruse —"

"Then we're no worse off than we were before. If anything, we stand a better chance of escaping with the Noble Blades on our side."

"What makes you think we're going to go along with this half-baked plan of yours?" Kelly said.

"What makes you think we're not? We owe them a debt of honor," Darrus said, and he turned to Derek. "It's your game, lad. What's the plan?"

"Sneak out of a city crawling with armed guards who've probably been ordered to kill us on sight, rescue a house full of civilians, and lead them to safety through a haunted forest and a cursed necropolis," Derek said.

"What a pity," Darrus chuckled. "I was hoping for something challenging."

NINETEEN
Faces of Evil

Felix, marginally more familiar with the surrounding environs than any of his allies, led the withdrawal from the city center, a painstaking process involving a great deal of sneaking and skulking. Patrols, while regular, were infrequent and light, suggesting that Derek's gambit was paying off and the path to the Pinceforth House would be unobstructed, or relatively so.

Their progress, slow to begin with, ground to a crawl as they reached the edge of the city center and cover became ever more precious, the densely packed buildings of central Woeste giving way to scattered homes. They traded the relative safety of shadow-soaked back alleys for wide-open backyards, across which they dashed one at a time in cautious fits and spurts, until they neared their objective: the Pinceforth House, which had no immediate abutters; two miles separated the house from its nearest neighbors, a farm owned by an elderly couple.

It was here, behind a storage shed toward the rear of the property, that the adventurers secreted themselves to plot their final push. At Felix's insistence, he struck out alone to make first contact, reasoning that he had the best chance of making it to the gatehouse unseen.

"Excuse me," Kelly said, indignant.

"Let him handle it," Darrus said. "Gods be with you, lad."

This he said to the empty air where Felix had been a moment earlier.

The thief covered half the distance by darting between the trees lining the side of the road, but then the sparse woods vanished entirely, forcing him out into the open. He threw his hood over his head and stepped out onto the side of the road as if he belonged there, as if he were merely another regular customer on his way to a night of tasteful debauchery. He kept his gait casual, easy — the stride of a man with no cares or concerns — and he forced himself to remain fixed on his destination and resist his natural instinct to scan his surroundings for possible danger. Excessive awareness of one's environment was the behavior of a guilty man.

"Well met, good sir," Felix said as, an eternity later, he reached Mavolo. "Is the Pinceforth House open this evening?"

Mavolo, ever savvy, replied, "We are, but I must advise you, we are particular with our clientele."

Felix closed the gap and in a hush said, "We have a problem," and then proceeded to summarize that problem.

Mavolo, unfazed, said, "What do you need?"

"I need you to keep an eye on things out here while we get everyone ready to move out. If you see trouble coming —"

"I'll handle it."

"Promise me you won't push your luck. These are dangerous people."

"I'll handle it," Mavolo said again with easy confidence.

"Thanks, brother."

Felix surveyed the road one way and then the other. As convinced as he could be there were no spies skulking in the trees lining the street, he raced back to fetch his friends. As a group, they sprinted back to the Pinceforth House and, once on the grounds, circled around to enter through the back, through the kitchen.

"Stay here," Felix said. "I'll grab the first host I see and —"

"No," Erika said. "For all we know, the Deathless Legion has infiltrated the house, too."

Felix bristled. "I know these people."

"You think you know them. It's been a while since you were last here. You don't know what —"

"*I know these people.*"

"I'm sorry, Felix, but she's right," Derek said. "We don't know how deep this goes. We can't afford to blindly trust *anyone.*"

"Oh, you mean like the necromancer there?" Felix said, jerking a thumb at Vladimir. "No one seems to have any problem trusting him to be on the right side."

"He's not really a necromancer," Darrus said.

"Uh-huh."

"This is straight talk here, friend; Vladimir is a highly skilled but simple sorcerer with a flair for theatrics. Having a 'dark wizard' among our ranks plays well with certain clients," Darrus explained, and he made a small gesture of presentation. "These grim trappings? It's all fiction. In truth, Vladimir is one of the most kind-hearted people I've ever met."

"I send most of my pay home to my widowed mother," Vladimir said.

"Aww," Winifred cooed.

"In other words," Felix said to Darrus, "you know him."

"Felix," Erika began.

"I'll find Kat. If there's anyone here we can absolutely trust, it's her."

"Erika, if there are any cultists hiding among the hosts, we need to weed them out. We can't do that without help," Derek said. "We have to reach out to *somebody*."

"Go," Erika said, but Felix was already gone.

While they awaited his return, the united parties began to strip the pantry of all provisions that would keep during their flight. Derek and Darrus planned the escape — an escape, they quickly realized, that would be as tricky and as treacherous as their flight from Woeste center. By Derek's best estimate two dozen people comprised the Pinceforth House's total staff, none of whom — save perhaps Mavolo — were fighters of any consequence. They were pampered civilians, wholly unaccustomed to extended periods of travel by foot through challenging environments. Some, he reasoned, would rise up and contribute as best as they could, if only toward maintaining their fellow evacuees' morale, but others were sure to lag and flag as they pressed on through one side of the Monolith Forest, across the Gray Necropolis, and out the other.

"Back," Felix announced, and he'd returned with one more in tow than anticipated.

"Dammit, Felix," Erika said.

"This is my home, young lady," Giuliana said. "If there's trouble, I deserve to know about it."

"We can trust her," Felix said.

"Don't have a choice now, do we?" Erika grumbled.

"No, you do not. Now, are you going to tell me what's going on?" Giuliana pressed.

"The short version? Rheagan Folstoy belongs to a cult of Habbatarr worshippers." The surprise that registered on Giuliana's face was both mild and brief. "They're after us and I wouldn't put it past Folstoy —"

"To use us against you," Kat correctly concluded.

"Let them come. I will not be scared out of my own house," Giuliana declared.

"I appreciate that, but this is not the time or the place to make a stand," Derek said. "We need to get everyone to safety."

"Liana, *please*," Felix begged.

Giuliana, her mouth bent into a hard frown, said, "What do you need us to do?"

"Get rid of all your patrons," Erika said. "I don't care how, but do not tell them the truth."

With a nod, Giuliana dismissed Kat to the task. "And then?"

"Then we make sure none of your people —"

Felix cut her off with a gesture. "Have you ever seen a brand on any of your hosts, on their inner forearm? A sigil that looks like a skeletal hand?"

"A brand? No," Giuliana said quite decisively.

"Are you sure? Are you absolutely sure?"

"I know my people, Felix — and you should

know better than to ask."

"I had to ask. Of course I believe you," he added as an apology.

"I don't," Erika said. "Show us your —"

Giuliana did not wait for Erika to finish. She pulled her shirt sleeves back and presented her arms. "Anything else, young lady?"

"You can stop calling me a young lady; I'm sixty-four."

"And I'm one hundred and seventy-three, so show your elder her due respect, *young lady,* and tell me what else we need to do."

"As soon as your patrons are gone, get ready to move out," Derek said. "We'll take care of provisions, you get your people packed up. Bare necessities only — clothes, blankets, some money, and weapons, if you have any."

"I'll start spreading the word," Giuliana said, and she left to do just that.

Several minutes passed before Kat returned, her expression harried. The patrons, she explained, did not appreciate being so rudely ousted from their evening of revelry and resisted all efforts to vacate the premises, but offers of a complimentary night or two in the future convinced them to leave willingly, if not happily.

The house now clear, Derek sent Winifred, David, Kelly, the Greens, and Vladimir to assist the hosts in their preparations. The remaining company made short work of clearing the pantry — mainly because it contained little in the way of food that would travel well. Derek, ever optimistic, believed it might hold them until they reached Licste, a small city abutting the western face of the Monolith Forest, if they maintained a smart pace throughout their exodus.

"Big *if,*" Erika said. "These people are civilians through and through. We push them too hard, we turn their escape into a death march."

"They're tougher than you give them credit for," Felix said.

"For their sake, I hope so."

Several burlap sacks full of food and three small casks of clean water joined a quartet of leather satchels and a small chest piled up in the center of the foyer. Erika scowled.

"What the hell is taking everyone so long?" she said.

"Patience, lass," Darrus said. "I'm sure they're doing their able best."

"Perhaps if we knew what we were packing for," Felisia said, adding her leather satchel to the pile. "Everyone's scared and no one knows why. Giuliana hasn't even told me," she added with a tiny indignant sneer.

"It's complicated," Derek said. "I promise, when we have time, I'll tell you everything."

"DEREK! ERIKA!"

They ran toward David's shout, galvanized more by his panic than his volume, and met the boy halfway up the main staircase as he thundered down, his face white.

"They're here!" he said, and he ran back up the stairs. Erika followed him while Derek and Felix returned to the foyer. Derek threw open the mudroom door just as Mavolo fell inside. He slammed the door closed behind him and threw himself up against it.

"Felix," he said.

"Yeah, we heard," Felix said. He and Derek peered out the narrow sidelights bracketing the front door. A line of floating lights, like will-o'-the-wisps hovering in the gloom of a primal swamp, lined the edge of the property, just outside the high iron fence — watching, waiting.

"Darrus, check the back!" Derek said. Darrus nodded and raced off, nearly bowling over Giuliana as she bustled into the mudroom.

"What is it?" she demanded.

"Bad news," Felix said, taking notice of one torch in particular. "I'm counting maybe twenty out front?"

"At least," Derek said, squinting to make out the shapes beneath the blazing torchlight. He pressed his face to the glass and took in the perimeter as best as the sidelights would allow. "Maybe another dozen or so that I can see at the edges."

"And I count another score at the back," Darrus said upon his return. "Surrounded, good and proper."

"Hope you're right about your friends being tough," Derek said.

"Yeah," Felix said. "Me too."

TWENTY
The House of Pain

"Giuliana," Derek said, "how many ground entrances does this place have? Three?"

"Four," Giuliana corrected. "This door, the one in the kitchen, the double doors leading to the patio, and one to the basement."

"Plus all the windows," Darrus said. "Too many access points. First floor is indefensible."

"Only if we let them get close enough." Derek threw the locks on the front door and shepherded everyone into the foyer, then locked that door behind him as well. "Giuliana, Felisia, Mavolo, make sure all your people are upstairs, someplace central, as far away from the windows as possible."

"My office," Giuliana said. "Felisia, come, let's —"

"No. I need to do something other than hide and cower," Felisia protested.

"I don't believe for one second you're capable of cowering," Derek said, and he leaned in. "Your friends are going to be scared, and they're going to look to you for strength. Be their strength. Please."

An argument formed on her lips, but she instead used them to give Derek a kiss for luck. "Stay safe."

"I'll do my best. Felix, get up there and tell the spellcasters to pick a direction and get ready to start throwing magic at anyone who tries to advance on the house. It's pretty clear they're going to try to burn us out."

"I think I can talk them out of that," Felix said before racing upstairs. He passed Derek's orders along at a shout and then made his way to a room overlooking the front lawn — Kat's room, he realized upon entering — where David stood vigil at a double-wide window.

"They haven't moved," he reported.

"That's because they're cocky idiots," Felix said, pushing the boy aside and throwing open the windows. "Hey! Folstoy!" he shouted at a specific torch, one that was noticeably closer to the ground than the surrounding flames. "Come on, man, I know that's you! There are only so many wheelchair-bound assholes in the world who want me dead!"

A throaty chuckle drifted up into the night air. "Oh, Felix," Folstoy sighed, "always so quick to make a bad situation worse, aren't you?"

"Hey, there you are! Brought some friends with you, I see."

"I did indeed — and all of them among the faithful, so don't waste your breath with some pathetic appeal to their humanity."

"Wouldn't dream of it. Say, can't help but notice you've got a lot of torches there. Makes a guy wonder if you're thinking about burning the place to the ground. Bad idea, man. Your precious mask might survive but the book definitely won't."

"But the book's in Giuliana's safe," David whispered.

"They don't know that, so shut up," Felix hissed back.

A low buzz, voices in guarded conversation, drifted across the front lawn, carried on a gentle summer breeze, but Felix could not pick out anything distinct, anything telling — but that they were conversing rather than acting? That gave him hope.

And that hope, for the moment, was rewarded. "We know you're not all alone in there, Felix," Folstoy said. "Turn over the mask and the book and I swear on my honor we'll let your whore friends go."

Felix's braying laugh drowned out everything after "on my honor." "If you think I believe that horseshit for one minute, you're a bigger idiot than I thought you were."

"We'll see who the real fool is," Folstoy said.

Felix seized David by the shoulders. "I'm not going to lie to you; they're getting in here sooner or later. All I need you to do is hold them off as long as you can and take out as many of them as you can — and when they get in, you fall back to help us guard the stairs. That's the only way up to the second floor so we can use it as a choke point."

David set his jaw and held his head high, hoping it would disguise his exhaustion. "I won't let you down."

With a smile no more sincere than David's display, Felix said, "I know you won't."

"Your friend is quite the orator," Darrus said,

grunting as he set down his end of the couch he and Derek had appropriated from the main parlor. They shoved the couch up against the patio doors and stepped back to take in the first piece of their makeshift barricade.

"As my mother would say, he's got a gift for gab," Derek said.

And Felix's gift was of the kind that kept on giving — in this instance, it gave his friends time to shore up the Pinceforth House's major vulnerabilities. By the time Felix rejoined his allies, three of the four doors leading outside had been nailed shut and had every available stick of furniture piled up behind them. That left the patio doors, two wide glass doors that invited breaching — and it was Derek's hope the Deathless Legion would take his bait and concentrate their attempts to gain entry there.

"You act like you have experience with sieges," Darrus said, catching himself too late. "Ah. Yes. I dare say the odds are a little more in your favor this time around."

"Maybe, but they still have the superior numbers," Derek said.

"Aye. They can wear us down or wait us out."

"They won't try to wait us out," Erika said.

"No," Derek agreed. "They have three objectives: recover Habbatarr's artifacts, kill everyone in the house, and clear out before they're noticed. They'll want to wrap this up as quickly as possible so they don't risk exposure."

"Our best bet is to use that against them," Erika said, "goad them into a hasty attack before they can plan things out."

"Let's see if we can make that happen," Felix said.

"Folstoy! You still out there?"

Folstoy gestured sharply. Ilfreda obeyed and pushed his chair up to the wrought iron fence that stood as the first feeble line of defense for the Pinceforth House. Greave and Mock broke off their debate over the best way to proceed with their hastily assembled siege and eased in behind their brother.

"Have you come to your senses, Felix?" Folstoy shouted. "Will you be giving us that which is rightfully ours?"

"Here's what's rightfully yours, you bloated, crippled, limp-dicked piece of shit!" Felix framed himself within the open window perfectly. Folstoy could clearly make out the two extended middle fingers held high above his head. "You think we're afraid of a bunch of withered old bureaucrats and their pet goons?"

"You'd be wise to be afraid, Felix. We are the Deathless Legion! Mighty Habbatarr guides our hand!"

"You are a bunch of desperate idiots who worship a rotting piece of meat. Habbatarr wasn't a god; he was a walking, talking corpse who was too stupid to stay dead — and we're the ones who put him down like a mad dog, so fuck Habbatarr and fuck you! You've got five minutes to clear out. That's how long it'll take us to get the fireplace going. If you're not gone by then, we start throwing your precious artifacts in, starting with the book."

"He's bluffing," Greave said, unconcerned. "If he burns the artifacts, there's nothing keeping us from turning the house into their funeral pyre."

"We can't risk it," Mock said. "To lose everything now —"

"Madam. Sir," Ilfreda said, causing Folstoy to
flinch. To call his attendant taciturn would be akin to
describing a hurricane as a spring zephyr. "The book is
as good as lost to you. Whether you act or hesitate, they
will burn it. The mask you might yet recover if you act
quickly — and refrain from turning the Pinceforth
House into a blast furnace."

"Your servant is wiser than she lets on," Greave
said with an admiring smile.

"Time's up!" Felix cried. "Have fun sifting
through the ashes, assholes!"

Mock surveyed the house and noted the absence
of smoke wafting from the central chimney. "We have
to move now."

"Agreed," Greave said, turning to her loyal soldiers within the city guard. "Hear me, Deathless Legion! The prizes we seek are inside! Short of setting
your torches to the house, do whatever it takes to force
your way in! Leave no one alive! Now go forth — for
the glory of our lord Habbatarr!"

A roar, fierce and triumphant, rose up from the
guard, and they shook their fists and waved their
torches in anticipation of the fight to come. Kyle
Broggart, a young man inducted only recently into the
fold, determined to show his worth to his elders, let
loose a war cry and raised his sword high as he
charged through the gatehouse, becoming the first to
set foot on the field of battle proper.

Kyle Broggart was also the first to fall. An arrow
bearing a wicked barbed head of Clan Boktn make

punched through his mail hauberk and drilled into his heart. He took several staggering steps before collapsing, as if his body could not quite understand that it was dead.

Two more arrows, loosed by Felix and Kelly Nightshadow, found homes in the next two guards through the gatehouse. They fell, their lifeblood spilling out of them. Their comrades in arms, heedless of their dying allies, poured through the gatehouse and sprinted across the great front lawn. The night flashed with daylight brilliance, a plume of white fire spraying the grass, instantly reducing it to ash — along with one unfortunate guard's tabard of office, a simple length of royal blue cotton embroidered with a silvery heart over the left breast. He flailed in a panic, slapping at the flames as they ate away at his gambeson and reduced a section of his hauberk to slag. His fellows avoided the fiery assault, narrowly, but made of themselves easy targets for the defending archers. Three more fell, one of them dead by the time he hit the ground, an arrow jutting from what was his right eye.

Those who survived their run through the killing box crashed into the front door as a living battering ram. It held against the first push, and the second, and the third. Sheltered from arrows by a small portico, Price Levarr, a captain of the city guard, ordered his people to throw their shoulders into it. On the fourth impact, the door shuddered. On the fifth, it began to pull away from the frame. Thrice more the guards hurled their bodies into the door, and at last, it gave way, only to run into a beaver dam of stools taken from the salon.

The main entrance a lost cause, Levarr ordered

his people to circle around to the back. He'd never patronized the Pinceforth House himself — a fancy, well-mannered whore was still a whore — but he knew this style of home typically had multiple ground-level entrances. It was vulnerable, somewhere.

Levarr and five of his people pressed close to the house as they slipped around the corner. Overhead, bizarre flares somehow bright and dark at the same time leapt out of a high window to slap away guards as they attempted to scale the iron fence. The men and women landed with a thud and a grunt that was audible even at a distance, but whatever this strange defense was, it was not inflicting any serious harm; after a moment of recovery, the guards returned to their feet and valiantly, perhaps foolishly, attempted the climb again.

A series of harsh buzzing sounds, each accompanied by a deafening crack, almost like thunder, greeted Levarr and his company as they reached the back lawn — a battleground, now littered with bodies. The dead lay in broken heaps, smoke drifting off their bodies. Those few who still lived, they lay sprawled on the ground, cowering from — what? Whatever had slain so many of their fellows had, for the moment, relented. One guard cautiously rose up to her hands and knees, glanced about furtively, then jumped to her feet, ready to renew her charge. An instant later, she was airborne, launched like a catapult stone by a finger of blinding white — a lightning bolt lancing down from the house. She crashed back to earth as limp as a rag doll.

"Stay close!" Levarr barked at his companions. He eased around the corner and dashed toward a broad open patio. Another lightning bolt, reflected in the patio doors, lashed out. Another man died with a scream.

Levarr peeked into the room beyond the double doors, past a flimsy barricade built of easy chairs piled atop a couch. A man, young and tall and broad, clad in brigantine and wielding a longsword, shouted something Levarr could not quite make out to someone he could not see, and then stepped out of the room.

"Get ready to breach!" Levarr said.

On his signal, the Deathless Legionnaires smashed the glass and barreled headlong into the low wall of furniture, shoving it out of the way with ease.

Levarr could not help but cheer. Victory was within reach — he felt that in his bones, as clearly and as vividly as he could feel the blight slowly, inexorably eating away at his innards. He knew the symptoms of the creeping rot very well; his father had succumbed to it a decade earlier. It was a slow, ugly demise that reduced the man to a shriveled husk, a stick figure shrouded in leathery, fish-white flesh before granting him the sweet mercy of death — and when Levarr first sensed the ache deep in his belly he knew, he just *knew* that he had taken his first step on the same grim path.

It wasn't that he didn't want to die that way; he did not want to die at all — so when Greave, somehow sensing his terror of the great unknown world beyond, spoke of her lord's power to defy death and his promise to bestow that gift upon his faithful, he threw in readily. He received the brand, taking it on his shoulder blade, and instantly his fear abated. Death, when and if it came, was no longer an ultimate end but, at worst, a transition to something greater. Something eternal.

Price Levarr cried out, a hosanna to his lord Habbatarr that was cut short by a sudden agony exploding in his gut — about where he felt the first hint of the creeping rot — but this new pain was sharp and intense and came with a vaguely unpleasant sensation of something hot and wet splashing down his legs. He fell back — no, someone pushed him away. It was the young man he'd seen a few moments earlier. His sword dripped with crimson.

The world tilted. Levarr lay there upon the floor, hands pressed over his belly to no avail, and watched helplessly as the young man and a dwarf in golden armor tore into his people, cutting them down, beating them down — and against all reason, Levarr's last sound was a gurgling laugh.

This was not his end, he thought. This was merely his transition. He would rise again. In Habbatarr's name, he would rise again.

He would become eternal.

Folstoy spat a curse at the house. Delilah Scheere ranted in Mock's ear, demanding that he do something to turn the tide of the battle, while Stripling did likewise inches away from Greave's face. A pair of city guards, one of them rendered lame from an arrow sunk deep in his thigh, staggered through the guardhouse and begged for help, for guidance.

"Enough! Silence!" Greave said, and her underlings obeyed. Then, as casually and calmly as she might ask a dinner companion to pass her the salt, Greave turned to Mock and asked, "Your followers. Do they all bear Habbatarr's mark?"

A thin smile spread across Mock's lips. "But of

course. And yours, I trust?"

"Of course." Greave extended a hand. "Shall we?"

"What are you two on about?" Stripling demanded.

"Silence, Lemuel. All will be made clear."

Greave and Mock took a minute to clear their minds. Their breathing eased into a steady, synchronous rhythm — in and out, in and out.

"*Esur'us au'm v'oruu reum,*" they said in perfect unison. "*Esur'us au'm v'oruu reum. Esur'us au'm v'oruu reum.*"

Folstoy broke into a heavy sweat, the night air suddenly hot and electric, and his belly grew queasy. He jammed the palm of his hand into his mouth and bit down to stop himself from purging his dinner. Benson Traymon was not so fortunate; he fell to his knees and wretched miserably. Mittle was dangerously close to joining him.

"What's happening?" Mittle moaned. "What in the name of the Gods is this?"

"Not the Gods, Jann," Folstoy said through gritted teeth.

Kyle Broggart, the first to die this night, was also the first to rise. His body seized once, violently, and he rose to his feet, slowly, like a drunkard picking himself off the tavern floor. Once erect he swung around, his movements jerky and imprecise, and he stared with lightless eyes at those who had been his masters in life — and remained so after the fact. Around him, Broggart's slain comrades flinched and flailed and rose up in defiance of their lifelessness, ready to fight once again — and this time, no arrow or spell or sword could stop their advance.

"In the name of *our* god," Folstoy said.

TWENTY-ONE
The Rise of the Deathless Legion

"Oh, you have got to be fucking kidding me!" Felix cried.

"Give me an arrow!" Erika said, holding out a hand. The incantation was growing to a crescendo. The arcane words, alien though they were to Erika's ears, were as clear as if she were standing next to the sorcerers chanting them, but their source remained indistinct. Any shot would be taken in desperation, with so little chance of ending the enchantment spreading across the lawn, raising up one by one all those they'd slain, but it mattered not if she had no arrows to loose.

"I'm empty," Felix said.

"So am I," Kelly said.

"Dammit! David! We need you!" Erika shouted.

David looked up at her from his spot at the foot of Kat's bed, where he'd collapsed minutes earlier, drained to the point of passing out. "I can't — I need to," he panted, but he nevertheless pushed himself upright, willing himself to ignore the many sleepless hours and the exhaustion of fleeing the city. Alas, his determination carried him but two steps before he staggered and fell into Kelly Nightshadow's arms.

"Kid's useless," she said.

"Take him to Giuliana's office," Felix said. Kelly threw him a sneer of protest but did as told, half-carrying the boy out into the hall.

Erika and Felix ran downstairs, intending to inform Derek of this latest development. The freshly severed flying head that greeted them as they reached the sunroom made it clear theirs was old news.

"Feisty sorts," Darrus remarked. His wind-up was impressive, the blow itself awesome. Captain Levarr's skull imploded with a wet, meaty crunch, and he fell again. Unconvinced this time would stick, Darrus swung twice more, reducing Levarr's head to pulp.

"Yeah, these guys are a little livelier than the ones we've encountered before," Derek said. "No pun intended."

Erika glanced past her fellow warriors and took in the haunting tableau beyond, of the dead rising to their feet to renew their attack. A thread of magical lightning, accompanied by a crack no louder than the snap of one's fingers, touched a zombified guard. He stiffened and staggered and then, no worse for wear, resumed his lurching march toward the house.

"Looks like the Greens aren't long for this fight," Darrus observed.

"Neither is David," Felix said. "Kid's wiped out but good."

"I say we tell the spellcasters to fall back to Giuliana's office, let them be the last line of defense," Erika said. "The rest of us can hold the ground floor as long as possible."

"You think that's the smart play?" Darrus asked. "Our unwelcome guests still have the superior numbers — and an annoying habit of not staying dead when they're told."

"Yeah, but zombies aren't creative thinkers," Derek said. "All they can do is follow simple orders."

"For example," Darrus said, eyeing the advancing horde, "'Storm the house and kill everyone inside'?"

"For example. The people controlling them are more dangerous, in their own way — but getting to them would mean fighting our way through all that," Derek said, gesturing with his sword, "and leaving the house unguarded in the meantime. Staying put is our best option."

"At least until we thin the herd a little," Erika said.

"Felix, get the spellcasters in position and send down the fighters. I want you, Winifred, and Kelly watching the other breach points to make sure no one slips in while we're, ah, thinning the herd."

"On it," Felix said. "Good luck."

Darrus gave his warhammer a flick, dislodging a chunk of brain matter. It hit the floor with a splat.

"I'll make my own luck, thank you kindly," he said. The first wave of the Deathless Legion, led by a woman with a savage electrical burn marring half of her face, thumped up onto the patio. "My friends. Shall we?"

Erika suppressed a grin. "Let's make a mess."

"Gods, do you ever do *anything* without arguing?" Felix snapped at Kelly. "Get your ass downstairs!

Now!"

"Kelly, please," Winifred said. "If we're to protect these people, we need to stand united."

Kelly glanced about the room and saw faces young and old, man and woman, staring back, wide-eyed and pleading. She threw Felix a snarl before storming out of the office.

"Sit tight, people," Felix said, "and don't leave this room."

Felisia dutifully closed and locked the door behind him.

Somewhere beneath her feet, all hell broke loose.

"What is going on?" Tasha Mayuse sobbed. "Giuliana, please tell us what's going on?"

"Not now, love," Giuliana said, clasping Tasha's trembling hands. "When this is all over —"

"When *what* is all over?! What is this? Why are these people trying to...oh, Gods," she wailed, and she fell to her knees, into Giuliana's arms, and wept.

"We deserve to know," Dale said.

From behind Giuliana's oaken desk, from the chair she would not even let Felisia sit in, David roused from a half-sleep and caught Giuliana's eye. Her brow creased, a silent question to which David shook his head.

This exchange did not go unnoticed. "What? Does this have something to do with him?" Dale demanded.

"Dale, stop," Felisia said.

"We deserve to know!"

A chorus of shouts echoing this sentiment filled the office, a generous space that felt less so for all the bodies packed therein. David pushed away an unwelcome flash of déjà vu and again, emphatically, shook his head.

"They want something I secured in my safe," Giuliana said, hoping her selective confession would mollify her people and quell the impending revolt.

"In your safe?" Dale said. "What?"

"You can't," David said, rising. His legs trembled, and he had to brace himself on the edge of the desk to remain upright. "Giuliana, *you can't*."

A startled shriek jumped out from the din of battle. Mavolo seized Felisia by the hair and held a dagger, curved and sharp, to her slender throat. The Greens and Vladimir snapped out of their own exhausted stupors but could only gawp uselessly at the scenario before them. Furl crouched between Adam's feet, claws out and ready to tear.

"Open it," he said, "or I open her."

"Mavolo? What are you doing?!" Kat cried.

"Open the safe," Mavolo repeated. "Do it."

"Release her!" Astra said, advancing. Mavolo wrapped a massive arm around Felisia's neck, locking her in place as a human shield against the sorcerer. His blade drifted down to her belly.

"Open the safe, Giuliana," he said. "Now."

Giuliana held her ground.

Mavolo cut deep. Felisia bit down on a scream.

Kat wailed Felisia's name and ran to her, a vain effort to catch her friend as she fell from Mavolo's grasp, dark blood turning her rich purple gown almost black. Striking with rattlesnake speed, Mavolo snared Kat and pulled her in to replace Felisia as his bargaining chip. Giuliana spat a curse in her native dwarven tongue.

"If I have to, I will carve my way through everyone in this room until you cooperate," Mavolo said, his manner easy and unconcerned.

David grimaced. If only they weren't so close together. If only he weren't so exhausted. But they were, and he was.

"Giuliana," he said. "Do it."

Giuliana's trembling hands twice dropped her key ring in the process of searching for the correct key, the one to the ponderous iron box that sat behind her desk. The key plinked out a discordant tune as Giuliana fought to guide it into the padlock. When at last she popped the lock, David stooped to take the book before she could.

"This is my fault," David said. "This is my responsibility."

If she was inclined to debate the boy, Giuliana kept her arguments to herself.

Slowly, David crossed the room, hugging the book to his chest. "Let her go. Take me instead."

"Give the book to her. She can carry it as well as you," Mavolo said.

David glanced down at Felisia. Her naturally porcelain complexion had turned chalky. Her breath came in ever weakening wheezes.

"You don't want her. You want me." Mavolo narrowed his eyes at the boy — a question, to which he received a most unexpected answer. "My name is Randolph David Ograine. I am the Reaper. I killed your lord Habbatarr."

The undead boast a strength that is not truly unnatural. Rather, they possess the same strength their

254

living counterparts possess but cannot access thanks to the body's natural warning system: pain. Pain prevents overexertion. Pain stops the living from pushing themselves so hard that they literally tear themselves apart. But if that innate barrier were to be removed? Strip away the capacity to feel pain, along with the instinct for self-preservation, and the resulting illusion is one of superhuman might.

Devoid of human limitations, the Deathless Legionnaires who fell in the front yard and rose again threw themselves heedlessly against the compromised front door, battering it and the hasty, haphazard barricade beyond to splinters at the cost of their own bodies, a cost they paid obediently and thoughtlessly — and, in the end, for negligible gain, for the bloody, broken things that lurched into the foyer fell quickly before Felix's flashing sabers. The one living man — one of the few remaining — who charged through posed little more of a challenge; one nimble parry and one precise counterstrike added him to the roster of the ignoble dead.

Felix finished separating the guard's head from his neck to prevent a resurrection and readied for the next assailant to step forward. A telltale creak of floorboards caused him to whirl about, sabers raised — and he froze, unable to make sense of the sight before him.

"Step aside, Felix," Mavolo said, careful to keep David in front of him. He squeezed the boy's throat, coaxing a strangled croak, and he waved his dagger, still slick with elven blood. "Step aside and let me pass."

"But — what — Mavolo, the hell?" Felix stammered.

"He's with them," David rasped. Felix blinked and shook his head as though clearing his head of a bad dream.

"Not yet I am not," Mavolo said, "but when they see the magnificent prizes I have? They will at last welcome me into the Deathless Legion."

"You aren't going to bring them jack shit," Felix said, ready to capitalize on the least little opening.

"Felix, get Winifred," David said. "Felisia's hurt, badly."

"David, I can't let this bastard — "

"You can't let Felisia die! Please!"

Mavolo squeezed again, cutting off David's air.

Reluctantly, so reluctantly, Felix eased out of Mavolo's path. Mavolo countered, the point of his blade hovering near David's temple as a warning. Felix backed out into the hall and leveled a saber at his now former friend like a damning finger.

"You're dead," he snarled.

"If only I feared death," Mavolo replied.

He waited until Felix had departed and then hustled his captive outside, into a night that had grown cold, a cold more appropriate to a late autumn evening, past a lumbering cluster of Deathless Legionnaires. The soulless shells paused to watch him pass with something that, on living faces, would have read as curiosity.

"Behold, my masters! What a trophy I have claimed for you!" Mavolo said, giving David a vicious shake that rattled his brain inside his skull and caused him to drop the book. It landed on its spine and fell open. "Pick it up," Mavolo said, releasing his charge.

David knelt, his knees creaking, his back protesting, his head full of wool. He blinked hard, and the pages before him came into focus. They were among the few he'd been able to interpret and put to use. Under much different circumstances, he might have laughed at the irony.

He gazed up at the looming giant. He was alone, isolated, close enough to touch. If the spell misfired — a distinct possibility — at least no innocent would suffer.

"I'm sorry," David said.

And then he said, "*Corin'es.*"

Mavolo died instantly and without a sound, save of course for the stomach-churning crunch of every last one of his bones instantly pulverizing.

Someone screamed — a man, David thought — and someone else barked an order: "Seize him!"

The secret lords and ladies of the Deathless Legion, in a mild panic, stepped through the gatehouse, though none of them were in much of a hurry to do any seizing. They spread out in a choppy line as if they couldn't decide whether to advance as a unit or try to surround their prey first. David, drained to the core, on the verge of slipping into unconsciousness, wrestled off his backpack, tore the flap open, and plunged his hand in.

The iron was warm to the touch.

The moment David pressed the mask to his face, he and it ceased to exist as two separate things. They became one — a single will, a single power. His voice rang out like a thunderclap.

"STOP!"

And they did, the Deathless Legion, transforming into a living statuary for a few fleeting seconds before the enchantment, tentative at best, began to lose its hold. Ilfreda flexed her fingers and strained to reach for her rapier. Greave, groaning like a woman in labor, took a faltering step, her hands grasping greedily for the prize this damnable whelp and his friends had stolen from the faithful — from *her*. It was hers. *Hers.*

"The mask is MINE!" she wailed.

David swooned. A gray fog settled over his eyes. Derek was little more to him than a shape, a blur as he hurtled past and brought his longsword up and around in a lethal arc. The blade cleaved easily through Greave's head, splitting it down the center to the base of her neck.

Erika, Darrus, and Kelly hurled themselves with equal savagery into the fray — such as it was. Mock managed to choke out a desperate cry for help before a pass of Erika's sica eviscerated him. His fellows died in rapid succession, many of them taking their death-blows in the back as they turned to flee.

Felix, denied his vengeance against Mavolo the turncoat, dashed past more readily available targets and sprinted toward Folstoy. The full moon of his face, locked in a perversely comical rictus of helpless horror, was such an inviting bull's eye.

Ilfreda sprang out, the tip of her rapier leading the way. Felix twisted away and lashed out with a saber, narrowly batting aside her opening thrust. He skidded to a stop, tearing furrows in the lawn, and leapt back toward his opponent. Ilfreda parried his wild slashes with contemptuous ease and returned with a series of quick pokes that put Felix in retreat. A sudden flick of her wrist sent the point of her blade skipping off Felix's chin. He countered the sweeping slash that followed, stopping the attack cold with one saber, smacking it away with the other, and then bringing both to bear on the towering elven woman. Ilfreda bit down on a grunt as she staggered back, an ugly gash bisecting the bridge of her nose and spilling red down her face.

Felix pressed his advantage and charged, his sabers scissoring the air in front of him. Ilfreda leapt clear only to spring right back, driving a high knee into Felix's sternum. He reeled, wheezing, and fell victim to a granite fist glancing off his cheek. Stars danced in his vision. Ilfreda drew back for her final strike, a lunging thrust straight into Felix's belly — a blow that would ensure a slow, painful death.

She roared.

And then her scream changed, rage becoming agony. Furl dug his claws deeper into Ilfreda's shoulders, her back, sank his fangs into the base of her skull as if biting an apple. She flailed and thrashed but the lynx would not let go — not until, quite by chance, she toppled over, dropping her full weight onto Furl. The cat, dazed and winded, scrambled out from beneath his prey.

Felix fell upon her, ramming a saber through her chest as though staking a vampire. He withdrew the blade and drove it home again and again, a maniac's scream shredding his throat. Spent, he rolled off her and sprawled on the lawn, gasping for breath. Furl crept past him, low to the ground, and gave Ilfreda an experimental swat. Satisfied, he sat up and seemed to smile.

"*Mrawr.*"

"Good job, cat," Felix huffed. "That'll show her."

David witnessed all this through a haze of waning consciousness. He wanted to sleep so very badly. The grass was so cool, so soothing, but the weight on his face had become unbearable. He dug his fingers under the edge and, with effort, pried off the mask — and for one horrible moment, he swore he'd just peeled the flesh off with it.

He gasped, but passed out before releasing the scream welling up within him.

TWENTY-TWO
The Road to Recovery

David's eyes fluttered open. At first, he couldn't make sense of anything that greeted him; nothing was as it was before — however long ago *before* was. Daylight streamed through a thin gap in the heavy curtains of —

He sat up, every last muscle in his body protesting, and looked around. He was in the cottage, in the shared upstairs bedroom. He sighed a tiny sigh. Familiarity brought with it a measure of comfort.

"Hello?" he rattled. He tried clearing his throat, but that made the dull burning sensation worse. A sandpaper tongue licked parchment lips. David swung his legs out of bed and sat there a while, building himself up before attempting to stand. He was somehow surprised when he did not instantly collapse to the floor.

He emptied his bloated bladder with an unselfconscious groan and got dressed, distantly aware of the sour funk clinging to him. Downstairs was empty but had not been so for long; dishes stained with egg and dusted with toast crumbs sat in a stack in the kitchen sink, along with a steel pot that yet held a single mug's worth of lukewarm coffee. Desperately thirsty, David downed it straight from the pot.

It struck him upon stepping outside how normal everything appeared to be, but the illusion fell apart a piece at a time with each passing second. Blemishes in the form of patches of charred grass and furrows of freshly disturbed earth marred the vivid green sea of the back lawn. As he approached the house, David could pick out windows in which squares of wood stood in place of panes of glass, and he shook his head in silent self-chastisement for not immediately noticing the silk bedsheets tacked in place over the gaping holes that used to be the patio doors. He brushed them aside and stepped into the sunroom. The furniture Derek and Darrus had placed to shore up the entrance, now a tangle of wooden frames and shredded cushions, sat in a sad pile against the wall.

Kat bustled past. She let out a small yip when David called out to her. She reappeared in the doorway, almost unrecognizable in a plain blouse and skirt. A scarf held her hair up in a frazzled nest.

"David!" She rushed to greet the boy with a hug.

"Hi. Good morning."

"Good afternoon, you mean." She stepped back and took David in, inspecting him. "How are you?"

"Good afternoon? I've been asleep all day?"

Kat's smile wavered. "You've been asleep since the night before last."

David met this news with a mildly curious, "Huh."

"Derek said you'd be all right once you got some rest, but we were so worried about you."

"Where is Derek?"

"He's, ahh — hm. That's a bit of a story. Winifred's upstairs tending to Felisia. She'll fill you in. I need to get back to work." She placed a gentle kiss on David's cheek. "Thank you for what you did that night. You were very brave."

David flushed, but not in response to Kat's sweet kiss. "Uh, yeah," he said, "about what I said?"

"You mean that ridiculous story you told Mavolo about being the Reaper? No one believed you, of course," Kat said, adding with a conspiratorial smile, "everyone knows Randolph Ograine died in Hesre."

David rapped lightly on the door before peeking inside. From her seat beside Felisia's bed, Winifred snapped out of her light doze and smiled, then lifted a shushing finger to her lips. David closed the door and crossed the room on tiptoes. Felisia, naught but a head poking out from beneath strata of quilts, did not stir. Her color was paler than normal but not distressingly so. It lent her beauty an almost angelic quality.

"Will she be all right?" David whispered.

"In time," Winifred said. "How are you?"

"All right," he replied, keeping his need for a drink of water and a bath to himself. "What did I miss?"

"Quite a lot."

To say Winifred debriefed David would be inaccurate; there was nothing brief about her tale.

A city guard patrol happened past the Pinceforth House minutes after Felix dispatched Ilfreda, and they immediately moved in to affect a mass arrest. Derek blurted out a hasty explanation that, naturally, was met with utter disbelief, but the guards' skepticism could not withstand the sight of one of their comrades shambling about the front lawn in a lazy circle, his intestines trailing behind him.

Folstoy, inveterate coward that he was, offered up an alibi that pinned his complicity on Greave and Mock — primarily but not exclusively. The entire council was corrupt to the core while he was but a hapless pawn acting under extreme duress — a claim his fellow survivor Jann Mittle vehemently disputed. Accusations and counter-accusations flew until their dueling tirades comprised a full confession of the councils' many, many foul deeds. The city guard clapped Folstoy and Mittle in irons and hauled them away, still screaming at one another.

The next order of business was to put the Deathless Legionnaires to rest for good. This was a grim but relatively easy task. With Greave and Mock dead, their puppets had lost their artificial will to press the assault or defend themselves against the warriors' merciful deathblows. It took until sunrise for the company, aided by several city guards, to clear the property of corpses, which were loaded into a convoy of open carts commandeered from nearby farmers — none of whom were happy to receive their property back coated in dried blood and viscera — and dumped into a paupers' mass grave just off the road leading to the edge of the Monolith Forest.

When the last cartload had rolled away, Olivia Urstalt, a captain of the city guard, asked a deceptively complex question: "Now what?"

Now what indeed? Woeste had overnight become a rudderless ship, the entirety of its city council dead or imprisoned and no one waiting in the wings to take the wheel, temporarily or otherwise. A hasty roll call revealed that the city guard's numbers had shrunken by a quarter, though not all of them were later accounted for among the slain, giving rise to the theory that those who survived the slaughter at the Pinceforth House had quit the city to avoid capture. With no better options presenting themselves, the city guard's commanders instituted a state of martial law until the mess could be sorted out. Precisely how they would accomplish this sorting out was a matter of speculation, for those commanders adamantly refused to share their thoughts with anyone outside their inner circle.

This secrecy only exacerbated the streak of general distrust already running strong through our heroes. Before disposing of the sack of flesh and pulverized bone that once was Mavolo, Erika checked him for the Deathless Legion's telltale brand but found nothing.

"So anyone could be a cultist and we wouldn't necessarily know," she said.

"Not until they acted overtly, no, which is why we decided to take matters into our own hands," Winifred said with a small frown that struck David as somehow apologetic.

"What? What did you do?" David said.

"We can't trust anyone in Woeste. We need someone from the outside to help us reassert control."

David blanched. "Oh, Winifred, no."

"Erika left yesterday morning," Winifred said, "to ask your father to intervene."

David anxiously counted the days until Erika and Kelly Nightshadow, who'd tagged along on the trip uninvited, returned from Oson, and he spent those days fretting that his father, who'd long held out hope of one day reabsorbing Woeste into the wardens' court, might decide to handle the matter personally. What then? He had no desire to reconcile with the man — the wound of Malcolm Ograine's betrayal had yet to scab over — but unexpected things happened in the heat of an emotional moment. The mere sight of his father could wash away his anger and cause him fall to his knees and beg to rejoin his estranged family.

What worried him all the more was the distinct possibility that any such pleas would fall on deaf ears and a hardened heart.

To distract himself from his woes, David threw himself into the imposing task of assisting in the repair of the Pinceforth House. The venerable manor house had taken considerable damage in the battle, and Derek and Felix were bound and determined to return the building to its original state, or as close to as their modest skills would allow. Darrus happily joined this effort, the Greens and Vladimir less so — at first, but soon the satisfaction of working alongside friends for a purely selfless purpose took over, and the chore of rebuilding felt not at all like a chore.

It was a methodical process — none of them were carpenters — but they'd finished their work to Giuliana's satisfaction and boundless gratitude by the time Erika and Kelly returned, riding up to the gatehouse late one afternoon, trailed by a full company of mounted soldiers and a Wensley Moste Grande bearing the Ograine family crest on its doors. David, who was in middle of helping Derek plant young new shrubs to replace those that had been trampled by the Deathless

Legion, ran back to the cottage without being told.

Derek rose, wiped his hands on his pants, and went to meet Erika. "Welcome back," he said. "How was the trip?"

"Uneventful," she said with a glance toward Kelly that suggested otherwise. She dismounted. "How are things here?"

"Pretty good. Almost got the house back in shape. Might even be able to open for business in —"

"I mean Woeste."

"Ah." Derek made a face. "There have been a few interesting developments."

"And we look forward to hearing all about them," a woman clad in light plate armor said as she dismounted.

"You remember Captain Greystone," Erika said through her teeth.

"Captain, hello again," Derek said, extending a hand turned a dingy gray from his afternoon of gardening.

"Mr. Strongarm," Helena Greystone said with all the distaste of a child beholding his dinner of raw chard. She cast her gaze toward the house and sniffed. "Tell the proprietor of this house she has a guest."

"Uh, I don't think she's really ready to —"

"That wasn't a request. It's been a long trip. Lord Houlte would like to retire for the evening."

"Lord Houlte?" Derek echoed, glancing back at Erika for an explanation that came in the form of a grimace.

"That would be me." A tall man with ebon skin, bright eyes, and a brighter smile stepped out of the Moste Grande and went right up to Derek, his hand out in greeting. "Morris Houlte. Delighted to meet you."

"Uh, hi. Derek Strongarm. I'm sorry, you are...?"

Houlte, quite casually, as if detailing what he'd eaten for lunch, said, "I am to be the new warden of Woeste."

TWENTY-THREE
All Politics is Local

"What a delightful old house this is," Houlte said in sincere admiration. "About two hundred years old, if I'm not mistaken?"

"About, yes," Giuliana said, leading Houlte and Greystone into the central parlor, the first of the house's many rooms to fully recover. "I regret it isn't as delightful in spots as it usually is."

"Mm, yes, Miss Racewind apprised me fully of the events preceding her unexpected return to Oson — but I believe I heard there had been some new developments in the interim?"

Derek did not right away realize Houlte had posed the question to him. "Oh, uh, yeah, a few."

"Sir, we can take this up tomorrow," Greystone said. "You should rest."

"Nonsense. I find travel invigorating," Houlte said. Giuliana invited him to sit. He accepted, becoming the first guest to enjoy the new couch since its delivery three days prior. "Now, Mr. Strongarm, what are these developments?"

"Sir, please. This matter is not for civilian ears,"

Greystone said, and she turned to Giuliana. "I must insist you leave us in private so we might discuss —"

"This is my house, young lady," Giuliana steamed, "and you do not get to tell me where I may or may not be within it."

Erika made no effort to mask her admiring smile.

"Furthermore, Woeste is my home. I've lived here all my life. I love this city and I have no intention of letting anyone simply stroll in and declare himself my lord."

"Madam Pinceforth," Greystone gnashed.

Houlte waved her down. "Captain, please. Madam Pinceforth is absolutely right; we are in her home, in the immediate and greater senses, and should show her all due respect as our host." Greystone, grudgingly, retreated to a corner of the room. "Mr. Strongarm? These developments?"

"There's been nothing too significant, but it's concerning nevertheless," Derek said. "Several more members of the city guard have disappeared, as have a number of citizens. We suspect they might be cultists who feared being discovered, which is a reasonable assumption considering Folstoy — the city councilor we captured — has been very chatty. He thinks if he gives up every cultist in Woeste it might save his own life."

"A shrewd gambit," Houlte remarked neutrally.

"Problem is, he only knows maybe half of the operation; he was one of Belinda Greave's underlings so he has no idea who was serving under Dunstan Mock. His people could still be here."

"People who, I understand, might not be so easily identified and flushed out. Miss Racewind said not everyone in the — what did they call themselves again? The Deathless Legion? — bore the cult's brand."

"We think the brand might be an honor reserved for those who've been formally inducted into the cult," Derek clarified.

"That doesn't make the aspiring cultists any less dangerous," Erika opined.

Houlte nodded and made a thoughtful noise. "It seems I will have my work cut out for me," he said, his smile returning. "But High Lord Ograine put his faith in me and I do not intend to let him down — him, or the good people of Woeste."

"Yes. About that," Giuliana said. "You claimed you're the new warden," she said, a question hiding in her words.

"I am to be. There is a process, of course —"

"Woeste doesn't have a warden. We haven't had a warden for more than a hundred years."

"And look how well that turned out," Greystone said.

Giuliana bristled. "Excuse me?"

"A malevolent presence was able to worm its way into the heart of your government. That wouldn't have happened if Woeste had been part of the wardens' court — as it should have been."

"Now, captain," Houlte said gently.

"What happened had nothing to do with how we govern ourselves, you hear me? *Nothing*," Giuliana said. "And I do hope you don't expect me to believe the wardens' court is beyond corruption. Our city's history proves otherwise."

"While true, Madam Pinceforth, in this rather specific case, the corruption is from within; therefore it cannot be purged from within. Rejoining the wardens' court is the best option."

"For who, exactly? Not for Woeste. I fail to see how stripping away our self-governance and forcing a complete stranger upon us is beneficial for anyone — other than High Lord Ograine. Another city under his thumb, that's all we'll be!"

"Madam Pinceforth!" Greystone exploded, striding out from the corner. Giuliana held her ground and met the captain with a determined glare. "This may be your house, but High Lord Ograine is your lord and you *will* speak respectfully about him."

"You better back off, Helena," Erika said.

"And you better learn your place before someone shows you where it is."

"Try it."

"Ladies!" Houlte said, his easy demeanor gone. "Our host has seen enough violence under her roof to last her a lifetime. Don't you agree?"

Erika and Greystone backed away from one another, but their hands remained on their weapons.

"Madam Pinceforth, you have your city's best interests at heart. I respect that, and I appreciate your passion, and I make you a solemn promise that my desire is not to silence the people's voices and supplant them with my own — or with High Lord Ograine's — but your city is in crisis. It needs strong leadership to endure, and it needs that leadership now. There is no other option than to rejoin the wardens' court."

His words were sincere, or at least effectively presented as such, and Giuliana's round, broad face softened. She folded her hands at her waist and nodded as if coming to a decision — which she had.

"There is another option, actually," she said. "We seat a new city council."

Houlte considered her for a moment. "Madam Pinceforth, let's speak plainly, shall we?"

"Oh, yes. Let's."

"Your city has been infested with a living blight that has struck the very heart of your community. Trust is at a premium. Do you truly believe your neighbors have enough faith in one another they would return control to —"

"That's what you don't understand, Mr. Houlte," Giuliana said. "The city council didn't *control* the people; they *were* the people — and I *do* have faith in them. Absolutely I do. If you think that faith is misplaced and Woeste would prefer to answer to Lord Houlte than to itself?" She smiled and spread her hands. "Then let the people decide how they wish to be governed."

Houlte rose. "I think it might be best if we sought accommodations elsewhere this evening," he said without malice, and Giuliana replied in kind.

"I agree."

With a polite nod, Houlte and Greystone took their leave, Giuliana accompanying them to the door in an illusory performance of her duties as a good hostess.

"What do you know about this Houlte guy?" Derek asked Erika.

"He's one of High Lord Ograine's most trusted diplomatic envoys. Smart, knowledgeable, personable, understands politics like few people I've met, and when he's properly motivated, he could sell legs to a snake."

"In other words, he's dangerous."

"Extremely."

"He doesn't know what dangerous is," Giuliana said, returning. "Dangerous is pissing me off."

"This is my fault," Erika said. "I shouldn't have suggested —"

"No no no, Erika, I'll have none of that. We all agreed this was the best course of action and we all expected this could happen." She smiled. "That's why I made plans of my own during your absence."

"Plans? For what?"

"For taking back my city," Giuliana declared. "Say hello to the first candidate for the new city council."

"Come in," Felisia said. She looked up from her book, a copper naughty that was disappointingly stingy with the naughtiness, and smiled. "Good afternoon, Mr. Strongarm."

"Madam Fairweather," Derek said, eliciting a sigh from the elf.

"I don't know if I'll ever get used to that."

"I think it suits you nicely. Much the same way 'Councilor Pinceforth' suits Giuliana."

"Too kind." She slid over and patted the edge of her bed. "Sit. How was the swearing-in ceremony?"

"You'd know if you'd gone," Derek teased.

"With everything I have to do to get ready for our grand reopening tonight? Can't spare the time, dear."

"Yeah, you look really busy."

Felisia swatted him with her book. "Cheeky boy. I needed to rest for a while. My constitution isn't quite what it used to be."

"You'll get there."

"I know. And I know I shouldn't complain, seeing as I was almost disemboweled," she said, a hand unconsciously straying to her belly. "Tell me about the ceremony," she said again, eager to redirect the conversation away from her brush with her own mortality.

Derek sat. "Not much to tell. Giuliana and the other new councilors took their oath of office, and their first official act was to pay us and the Noble Blades for our service to the city, which I thought got the new administration off to a strong start," he joked. "Um, what else? Oh, Houlte gave a nice little concession speech. He promised High Lord Ograine would respect the people's will, and the soldiers he's leaving behind until the city guard situation is figured out will answer directly to the new council. They have a have a hell of a long haul ahead of them, but I think everything will work out."

Felisia's smile turned melancholy. "But you won't be staying to find out, will you?"

"We're planning to head out in the morning with the Blades. We have some business of our own to wrap up, so..." He ended the thought with a shrug.

"I don't like goodbyes."

"Not too fond of them myself."

"You'll of course join the celebration this evening?"

"Wouldn't miss it."

"Derek? Would you spend the night with me?"

His cheeks flushed pink. "Felisia —"

"Not like that. I just — I would like to spend the night with you."

"Okay." He stood and held out a hand. "Ready

275

to get back to work?"

"Say it again."

"Are you ready to get back to work, Madam Fairweather?"

Felisia smiled. "Absolutely."

TWENTY-FOUR
A Parting of the Ways

The Pinceforth House reopened in understated fashion, opening its doors to a select guest list that included our heroes, naturally; a handful of longtime clients in excellent standing; the Noble Blades; and as a conciliatory gesture, Morris Houlte and Captain Greystone. The former attended gladly, the latter for the sole purpose of watching Houlte's back. Felisia's first night in charge of the house was, by all measures, a rousing success — as was Kat's first night assuming Felisia's former position as concierge, as evidenced by the many hours of laughter and revelry and, as the night grew long, moans of delight drifting from beneath certain closed doors.

David spent the evening tucked away in the cottage, away from Houlte, who, unlike Greystone, was not part of the conspiracy of silence surrounding his alleged demise, but he accepted this gracefully. Beyond the luxurious beds, the Pinceforth House had never held for him the same appeals it had for his elder companions — each of whom, at some point during the night, stopped in to check on the boy.

"How are you doing?" they all asked, and each time David replied with a smile, "I'm good."

Sometime around midnight, he nodded off on the couch in the cottage's small living room and slept well.

He awoke the next morning a little after sunrise when Derek crept in to begin packing. To apologize for waking him, Derek prepared a breakfast of sausage, scrambled eggs, toast, and coffee, and once the plates were bare, they gathered up their belongings, loaded them into their packs, and set those by the door in anticipation of their departure.

"I think we got everything," Derek said.

"Almost everything," David said.

From a heavy steel lockbox hidden beneath the floorboards of the cottage, beneath the sitting room table upon which David had labored and researched — and on more than one occasion slept under — he retrieved a package wrapped in an old, threadbare shirt. He carried this package to a small fire pit behind the cottage, a shallow hole lined with rocks stacked in a ring to form a low, wide chimney. David unwrapped the parcel, placed the mask of Lord Kilnmar upon the packed ash left behind by countless previous fires, and took several steps back.

"*Igi au'sum*," he said.

Derek squinted against the gout of flame that leapt from David's outstretched hand and splashed down upon the mask. Within seconds, the black iron glowed a dull red, and then a vivid orange, and then a radiant white.

"It's not melting," Derek observed. "Dammit, we are going to have to throw this stupid thing into a volcano, aren't we? Son of a — oh, wait, no, there it goes," he said as the center of the mask fell in upon itself, as though made of wax. "All right. That's one fewer dangerous magical artifact in the world," he said brightly. "I'd call that a good start."

"Yeah," David mumbled.

They stood there a while and watched the ancient iron melt into a molten puddle. David then abruptly ducked into the cottage, returning right away with his pack in hand. He dug into it and removed Habbatarr's book, which he then carried to the fire pit.

"David?" Derek said.

"Every academic in Woeste knows this book exists because of me. Word will spread. The Deathless Legion will come looking for it, eventually," David said, though something told Derek the boy was not speaking to him. "I can't let them get their hands on it. It's too dangerous. Destroying it is the smart thing to do."

There was conviction in his words, and yet he stood there, the book in his outstretched hands, conflict playing across his features.

"What do I do?" he asked.

Derek knew what he wanted to say.

Instead, what he said was this: "It's your decision."

An eternity followed.

David knelt and fed the book into the fire. It caught instantly, hungry flames devouring the desiccated pages. David drew a breath, almost a gasp, as a sense of relief washed over him and swept away a weight he hadn't realized he'd been carrying.

Derek laid a hand on the boy's shoulder. "For

what it's worth? I'm really proud of you."

David smiled.

It was worth the world.

Felisia kept her goodbyes short and sweet. She saw her friends as far as the foyer and said her farewells, with only Derek receiving more than a thank you and a hug — and even then the kiss was brief. Her duties as madam completed, she returned to her bedroom to sleep away her melancholy.

Kat accompanied her departing guests to the gatehouse, where she made Felix swear to all the Gods above and below that he would be more diligent in writing to her. She remained there, her tears flowing freely, until the adventurers disappeared down the road.

"I think a good breakfast is in order," Darrus said. "What say you, my friends?"

"Sounds like a fine idea," Derek said. "One last meal together before we go our separate ways."

"It doesn't have to be." Derek raised an eyebrow. "We work rather well together, lad. Imagine the glorious things we could achieve were you and your comrades to join the Noble Blades."

"Is that a formal invitation?"

"It's an idea I've released out into the world. What becomes of it?" He rolled a shoulder — a lazy half-shrug.

Derek turned to each of his friends, read their expressions, and said, "I don't think your reputation would survive us."

Darrus laughed. "Some days I'm astounded our reputation survives *us*. Ah, well," he sighed. "Tell me, have you any great plans for your reward?"

Derek shook his head. "Money's already spent."

"Already? Ha! And am I wrong in thinking your largesse benefited a certain house of hospitality?"

"You could say that, yeah," Felix said.

"Oh?" Darrus said, and then he understood. "Ah. You spent your pay on the tools and materials to repair the Pinceforth House."

"All that damage was our fault. It was the right thing to do."

"Aye. That it is."

"Oh, Darrus, no," Kelly whined.

"Hush, girl. We owe these good people a debt gratitude alone cannot pay. Besides, are we not the Noble Blades? We certainly can't let anyone be nobler than us, eh? Bad for business," Darrus said, slipping Derek a wink.

Darrus's generosity carried over through breakfast, which he paid for in full out of his own pocket before personally wishing each of his new friends all the best in their future adventures — adventures that would require more than one good man's heartfelt blessings. They would challenge our heroes in body and spirit, push them to their limits and beyond, and threaten not only their lives, but the lives of every living soul in all of Asaches.

But these are tales for another time.

For now, my friend, I bid you farewell.

An *Adventures of Strongarm & Lightfoot* Side Quest: Companionship, Compassion, Restraint, and Other Things Erika Racewind Dislikes

You might have noticed late in my tale a passing moment between Erika Racewind and Kelly Nightshadow upon their return from Oson, and that caused you to think to yourself, "What's that about?"

It is about this, a series of decisions made over drinks in the salon in the wee hours following the Deathless Legion's assault on the Pinceforth House and the aftermath thereof, when our heroes and their allies were near collapse from exhaustion and perhaps not as clearheaded as they should have been when deciding the fate of a city.

"I have to admit," Derek said, "I am not enamored with this plan."

Erika leaned on the bar, her back groaning, and tossed back her whiskey. A more conservative sort might have argued that dawn was too early to be indulging in spirits, but after spending an entire night fleeing from the city guard and then fighting off the

Deathless Legion — twice over, in fact — our heroes would probably tell those people to keep their opinions to themselves, thank you very much.

"Neither am I, really," she said, "but we have to face facts: this is something we can't handle ourselves — and we definitely can't trust anyone in the city guard."

"Why not?" Kelly said. "The Deathless Legion's been exposed. You really think any cultist with half a brain is going to stick around?"

"We can't be certain they won't," Darrus said, pacing about, hands folded and head bowed in thought. "Not unless we personally strip every last man and woman to their skin and search them for the brand."

"Even then," Erika said, recalling how her inspection of Mavolo's remains came up empty. "No, our best bet is to involve High Lord Ograine. People trust him, he has the resources to help us reestablish order..."

"And a golden opportunity to reassert his authority," Felix said. "You know he'd jump at any chance to bring Woeste back into the wardens' court."

"I know." Erika turned to Giuliana, who'd spent this impromptu meeting of the minds tending bar and keeping her peace. "This is your call, Giuliana."

"Mine?" She chuckled humorlessly. "What makes this my call, dearie?"

"Woeste is your home. You have as much right to make the decision as anyone. Certainly more right than I have."

Giuliana took a slow sip of her wine. "Do you truly believe petitioning High Lord Ograine for aid is our best option?"

"I do. It's not an ideal option, I won't lie about that, but yes, I think it is our best option."

Giuliana nodded. "Do it."

"Let me grab a few hours of sleep and I'll head right out."

"I'll go with you," Derek said, but Erika shook her head.

"You're more valuable keeping things here under control. Oh, don't give me that look. It's a straight ride from here to Oson; I'll be on the Grand Avenue the whole time. I can handle this by myself."

"All right," Derek relented.

"Stay out of trouble anyway," Felix advised.

Erika raised an eyebrow. "Don't you mean, 'Be careful'?"

"You heard what I said."

Erika returned to the guest cottage, stripped out of her leather armor and her boots, and fell asleep immediately upon flopping face-first onto the downstairs couch. Derek roused her around noon, during a break from helping Giuliana assess the extent of the damage to her property — which was significant but, all things considered, could have been so much worse.

Once fully re-dressed, Erika dallied long enough to raid the Pinceforth House kitchen and throw together a sandwich, which she wolfed down during her hike to the closest public stables. Their own horses were still missing from the previous night, when a city guard took them away with the false intent of securing them nearby, but Giuliana promised that strategically dropping her name would convince her old friend Nicholas Strige to lease one of his fastest horses.

Kelly Nightshadow, however, had to rely on a more monetary brand of influence to secure her mount.

"What the hell are you doing here?" Erika said upon finding the Noble Blade sitting on the small porch outside Strige's office, munching on a green apple.

"Riding with you to Oson," she said cheerfully. "Someone has to watch your back."

"No, someone doesn't."

"Your bumpkin friend didn't think so."

"His name is Derek," Erika said, bristling, "and maybe you missed the part where he didn't insist on coming with me. I don't need a partner for this. Go back to the house and help them."

Kelly took one last bite of her apple and tossed the core away. She then stood, made a show of stretching out, and strode up to Erika to stand nose-to-nose with her. "I'm going with you. You have a problem with that?" She stepped back and spread her arms. "Do something about it."

"Oh for Gods' sake," Erika sighed. "Fine. Whatever. But I'm warning you now, if you fall behind or get in trouble? I'm not going to waste my valuable time —"

"Don't worry about me," Kelly smirked. "I'm one of the Noble Blades. I can take care of myself."

A dozen responses, none of them kind, swirled around in Erika's head. She dismissed them with a wave, as if shooing away a bothersome fly, and stepped into the office to claim her horse.

The Grand Avenue was unusually light on traffic of the foot, horse, and carriage variety that afternoon, with travelers neither approaching nor leaving

Woeste in any appreciable volume. Several minutes, sometimes as much as an hour, would pass when Erika and Kelly were the only ones on the road — but for Erika's tastes, the Grand Avenue was still too heavily populated.

"You don't talk much, do you?" Kelly said.

"Nope."

"Good. I prefer it quiet. The rest of the Blades can't see fit to go anywhere without singing or telling stories or nattering on about something. Don't get me wrong, now; they're my friends and I respect them, but all that constant blather gets *so damned annoying*."

"I can imagine," Erika said dryly.

"Shouldn't we pick up the pace a little?" Kelly said a few annoyance-free minutes later. "At this rate it'll take us all month to get to Oson."

"Our pace is fine as it is."

"These are good horses, Erika — fresh and young and strong. We can push them."

"We *can*," Erika agreed. "We *won't*."

Kelly harrumphed. "For someone on an urgent mission, you don't seem to have much of a sense of urgency. Come on, let's put the spurs to these beasts, eh?" She scowled and snapped, "What's so funny? Are you laughing at me?"

"I'm thinking of a dumb joke Felix likes to tell. An old bull and a young bull are standing at the top of a hill, looking down on a pasture full of cows. The young bull says, 'What do you say we run down there and fuck a couple of those cows?' The old bull says, 'What do you say we walk down and fuck them all?'"

Kelly wrinkled her nose. "I don't get it."

"Didn't expect you would," Erika mumbled to

herself.

The Dragon's Grave Inn, one of several such establishments along the Grand Avenue, was so named because it was constructed long ago on the very spot where the great dragon Graltgrrongk fell following an epic battle with the hero Catherine Sharpsteel, the Bloodstained Queen. According to the story, the rampaging Graltgrrongk reduced a village within the minor city-state of Wesrouh to ash, leaving behind a lone survivor — a young girl who would in time grow to become the invincible, implacable knight-errant Catherine Sharpsteel. Her legend ended when she met Graltgrrongk on the very spot where she arose from the ruin of her village, forty years to the day of her rebirth in fire and destruction, and unleashed upon the monstrous dragon a lifetime of rage and wrath.

Some say she limped away and died of her mortal wounds but passed into the next world happy, knowing she would again be with her family. Some say she survived but hung up her sword, having no more reason to lift it in battle now that her lifelong foe had been vanquished. Regardless of her ultimate fate, Catherine Sharpsteel, the Bloodstained Queen, would be forever remembered for bringing down one of the greatest terrors to ever threaten Asaches.

According to the story.

Which is complete nonsense.

It is true a dragon died more or less on the spot upon which the Dragon's Grave Inn was built, but it was not the dragon Graltgrrongk, nor did he die in combat with anyone, much less Catherine Sharpsteel, who had quietly retired a year earlier and was at the time giving birth to her first daughter, Teresa. The creature was a lesser-known beast named Threshmakalt, who simply dropped dead of extreme old age. A warrior who found the body some hours later, a wandering mercenary named Katherine Silversword, took advantage of the situation to inflate her own reputation and laid claim to slaying the monster in battle. She boasted of this fraudulent achievement far and wide, but it did not take long for unreliable storytellers (unlike yours truly) to misremember certain details and embellish upon others until it became the tale people know today — a tale the current owners of the inn are happy to capitalize on to justify overcharging for their unremarkable food, drink, and lodgings.

"Why are we stopping?" Kelly said. "We still have a few hours of daylight ahead of us."

"Have you ever traveled the Grand Avenue before?" Erika asked.

"Of course I have."

"Then you know the next inn is a good four, five hours away, which means we wouldn't reach it until after dark."

"If we crawl along like a couple of tortoises, sure, but if we put these animals to work —"

"A horse can only sustain a full gallop for two, maybe three miles. Any time we'd gain by pushing them, we'd lose because we'd have to stop and let them rest — and there's no guarantee we'd be able to exchange them for fresh horses when we arrived at the inn, because the Wandering Bear is a smaller establishment that doesn't have a public stable." Erika dismounted. "But you know all that."

Kelly jumped down from her horse and followed Erika inside without ever confirming or denying this.

An inn with a sleepy atmosphere is not necessarily a bad thing. A sleepy inn is warm, cozy, comfortable, inviting, and less likely to erupt in a drunken brawl. In the case of the Dragon's Grave Inn, however, its sleepiness was almost literal. Three fellow travelers occupied a table near the fireplace, which sat cold and dark, and two women in white aprons stood at the bar chatting with the tavern keep, a portly man whose hair had fled the top of his head and reestablished a base camp inside his ears.

"Looks like we won't be seeing much action here tonight," Kelly said, disappointed.

"Good," Erika said. She strolled up to the bar and eased onto a stool. It felt so good, sitting on something that wasn't a hard leather saddle. "Two rooms for the night and stabling for our horses."

The tavern keep, Sebastian Monns by name, gave her a look with which she was well acquainted, a sidelong squint that betrayed his suspicion toward his new elven customer. He then glanced past Erika to take in the empty tavern and decided the need to turn a profit for the night outweighed any reservations he had about renting her a room.

Erika laid out enough gold to cover the rooms, the stabling, a hot meal, some cold beer, and his discomfort. Monns dismissed one of his barmaids to tend to the horses, the other to fetch the food, and turned to pour out two mugs of lightly chilled stout, which he handed to the women without a word of thanks for their patronage. He then stepped out from behind the bar to spend some time chatting with his other customers.

"Gods, the balls on this guy, charging that much for room and board. Talk about highway robbery," Kelly griped.

"When you're the only game in town, you get to set the prices," Erika said. "Just be grateful it's so slow in here, otherwise he would have sent us packing."

"Why?"

Erika gestured in the general vicinity of her snow-white elven face. "He might not have said, 'I don't serve your kind here,' but he was definitely thinking it — and mark my words, slow night or not, I step one foot out of line, he'll tell me to leave."

Kelly snorted. "I'd like to see him try to kick us out."

"I wouldn't. All I want is to eat and go to bed." She leaned in. "You are not going to ruin that for me. Do you understand?"

"You don't have to talk to me like I'm a child."

Erika took in her uninvited traveling companion, really took her in for the first time, and could not help but pity her, for the only thing remotely adult about Kelly Nightshadow was the hard stare she leveled in return. She had the eyes of an old, old woman, weary and sad, but that was where any illusion of adulthood ended.

Two plates piled high with sliced ham and wedges of red potatoes generously dusted with herbs appeared in front of them. The barmaid offered the women a small, polite nod, then returned to the kitchen.

"You should eat," Erika said. "We have a long ride ahead of us."

"I'm not a child," Kelly said.

"I know."

Erika awoke with a start, jolted from a sound sleep by a crash and an explosion of voices. She listened for a moment, waiting for the sound to repeat, then closed her eyes and lay back on her pillow and promptly returned to the dreamlands.

And then an insistent pounding at her door rudely pulled her back into the land of the living. She opened the door to find Monns standing in the hall, red-faced and pop-eyed. Even his ear hair seemed to be rigid with anger.

"I want you out," he demanded. "Now."

"Huh? What? Why?" Erika said, squinting against the light being cast in her face by an oil lamp. "I didn't do anything."

"No, but your young friend —" Monns snarled, leaving his thought incomplete. "Get that little hellion out of my tavern."

She hissed through clenched teeth and said, "What did she do?"

"You can ask her yourself. Get your things and go."

Monns left his lamp behind so his no longer valued customer would have light enough by which to get dressed and pack — which she did, cursing under her breath all the while. She stomped downstairs, back into the tavern, and found Kelly leaning against the wall near the front door, her left eye a bloated, blackish-blue mass. Her good eye stayed focused on the floor.

Monns thrust Kelly's pack into Erika's arms and repeated his order to vacate the premises. Before closing the door, she caught a glimpse of an overturned table and a man, one of the travelers she'd seen upon their arrival, pressing to his nose a rag soaked through with blood. His companions paused long enough in their fussing and fretting to throw matching icy glares at Erika's back.

"What did you do?" she said.

"He started it," Kelly whined.

"And yet he's not the one getting thrown out in the middle of the night. *What did you do?*"

"He — those guys — they invited me to play some cards with them," Kelly said, her breath thick with the sickly-sweet scent of high-end rum. "They lost. A lot. They didn't like it. He got in my face. The guy. I defended myself."

"So you didn't throw the first punch?" Kelly shrugged. "Oh, bloody hell."

"Where're you going?" Kelly said, chasing after Erika with her arms outstretched to help maintain her balance. "You're not going to leave me here, are you?"

"I'm getting our horses."

"Where're we going to go?"

"To the next inn."

"Now? But it's the middle of the night. You said —"

"It's not as if we have any other choice."

"But you said the next inn is hours away. It'll be dawn by the time we get there."

Erika rounded on her. "Maybe you should have thought of that before you got into a pointless bar fight! And I swear to the Gods, if you say 'He started it' one more time —"

"All right, okay." Kelly raised her hands as if in

surrender. "Look, can't we just make camp some-where?"

"We could if you weren't too drunk to keep watch."

"I'm not *that* drunk."

That she said this while listing to one side like a sailboat caught in a stiff crosswind rather undermined the plausibility of her claim.

The first rays of the rising sun were tinting the horizon by the time Erika and Kelly arrived at the Wandering Bear Inn — so called because the proprie-tress, Lenka Proset, spotted a large black bear wander-ing by while the building was under construction and thought the Wandering Bear Inn would make a cute name for her new business.

Sorry, folks; not every story is a winner.

Erika tied the horses up in a structure too large to be a shack but too small to be a proper stable, but the close quarters was a negligible issue; there were no other mounts tethered within.

The tavern was just as empty. No one greeted them at the door. Every table was vacant and the bar was unattended. Erika called out, then again. A third hail summoned from the kitchen an old man who moved at a brisk waddle.

"Hello!" he beamed, a grin hiding beneath a wiry snow white mustache better suited for a walrus than a man. "Welcome to the Wandering Bear Inn. I'm Gus. How may I be of service, ladies?"

"For now, we just need some feed and water for our horses, two rooms for us, and some peace and qui-et," Erika said, casting a sideways glare in Kelly's direction.

"The first two I can provide happily." Gus's smile weakened. "The third I can also provide, though not so happily."

"We've noticed the Grand Avenue's a bit on the quiet side. Any idea what's going on?"

"Well, according to a couple fellows who stopped in last night, there's some kind of kerfuffle at the Ulstar Gate."

Erika frowned. "Tolljackers?"

"Sounded like."

"Tolljackers?" Kelly asked.

"Highway bandits who take over the old toll-gates and shake down travelers," Erika explained.

"Happens from time to time. After a day or two they clear out and everything goes back to normal," Gus said. "Until then, folks usually take the Travelers' North Highway to go around them."

Erika paid for her room, adding a generous gratuity out of pity, and trudged upstairs. Kelly threw her money on the bar and ran after the elf.

"What are we going to do about the tolljackers?" Kelly asked.

"*We* are going to do nothing. You heard the man; it's a hit-and-run game. They'll probably be long gone by the time we reach the gate."

"And if they aren't?"

Erika stopped at the top of the stairs and glared down at the girl. "Are you *looking* to start another fight?" she asked, somewhat rhetorically.

"It's a fair question. If we ride out to the gate and the tolljackers are still there, we either have to pay them, which is horseshit; fight our way past them; or turn around, backtrack to the nearest crossroad, and take the Travelers' North Highway around them — which will add, what? A couple of days?" She shrugged. "Besides, innocent people are getting accosted and robbed. Are we really going to let them get away with that?"

It was bad enough when Felix presented an argument she could not refute. That Kelly had her so neatly cornered made Erika want to kick the girl down the stairs out of spite.

"Go to bed," Erika said.

The Gods saw fit to show our beleaguered heroine a little overdue mercy and allowed her to sleep without interruption. She slept soundlessly and dreamlessly and awoke a few hours before sunset, her stomach gurgling impatiently. She dressed and went downstairs to find Kelly sitting at the bar, regaling none other than Lenka Proset herself.

"Erika!" Kelly cried, raising her mug in toast. "There you are! I thought you were going to sleep the whole day away."

"I *did* sleep the whole day away," Erika pointed out. "How long have you been —" She almost said "drinking," but the glassy glaze over Kelly's eyes answered that question. "Awake?"

"Couple hours?"

"And she's spent the whole time spinning a lot of tall tales," Lenka said with good humor, "claiming she's one of the Noble Blades."

"Tell her, Erika," Kelly said. "Go on. Tell her. Tell her. Go on. Tell her."

"She's one of the Noble Blades," Erika confirmed, if only in the thin hope of shutting Kelly up.

"That's right! And you know who she is?" Kelly posed to Lenka.

"Kelly, stop."

"What? You embarrassed or something? You —" She thrust her mug at Erika's face, nearly popping her in the nose. "— need to stop being so modest."

"And you need to sober up." Erika took the empty mug away and relayed it to Lenka. "Could you fill this with water, please?"

"Let's get some food into her, too," Lenka said, toddling off to the kitchen.

"Why do I need to be sober?" Kelly said, teetering on her barstool. Erika pushed her back upright. "Are we leaving?"

"No, we are not," Erika said. "The next inn is on the other side of the Ulstar Gate. Even if we left right now, we wouldn't reach it until morning. We're going to stay right here for tonight, let the horses rest up, and set out at first light so we can maybe make up for all the time we've lost because of your antics."

"Me? I wasn't the one who slept all day."

Erika's hand curled into a fist, and not involuntarily. Kelly jumped to her feet, sneering, eyes blazing — but not, Erika realized, for her.

"Well, look who it is, will you?" someone said, his words strangely mushy, as if he was speaking through a head full of mucous — or a recently broken nose. Kelly's gambling partner of the previous evening stepped forward, granting her a clear look at the vivid blackish-blue stain splashed across the center of his face.

"Sit down," Erika whispered.

"We can take these assholes," Kelly said, not whispering.

"I said *sit down*."

Kelly, grudgingly, obeyed.

"We have no quarrel with you," one of the men said, a fellow who gave the impression he was quite the physical specimen back in his salad days. That salad had long ago been replaced entirely by pork.

"But I have unfinished business with her," Kelly's friend said as he and his companions spread out, surrounding the women as best as three men could surround anyone.

"Gentlemen, I understand you'd like to knock some sense into my friend. Believe me, I understand," Erika said with an accusing glance over her shoulder. "But if anyone's going to do that, it's going to be me."

"Woman, if you don't step aside, we'll have to go through you," said the third fellow, a broomstick of a man.

Erika took a step toward him. He took a step back. His friends took two.

"That's right; you *will* have to go through me. Do any of you really want to do that?"

None of them moved. None of them answered.

"I thought so. Here's what's going to happen: you three are going to plant your asses at that table —" She indicated the table farthest from the bar. "— and pretend we don't exist. We'll sit at the bar and do the same. Everyone wins, especially the nice woman who runs this establishment."

"What was that?" Lenka said, setting down on the bar two bowls filled nearly to overflowing with her famous savory venison stew.

"Nothing. Saying hello to your new customers."

"Oh! Hello, gents! I'll be right with you. I just have to get these ladies some water and...?"

"Same for me," Erika said. "I think we've done enough drinking for one night. Haven't we?"

"Guess we have," Kelly grumbled.

Erika eagerly tucked into her third bowl of stew while Kelly continued to pick listlessly at her first, which had grown cold and congealed. Every so often she'd glance over her shoulder at the men — during the course of their idle chitchat with Lenka they'd revealed themselves to be traveling merchants — and Erika would call her attention back to her meal. She'd force down a spoonful or two and fume quietly until it was time to cast the evil eye once again.

"Will you knock it off?" Erika said. "They're leaving us alone."

"They keep looking at us," Kelly said.

"Maybe that's because you keep looking at them."

"Mmrr." Kelly ate a spoonful of her dinner, grimaced, and spit it back in the bowl. "I'm going to go check the horses," she announced.

"You do that."

Kelly stalked off, and the moment the front door banged shut Erika felt a knot at the base of her skull unravel. The release was nigh orgasmic; she shuddered and let out an involuntary sigh of relief.

"Are you all right, dear?" Lenka inquired, appearing behind the bar with two fresh tankards of cold water.

"I'm fine. The day's catching up to me is all."

"I didn't realize sleeping all day could be so exhausting."

"It's my traveling companion who's exhausting."

Lenka nodded as if she understood completely. "She strikes me as a handful and then some, that one."

"That's for sure."

"She's so angry, poor thing," Lenka said with a sad shake of her head. "Oh, she put on a nice little act for me, so brave and boisterous, but I could see it in her eyes. She's carrying a weight."

"I've known a lot of people who carry weights. They didn't go dumping it on others."

"Not everyone is as strong as you, dear."

Erika frowned.

"I can see it in your eyes, too," Lenka said, a solemn note tempering her merry demeanor. "You know how to carry your weight. Not everyone is that strong."

Erika finished off the last of her stew and pushed the bowl away. "I think I've had enough."

"Very good." Lenka looked past Erika, made a curious noise, and disappeared into the kitchen.

Erika turned. The tavern was empty.

Cursing, she ran outside, ran toward the tiny stable, toward the sound of fighting, and launched herself at the first form she saw. The portly merchant took the point of her elbow on the side of his face and staggered away, stars dancing in his vision. The skinny one caught a thunderous kick to the chest that sent him flying, which left the man with the broken nose, who had Kelly in an awkward headlock and was raining hammer blows onto her back. Erika seized him by the blackened bulb that was once his nose, pinching it between her thumb and forefinger. His eyes doubled in size, and he let loose a thin, high squeal — the closest to a scream he could manage.

"You're going to leave now," she said. "You're going to go back inside, pay for your meals, and then you're going to leave. Do you understand?"

The man squeaked in the affirmative. Erika released him. His face remained locked in a rictus of blinding agony.

"Go."

Erika graciously granted the men enough time to recover from her brutally efficient beating and then bent to pick up Kelly from the ground. She slapped Erika's hands away.

"Get off," Kelly slurred. "Can get up myself."

After Kelly tried and failed and tried and failed and tried and failed to do so, Erika grasped the girl by the arm and hauled her upright. She expressed her gratitude by shoving Erika away with a curse.

"What the hell is your problem?" Erika said. "You didn't come out here to check the horses; you deliberately baited them, didn't you?"

"Those assholes jumped me!" Kelly said with a newly developed lisp, courtesy of a badly swollen lip.

"You spent the entire night needling those guys, and then practically challenged them to come outside and finish what *you* started, so don't you dare act like you didn't bring this on yourself. That's it," Erika said, throwing her hands up, "I'm done with you. Tomorrow morning, you're getting on your horse and riding back to Woeste."

"What? You can't — "

"This is not up for debate. You've been a pain in

my ass from the start and I've had it, you hear me?"

"You can't send me away," Kelly said, her voice cracking. "You need me!"

"I do not need you!" Erika roared. "I never wanted you in the first place!"

Kelly blinked, and when she opened her eyes, that strange illusion of age beyond her years had vanished, and she looked for all the world like the child she was — a desolate, broken child at that.

"Fuck you," she hissed. Tears slid down the swollen landscape of her face. "Fuck. You."

She spun on her heel and stormed off into the night. Erika on impulse almost went after her.

And then she remembered: she didn't care.

Erika awoke at the crack of dawn. Her first act upon sitting up in bed was to curse Derek for inflicting such a horrible habit upon her.

Dressed and packed, she went downstairs to square her bill and get back on the road. Gus stood behind the bar, a book in one hand and a mug of warm milk in the other — his standard ritual to calm his mind and relax his body before going to bed and handing the inn over to Lenka for the day. The Prosets saw little of each other, but this arrangement had served their marriage well for more than twenty years, and they were of no mind to rock such a steady boat.

"Good morning," he said. "Hope you slept well."

"Like the dead."

"The dead don't wake up."

"Or ask what's available to eat."

Gus set his book down. "Still got half a pot of

venison stew left over from last night."

"Trade you." Erika flicked several coins onto the bar. "I'll take a bowl of stew and some coffee, you can have that."

"Sounds like a fair deal to me," Gus said, scooping up the coins. He returned a few minutes later and presented Erika with her piping hot breakfast. "You heading out this morning?"

"Hm-mm. Still have a long ride ahead of me."

"You're going to Oson too, yeah?" Erika froze, her first spoonful of stew hovering in front of her open mouth. "That's where your friend said you two were going."

"She left already?"

"Hour or two ago."

Erika pounded down the coffee, scalding her mouth, and ran out of the tavern.

An hour or two. Enough time to reach the Ulstar Gate.

For several generations, the Grand Avenue generated significant revenue in the form of modest tolls collected from travelers at strategically located tollgates. The gates, stone structures resembling castle gatehouses, were treated much like military outposts and were in fact manned by a small division of the Oson army called, appropriately if unimaginatively, the gatekeepers, a dozen or so of whom would be stationed at a given gate for months at a time to collect money, patrol the area, and aid travelers.

This system worked exceptionally until economy-minded — which is to say, frugal — travelers took to avoiding the tollgates by blazing what is now known as the Travelers' North Highway. Income dropped, and within a decade or so, the cost of sustaining the tollgates tipped the scales unfavorably compared to the money they took in, and the practice was discontinued in favor of other methods of revenue collection.

It didn't take long for gangs of enterprising bandits to avail themselves of the abandoned infrastructure and take to periodically hunkering down inside the miniature fortresses and holding travelers for ransom. Tolljacking has proven to be a difficult crime to quash due to its hit-and-run nature; savvy tolljackers typically squatted in a gatehouse for a day or two at most and dispersed long before any soldiers arrived to clear them out.

(In case you're wondering: yes, it has been suggested to the wardens' court that the tollgates should be removed entirely in the interest of foiling the practice — many, many times it's been suggested, but the wardens insist the gates might become useful again one day and should be left in place, just in case. Critics suspect this is mostly an excuse to avoid spending money on their demolition. Those critics would be correct.)

Erika guided her poor exhausted steed to the side of the road and jumped off. The animal sputtered, as if in equal measures relief and frustration. Erika gave him a gentle pat on the flank and left him there, trusting that after such a demanding morning he wouldn't be inclined to wander off.

She strung her longbow and covered on foot the remaining distance to the Ulstar Gate, one of the largest tollgates along the avenue. Two fat turrets, each thirty feet high, sat on either side of the road. A wide arch that doubled as a footbridge between the towers loomed over the Grand Avenue, supported in the middle by a thick central column. Lengths of rusted chain, symbolic barriers at best, stretched across the two lanes this column created. The entire structure sat atop a rise that was too long and too broad to qualify as a proper hill, but the drop-offs on either side of the avenue were steep and effectively prevented travelers from circumnavigating the gate.

As she drew closer, Erika spotted someone moving across the bridge, pacing deliberately — a sentry. The figure, spying her, stopped and brought up a heavy crossbow, resting its tiller in the crook of his elbow — a display intended to alert rather than threaten.

He whistled through his teeth, the sound clear and shrill in the still morning air. Two more bandits emerged from the left-hand tower, the north tower, and joined him on the bridge. In unison, they raised their own crossbows to mimic their leader.

"Morning, boys," Erika called out. "Don't suppose you saw a friend of mine who might have come by earlier? Young, golden skin, dark hair, kind of mouthy."

"Maybe we have," shouted the middle bandit, the whistler. His voice carried down the road, strong and clear, before evaporating into the world beyond. "Maybe we haven't."

"She still alive?"

"Maybe she is. Maybe she isn't."

"For your sake, she better be."

"You threatening us?"

"Yep."

The whistler laughed. "We outnumber you, you know."

"Three against one feels like even odds to me."

"Odds ain't that even, missy." The whistler lowered his crossbow but did not bring it to bear on his target — yet. His comrades did likewise. "Stop right there."

Erika kept walking.

"I said stop."

Erika kept walking.

The whistler shouldered his weapon and took aim. "I said stop!"

Erika kept walking.

"Dammit, woman, you stop walking right now or I will kill you where you stand!" the whistler shouted. His companions shouldered their crossbows to lend his threat further weight.

Erika stopped.

She stopped long enough to gauge the remaining distance between herself and the gatehouse — two hundred feet, give or take — to note the entrances at the base of the towers, to get a feel for the breeze, its direction and strength, to remind herself that the two imbeciles flanking the whistler were brandishing crossbows that weren't even cocked, much less loaded.

And then she moved.

The whistler panicked and squeezed off a wild shot. The bolt unerringly struck the spot where Erika had been a heartbeat earlier. Her return shot found its target, sinking deep into the whistler's side. He staggered back, his face a pale mask of shock, and fell out of sight.

Erika dashed beneath the shelter of the bridge, leapt over the chain, and nocked a fresh arrow as she took position behind the central column.

She waited.

The door at the base of the north tower cracked open, cautiously, and a moment later swung wide. One of the whistler's men, a lanky fellow with a shock of bright red hair, emerged and immediately checked his right flank — and thus never saw Erika on his left. He pitched onto his face, an arrow jutting from between his shoulder blades.

Her position given away, she took cover behind the central column and let the bandits pouring forth from the tower exhaust their crossbows. Two bolts sailed past her harmlessly. She counted two more pinging off the stone.

Erika nocked an arrow and dared to poke her head out. She caught a fleeting glimpse of two bandits, women both, darting behind the other side of the central column, moving into position for an ambush from behind. None of her other foes were within sight.

She sprinted across the road to the north tower and tested the door there, a secondary entrance, only to find it barred from inside. She had time enough to spit a curse before her two stalkers sprang out, their crossbows primed and ready. They fired in unison. Erika threw herself out of the bolts' lethal path.

The heavy crossbow comes with many benefits. It is a powerful weapon, capable of launching a bolt hundreds of yards. At close range, it can drive its projectile through plate armor. And unlike a longbow, a crossbow can remain drawn for extended periods of time, ready to fire, without any stress upon the archer. However, once it's been fired, it takes time to get it ready again — time enough for a skilled archer using, for example, a longbow of elven make to nock and loose several arrows.

One of the bandits, thinking herself faster than she really was, stepped into her crossbow's iron stirrup and, with a grunt and a heave, set the bowstring. By this time, her partner was on the ground with an arrow in her chest, and Erika had nocked the arrow that would an instant later penetrate the bandit's brain through her eye socket.

A flash of motion at the edge of Erika's vision alerted her to her final enemies. The bandits sprang out from behind the cover of the north tower and fired. She dove, tumbling beneath the bolts, rolled back up to her feet, and loosed two more arrows. One struck home. The other sliced through the empty air as its intended target, a stout bandit with a wiry black beard, scrambled clear and ran back into the tower. Erika gave chase.

The tower door slammed shut. Erika heard the bump and thump of the bearded bandit desperately trying to fumble its crossbar into place. She took a step back to give her kick more power. The impact carried through the door and threw the bandit back into the tower, arms pinwheeling.

Erika's bowstring snapped one last time.

She backtracked along her trail of devastation, checking each of her foes to ensure they were down for good. They were.

A sweep of the north tower turned up no more bandits lurking within, waiting to jump her. Nor did it turn up Kelly Nightshadow.

Erika emerged onto the bridge. The whistler, alive but in agony, had managed to crawl over to the south tower, leaving behind a snail trail of blood. She crossed over to him and knelt down to grasp the shaft still protruding from his flank.

After he finished screaming, Erika asked the whistler, very calmly, "Where's the girl?"

"Inside," he panted. "She's inside."

"Is she alive?"

The whistler nodded.

"Did you violate her?"

The whistler shook his head.

Erika thanked him for this good news by granting him a quick and painless release.

Relatively painless, I should say. She was still Erika Racewind.

She located Kelly Nightshadow on the top floor of the south tower, the former barracks for the gatekeepers, wrists and ankles bound together behind her back, a rag stuffed in her mouth. A flash of panic turned to relief upon realizing who had entered. She then looked away to hide her shame.

Erika severed Kelly's bonds then stepped back and granted her the time she needed to massage the feeling back into her extremities. She refused Erika's hand when offered and stood on her own power. This took a while.

"Are you all right?" Erika asked. Kelly gave a small nod. "Good. Now, are you done trying to prove yourself to me?"

Kelly scowled. "I am *not* trying to —"

"Yes you are. I can spot the chip on your shoulder from a mile away. You are absolutely hellbent on showing me how smart and how tough you are, and it almost got you killed — and for what? My approval? My respect?"

"You wouldn't understand," Kelly muttered, stalking off to sulk.

"Try me."

"You wouldn't understand. How could you?"

"Kelly," Erika said gently. The girl turned. "I was a reckless idiot once too."

The young rogue searched Erika's face for any hints that this was an empty platitude meant to ease her humiliation. Oh, she searched.

"I'm not trying to impress you," she said.

"Who, then?"

"...Darrus."

"Darrus? Why do you need to impress him? You're already one of the Noble Blades."

"The only reason I'm with the Blades is because Darrus feels sorry for me," Kelly said in a tiny voice.

Prior to joining the Noble Blades, Kelly said, she traveled with another party of much less famous, much less successful adventurers. Whether it was fate or chance that led them to one day cross paths with the Noble Blades is a matter of opinion, but cross paths they did, down in the depths of a nameless ruin said to hold in its bowels a priceless treasure — precisely the kind of vague, unsubstantiated rumor that attracts adventurers of the brave, foolhardy, and desperate varieties.

The Noble Blades encompassed the first quality, Kelly and her companions the third. It could be argued both groups shared a common ground with the second.

It was there in the bottommost reaches of the ruin, in a vast subterranean chamber, that Kelly Nightshadow's life took its unexpected turn.

Until this point, the two parties had penetrated

the depths of the ruins on separate paths, wholly unaware of one another's presence until they simultaneously stumbled across the chamber and the enormous sarcophagus therein, adorned with undecipherable runes, perched on a high dais, surrounded by the remains of a score of adventurers who managed to survive the catacombs only to be felled by forces unknown within arm's reach of their reward. Kelly, overeager to lay claim to the prize and heedless of the grim warning presented by the littering of corpses, dashed in and in doing so stepped on a spring-loaded flagstone, thus triggering a simple but highly effective booby trap. A massive stone slab, too thick to shatter and too heavy to lift, fell down over the entrances, sealing the adventurers in, and a sluice gate in the ceiling opened to let in an underground river.

The chamber began to fill rapidly. It took less than a minute for the water to rise to Darrus's waist.

Kelly, a self-educated scholar of traps small and large, recognized Tolliver's Drowning Pool immediately and knew that once the water reached a floatation switch set into a deep recess in the ceiling, the sluice gate would close, and grates in the floor would open to drain the water. She located the switch easily and pointed it out to her teammate Rayne Swifthand, an ace archer, who triggered the switch with his first arrow.

Instead of hailing Kelly as their savior, her friends, there in front of the Noble Blades, unceremoniously ejected her from their ranks. That she saved everyone's lives was secondary to the fact she caused the life-threatening crisis in the first place, and they damned her as a careless, impulsive idiot who would one day get them all killed were she allowed to remain in their company.

(That accusation would come back to haunt Kelly's erstwhile companions three weeks later when, during a dungeon dive, they set off a Toadstool's Breath trap and asphyxiated in a cloud of toxic fungal spores.)

"Darrus insisted on buying me a drink to thank me for saving the Blades," Kelly said. "I thought that was going to be that, but he invited me to travel with the Blades 'until the world shows you where you're supposed to be,'" she said, mimicking Darrus's brogue with admirable accuracy.

"And then he asked you to join them," Erika said, but Kelly shook her head.

"He never asked me to leave. There's a difference."

"But he never asked you to leave."

"...He might."

Erika, nodding, said, "You're right; he might. If you keep doing stupid shit like provoking pointless fights with random strangers and charging headlong into dangerous situations then yes, he very well might decide you're too much of a pain in the ass and send you walking. And you'd deserve it for behaving like a huge idiot."

Kelly frowned. "You suck at comforting people."

"I'm not trying to comfort you; I'm trying to save you from yourself. Your antics are going to get someone killed — maybe you, maybe one of your friends. Is that what you want?"

Kelly's eyes dropped to the floor. She shook her head.

"Good," Erika said, solemn. "Because that is the

worst thing in the world to have to live with."

"Did you —?"

Erika didn't let her finish the question. "You want to impress Darrus? You want to be worthy of the Noble Blades? Then grow up. Grow up, do your job honestly, to the best of your ability, and stop trying to prove yourself to the entire world."

With that, Erika spun on her heel and marched away. Kelly slumped against the wall, tears imminent.

"Well?" Erika said from the doorway. "Are you coming or what?"

"What? You still want me to —?" she said, stopping there. If she didn't ask, Erika would have no reason to answer.

Kelly freed her horse from its prison in the small stabling area in the base of the south tower while Erika ran to fetch hers. She found the animal right where she left it, munching grass and happily oblivious to the mayhem it had missed out on.

They still had several days ahead of them on the Grand Avenue, and several more for the ride back, and no guarantees that it would all bear the intended fruit. High Lord Ograine owed Erika no favors — not in the legally binding sense — so her plea might well fall on deaf ears. She then glanced over at Kelly, beaten and bruised, ragged and bedraggled, but tall in her saddle, her head high, and decided that however their mission of mercy might play out, something good might yet come of all this.

"Ready to ride?" Erika asked.

"Ready when you are, Miss Racewind," Kelly said.

Miss Racewind, Erika mused.

Yes, indeed; something good might yet come of all this.

ABOUT THE AUTHOR

Michael Bailey was born in Falmouth, Massachusetts and raised on a steady diet of comic books, *Dungeons & Dragons*, Saturday morning cartoons, sci-fi television, and horror movies...which explains a lot.

An effort to parlay his love of geek culture into a career as a comic book artist failed when he figured out he wasn't that good, so he turned to writing as means of artistic expression. Since then, Michael has written several scripts for New England-area renaissance faires, as well as a number of articles based on faire culture for *Renaissance Magazine*.

In 2013, Michael left his job of 15 years as a reporter and blogger for his hometown newspaper, the Falmouth Enterprise, to pursue his writing career. His debut novel, *Action Figures – Issue One: Secret Origins* made its debut in September 2013.

Michael lives in Massachusetts with his wife Veronica, four cats, and an English bulldog.

Visit Michael online at www.innsmouthlook.com, and find him on Facebook, Twitter, Tumblr, Instagram, Pinterest, and Goodreads.

16808853R00175

Made in the USA
Middletown, DE
26 November 2018